The
MEDUSA
Situation

Gabiann Marin

Clan Destine
PRESS

First published by Clan Destine Press in 2024

Clan Destine Press
PO Box 121, Bittern
Victoria, 3918 Australia

National Library of Australia Cataloguing-In-Publication data:

Marin, Gabiann

THE MEDUSA SITUATION

ISBN: 9781922904744 (paperback)

ISBN: 9781922904751 (eBook)

Cover Illustration by Trudi Canavan
Cover Design by Willsin Rowe
Design & Typesetting by Clan Destine Press

Clan Destine
P R E S S

www.clandestinepress.net

This book is dedicated to the Nine Muses of old – capricious, maddening and wise – who took me down the myriad twisting pathways of inspiration and creativity which eventually led to the creation of this book.

But primarily it is dedicated to the lesser-known 10th Muse, who always found me, took my hand and guided me back when I got lost.

Neal, my beloved,
the unsung Muse of practicality and support,
I love you with all my heart and
this book would not exist without you.

I

Unexpected Visitors in Marrickville

APPLAUSE EXPLODED AS THE YOUNG WOMAN TOOK THE STAGE. SHE looked around with wide eyes, her innocent expression undermined by her high hemline and massive coiffure of blonde ringlets. The camera cut to Dionysus, infamous wine and debauchery enthusiast and television host, who gave the woman an inauthentic smile before introducing her to the audience.

'Hello Helen, and welcome to *Oh My God!* It's great to have you on the show.' His smile turned into a wolfish grin. 'Many of our viewers will know you as the face who launched a thousand ships, the woman who sparked the greatest war of ancient Greece and, of course, the authoress of the bestselling book, *50 Shades of Troy.*'

Helen nodded fervently. 'It's great to be here, Dionysus.'

'So, you're here to confront your partner, Paris, who you believe abducted you and started an entire war, simply for the sake of his own ego?'

'That's right, Dionysus. I want to know: did he ever really love me? Or was the whole thing just a ploy to get into the history books?'

The goddess Hera, watching from her sitting room in an inner west suburb of Greater Sydney, could see how Dionysus enjoyed the anticipation of ambushing this young woman on interdimensional television.

If asked, Hera would never publicly admit to watching the *Oh My God!* talk show. It was awful television, even by Mystic TV standards, and she had refused to appear on it several times herself, despite Dionysus' entreaties and offers of substantial amounts of existence points. Hera had her own ways of dealing with her husband's many infidelities, and none of them included her public humiliation on Mystic Television.

But there was a part of her that could not resist watching other people's embarrassment and stupidity. Something she shared with a great majority of the Deity Channel's watching public, if *Oh My God!*'s ratings were any indication.

Nevertheless, Hera had a bit of sympathy for the blonde-haired woman who sat there in the spotlights. Abuse and humiliation were hardly something new for Helen of Troy. Hera noted that Helen still held onto her legendary beauty, but now it had been tarnished by modern versions of what that meant. Her face was distorted by several unnecessary surgical procedures, including a ridiculous trout pout and unnaturally large bosoms straining against gravity and the Lycra of her unbecoming strapless dress. Several tattoos could be seen on her arms and shoulders, including the name Paris in highly ornate script across her left clavicle.

Onscreen, the camera switched to a close-up of Dionysus, who was making a show of looking at the palm cards he carried in his left hand.

'Well, we have a number of people who say not only are you responsible for all the carnage of Troy, but that you are also a cheating, double-crossing little harlot.'

The audience went wild, hooting and hollering as Helen's face fell into an almost comical look of indignation. 'Who said that!? Cassandra? She doesn't know anything!'

'Indeed! Let's meet your sister-in-law Cassandra and see what she has to say.'

A sliding door opened and a tall brunette came running out, face contorted with rage as she screamed at the blonde.

'You rotten bitch! I told you something bad would happen if you ran off with Paris!'

Helen was up in a flash and the two women were upon each other, pulling hair, long fingernails digging into exposed flesh, dresses hiking up dangerously close to panty lines as the audience screamed and cat-called in enthusiastic approval. After a minute, two large ogres, both wearing black security shirts, appeared from the wings and pulled the women apart.

Cassandra and Helen sat on either end of the stage, a single empty chair between them. It didn't take a genius to work out that this empty seat would soon be filled by the aforementioned Paris. Hera particularly hated that little troll-faced mortal, and not only because he had decreed Aphrodite more beautiful than her in the infamous beauty contest that had started it all. Aphrodite had cheated, of course, and honestly Hera cared little about conforming to mortal beauty standards, but she would never forgive how the war he had wrought had so splintered her family. They may not have been the most functional of Deity dynasties to begin with, but it was the scars and fractures created as the Olympians chose different sides in that infernal conflict that had really cemented so many of her family's continuing feuds. Why any of them had sided with that weedy little mouth-breather was beyond her.

'Cassandra, you say you had a prophetic warning of the war and Helen's place in it, but she didn't listen to you,' Dionysius prompted.

'Yep, that's right, Dion' Cassandra agreed. 'She's a selfish cow!'

The audience sucked in its collective breath, several then oohing and aahing at this accusation. Still others clapped in agreement and hollered their approval. Egged on by the audience, Helen was up again and running at Cassandra, knocking her backwards on her chair. The two went down screaming.

'You go, girl!' a young nymph called out from the second row of the studio seating as the ogres again pulled the warring women apart. Dionysus, seemingly unfazed by all the hysteria, flipped through some of his notes and nodded.

Hera could understand Cassandra's point – Helen's involvement with Paris had been a massive mistake – but she also couldn't help feeling a lot of sympathy for poor old Helen stuck with this idiot and blamed for everything. Paris would never have gotten the time of day from someone as beautiful as Helen if Aphrodite had kept right out of it.

'Well, as you know, we have Paris backstage, and he has a revelation he wants to share with Helen – when we come back.'

Helen blinked up in surprise and Dionysus smiled smugly.

Then the show cut to the usual advertisements for Hebe's cut-price facelifts and the all-you-can-eat night at Valhalla's warrior buffet, the commercials so loud the sound waves coming from the television were almost visible. The noise would deafen most people, but Hera's husband, Zeus, slumped in the armchair to the left of her in front of the TV, continued to snore loudly, undisturbed. She sighed, got up, and headed to the kitchen to make herself a cup of tea. A few minutes later she settled back into her usual place on the sofa, steaming cuppa and a full packet of Tim Tams in hand, to watch the conclusion of the show.

She had missed a bit while in the kitchen and now Paris was onstage. He looked as he almost always did, weedy and recalcitrant, dressed in a pair of black denim jeans and a ripped Iron Maiden t-shirt. He was sitting slumped and uninterested between the still-sniping Cassandra and Helen. His lack of engagement with the two women was a bit of a disappointment and the show was struggling to keep up its usual feel of unrestrained chaos and general hysteria. Just when she considered flicking the channel to Judge Janus repeats, Dionysus gave the audience a wicked wink and called out the name of Oenone, Paris' ex-girlfriend. The one he had abandoned for Helen. Hera perked up. Now it was getting interesting.

The willowy sea nymph appeared from backstage and Paris suddenly became much more animated. He stood and hugged Oenone, declaring he wished he had never left her for a frigid bitch like Helen, who brought nothing but drama. As if on cue the outraged Helen jumped up and flung herself at her ex-lover, slapping him around the face as she cried out her betrayal.

'You told me that was over!' Helen wailed.

Hera grinned, pleased. She knew Oenone from pottery class and was pretty sure the nymph had no interest in getting back with Paris, considering she had moved in with a Chinese water god several hundred years ago. Dionysus must have offered her a huge cache of existence points to humiliate herself and take part in this orchestrated farce, but it was going to be pretty sweet watching her shatter Paris' dreams of a reconciliation.

Hera was just settling back in her sofa, savouring the taste of her melting Tim Tam enjoying the assured public rejection and humiliation of Paris, when a hard rapping on the front door broke her concentration.

At first she chose to ignore the interruption; whomever it was would go away eventually and things were starting to get interesting now that Paris was sobbing and Dionysus had announced yet another wronged woman guest: a dryad who claimed Paris was the father of her young child. Hera thought the child had a nose that looked suspiciously like Zeus', but before she could see the baby more closely, the knock on the door repeated, louder and more insistent than before.

Hera muted the television and yelled across the room. 'Go away!'

Another, louder, knock came in response. Hera got up and strode to the door, annoyed enough to smite any Jehovah's Witness or door-to-door salesman with a mighty burst of divine retribution. She kicked a washing basket full of unironed clothes out of her way, spilling the shirts, trousers and dresses onto the floor.

As the clothes fell, Hera found herself hesitating. You never knew who was still around these days. There were more than a few who might come around for a bit of biffo, now that the King and Queen of Olympus weren't quite as powerful as they once had been. Goddess knew Zeus had made his fair share of enemies – both divine and mortal. If truth be told, she had made one or two enemies herself.

Maybe she was better off ignoring this unexpected visitor.

The thought upset her in a strange way. Back in the day no one dared approach her home unannounced. Hera had been a force to be reckoned with, the undisputed Queen of the Greek Pantheon, governing over the greatest civilisation ever to emerge from that old primordial soup they called human existence.

As a goddess and a queen, people treated her with respect – not like now, when they apparently just turned up and knocked at her door in the middle of the day like she was some inconsequential, common mortal. It was unforgivable. She should smite them here and now, on principle. Trouble was, Hera hardly had the energy for even the occasional bit of divine vengeance or almighty smiting any more. She was not a young goddess, if she had ever been, and – although she was still prone to bursts of ferocious anger – actual wrath seemed like too much bloody effort these days. Fact was, she had softened with age, lack of power and, she hated to admit it, a touch of arthritis.

It was no surprise that she had let herself go a bit. So what? She and Zeus had removed themselves from the other gods decades ago and tried to settle into a somewhat mortal, immortal existence, precisely so she wouldn't have to deal with the stupidity and politics of the Divine Realm and the hundreds of other forgotten and fallen deities.

At first she and Zeus had settled in Greece, but it was hard seeing their previous worshippers move on to another, less interesting, god. So they had made the journey to Italy and then Greater Europe. But, as the decades and then the centuries passed, they found the constant human squabbling more than a little annoying. Through the Crusades, the Napoleonic and then the Crimean wars, Hera found that the Europeans quickly became tiresome. War, Hera realised, wasn't quite so much fun when one was not safely tucked up on Mount Olympus, watching from afar and occasionally interfering for her preferred side. So, as Mussolini cosied up to Hitler, Hera and Zeus migrated with many of her former country folk to the land of Australia.

As the decades passed they were kept relatively well off by the constant historical and narrative interest in their old stories from Rome and Greece, so even the ever-rising cost of living didn't hit them too hard. She sometimes missed the excitement of the grand old cities like Paris, or Prague, but was surprised that she never felt any urge to make her home on the Divine Realm where many of the other old gods had chosen to retire. She liked her new home in the antipodes, the weather was good and most of the dysfunctional drunkards, cheaters and liars who made up her extended family rarely bothered to visit.

Zeus, less willing to relinquish his old glory days, occasionally invited around the odd relative – usually a cousin, in-law or, if she was particularly unlucky, one of their rotten brothers. Hera usually managed these visits by drinking herself into a comfortable fog before the familiar family rivalries were aired. She never felt she missed much because, almost without exception, these impromptu family visits always devolved into the same clumsy fist fights, unnecessary insults or regrettable sexual encounters as they had in times gone by, before everyone eventually made up and declared drunken anticipation at meeting up again sometime in the unspecified future.

So, sure, occasionally she missed being a powerful goddess, but mostly she was happy to turn her back on that old existence and sink comfortably, if not contentedly, into her new suburban life of marital squabbles, daytime television and barely acknowledged regret.

A third round of knocking. Hera scowled and glanced at Zeus, wondering if she should let him deal with it. But he was drooling in his sleep, his singlet top stained with anchovy butter, and the air around him dull with the aroma of sweat and past glory. *Greek god my arse*, she thought, irritated.

Another round of knocking. This time insistent and uninterrupted. Whoever it was, they were getting on her tits and she thought maybe she would indulge in a bit of divine smiting after all, if for no other reason than to prove she still could.

She swung the door open.

'I said *Go Away!*' she said angrily, before she even registered the women standing on the doorstep. Only they weren't women. They were gorgons.

Two of them in fact. Topping seven feet tall, dressed in long green gowns, their serpent hair hidden under large floppy hats and dangerous eyes masked behind aviator shades, the sisters looked less like monsters and more like eccentric bag ladies.

The older, and shorter, of the two, Stheno, didn't waste any time, pushing her way inside as soon as Hera opened the door, followed immediately by the youngest of the three sisters, Euryale. Medusa, the most famous of the Gorgons, did not seem to be with them.

Hera made a concerted effort to calm her anger. She wasn't exactly afraid of the gorgons, but, all the same, she didn't really have any desire to start a fight with them. Mystics or mortals she would happily turn into toads, but monsters had at least some of her grudging respect.

Euryale closed the door and locked it, then looked out the window before drawing the blinds quickly. Whatever their business here, she clearly didn't want anyone else knowing about it.

As Euryale fixed the blinds closed, Hera noticed the piles of unfolded clothes and yellowing newspapers that filled the family room, the outcome of her continuing war of attrition with Zeus. His seeming inability to do even the simplest chore had been fine while they lived on Olympus. There were hundreds of servants waiting impatiently to scoop up the random dropped grape or mop up the spilled wine from their drunken parties. But here, on the Mortal Realm, there was no one to pick up after them.

Zeus, of course, expected her to do it, often mentioning she was the goddess of marriage, which meant she should rightly do all wifely duties. To which she usually responded by smashing a few plates and screaming that she was a goddess, not a maid, and he could pick up his own dirty underpants. Then they spent about a decade not speaking to each other as the unwashed china and silverware crusted over in the abandoned, moulding sink.

Up until a few decades ago, when Zeus ran out of cutlery or clean laundry, he would invent some pretence to invite over their sister Hestia, the goddess of the hearth. Hestia had an almost pathological need to clean, so the house was usually spotless in the time it took them to make her a cup of tea. But Hestia wasn't stupid and soon demanded payment for her cleaning duties, which Zeus, being an infamous miser, refused to pay. So Hera and Zeus were now back to ignoring the mess and secretly hoping that the other would give in eventually, while knowing that neither of them probably would.

Over in the corner, a half-full beer can fell out of Zeus' slack hand and spilled over their Persian rug. Hera waited a few moments for Zeus to react, but he did not stir so, not wanting to appear too slovenly in front of her uninvited guests, she went over and picked it up, accidentally on purpose dribbling some of its contents across his snoring face. Zeus snorted and grimaced but didn't quite awaken.

'We need to talk,' Stheno said, and then nodded at the sleeping Zeus. 'In private.'

'Nothing wakes him up after a few beers.'

'Even so,' Euryale said, gesturing Hera towards the back of the house.

Hera noticed that the snakes under the gorgon's hat were hissing angrily, a sure sign that she was definitely upset about something despite the fact that her face behind those huge sunglasses remained as still and emotionless as a marble statue. It would probably be quicker, and less dangerous, to listen to them than toss them out.

She picked up the remote and snapped off the television. She knew the show would end in the usual predictable way. The paternity test would be inconclusive. Paris would end up abandoning both Helen and Oenone once again so he could whisk the pining dryad off for some hanky-panky. The audience would of course then blame all of this behaviour on the women, simply because men were never, ever held accountable for anything. But Helen would end up having the last laugh as sales of her book would go through the roof. The formula was pretty much the same every episode – just the humiliated participants changed.

Hera led the two sisters into the kitchen. Again Euryale closed the door while Stheno checked that the room was empty.

Satisfied that they were alone, Stheno and Euryale sat down at the cracked linoleum table, waiting for Hera to join them. Hera moved the dirty dishes over to the already teetering pile in the sink and then sat across from the sisters, conscious that behind those ridiculous glasses were gazes so powerful one glance would turn her instantly to stone. Even as a goddess she was not immune to the power of the gorgons. As far as she knew, no one except the gorgons themselves were impervious to their deadly stare.

As if reading Hera's thoughts, Stheno leant forward, her glasses slipping slightly down the bridge of her nose. Hera narrowed her eyes and tensed; she knew she should shut her eyes or turn away, but it was not in Hera's nature to back down, so she stared back. Stheno, apparently unwilling to push the goddess further, shoved the glasses back up on the top of her nose and pulled away, allowing her sister to take the lead.

'We need your help,' Euryale said.

'My help? Aren't you two of the most powerful monsters in the whole of Monsters' Realm? What on earth could I do for you?'

Euryale and Stheno exchanged a look. 'Medusa's head has been stolen,' Euryale stated frankly.

Hera sighed heavily. 'Not again.'

The sisters looked troubled and nodded.

'We have looked everywhere. Medusa is beside herself,' Euryale added. 'When that bastard stole her head the last time, she didn't get it back for years.'

Hera knew the story – how Medusa's head had been lopped off a few millenia ago by the Greek hero Perseus. 'Hero' in this case meaning a man who crept up on a sleeping creature and hacked off her head for no better reason than a human king had asked him to. Apparently, that passed as a heroic act back in the day. Hera supposed it probably still would. Humans were funny that way.

Perseus had ended up terrorising the human realm for years as he haphazardly paraded around with the severed head, petrifying gods and titans and mortals alike. The Divine Realm couldn't let this stupid young man just wander around with a weapon of such power, even though he used it mostly to bully people into buying him drinks in local taverns, so they had asked Athena, the warrior goddess, to get the head back. Of course Athena had been successful; insisting that Perseus give her Medusa's head as an offering if he didn't want his own head taken off with her mighty sword.

But once she had it, Athena wasn't sure what she was meant to do with the trophy, until the disembodied head had unexpectedly spoken up and told her that Medusa was not, as they had all assumed, actually dead.

Despite the decapitation, Medusa had continued to live on as disconnected mind and body, waited on by her two dutiful sisters as they hoped for the head to be returned. Athena agreed to return Medusa's head but worried how the gorgon would manage carrying it around without it constantly falling off. A gorgon's head tumbling off and rolling away unexpectedly could provide another opportunity for Perseus, or some other idiot teenager with a need for fame and glory, to nab it again. That was not something anyone in the Mystic Realms would be too pleased about.

Finally Hera's son, Hephaestus, himself no stranger to disability, agreed to fashion a lovely iron collar that would snugly hold Medusa's head securely on her neck. With her head firmly back on her shoulders, Medusa and her sisters had once again returned to their isolated island. They agreed to post extra security should another 'hero' come looking to make his name and they had stayed out of trouble pretty much ever since. This was of course, back before the creation of Monsters' Realm, after which the gorgons were relocated to one of the safest and most heavily protected islands in all the seven realms.

'She never really got over that whole Perseus ordeal,' Euryale said. 'For it to happen to her again – it's horrifying.'

'We are in a new era now, Euryale; that sort of thing doesn't happen in the 21st century. Not with the EBCU and all the compliance and divine behavioural committees. She probably just left it somewhere,' Hera replied. 'Have you checked the back of the kitchen cabinet?'

Hera knew Medusa had been known to detach her head from its collar to look around corners and under low furniture. It was a handy thing to have a head you could dislodge at will. Trouble was, Medusa's mindless body might have a difficult time always remembering where the head had been put down, and wander off without it.

'We didn't lose it,' Stheno hissed.

Hera thought this may have been an annoyed hiss, but it was difficult to tell. Hissing tended to sound annoyed and gorgons tended to hiss an awful lot – part of the reason they were seen as bad tempered, she supposed.

'Do you know how messy it is to feed someone through their neck?' Stheno complained from the corner of the room. 'It's a nightmare.'

Hera shook her head. She really didn't understand why they were coming to her. 'I'm sure you could get some kind of tube or something; medicine is quite amazing nowadays.'

Euryale inched a little closer. 'You don't understand. It's not just about us. As you know, Medusa's head, if it fell into the wrong hands, could threaten everyone – even the gods themselves. It is in everyone's interest to find it before something bad happens.'

'Nonsense,' Hera said. 'No one could get into Monsters' Realm. She's just misplaced it. It'll turn up.'

'I am telling you, Queen Hera, it hasn't just been misplaced. Medusa doesn't leave our cave and we have searched everywhere. There is no other explanation other than someone has taken it.'

'Hera,' Stheno added, 'you have to track it down.'

'There are many more powerful deities than me,' Hera replied, surprised. 'Why don't you ask Poseidon? Or Zeus?'

Stheno hissed angrily, but Euryale retained her calm expression. 'Those idiots couldn't find the Parthenon with a map and a tour guide. We all know who the real brains of Mount Olympus was.'

Hera appreciated the flattery, self-serving as it may be, and she knew there was truth in it. After all, it was not the male gods but she and the other goddesses who had guided or punished the human heroes and aided the efforts of mortal and immortal alike. Her brothers had spent most of their time as divine beings fathering illegitimate children and drinking copious amounts of fermented nectar. But that didn't mean she was going to get involved in this. The head was probably just misplaced, regardless of what the sisters said. And if it had been stolen, well, now that was a problem for the new gods.

Hera had retired long ago, so what possible reason could she have to go traipsing across the known realms looking for some idiot, possibly brandishing a gorgon's head that could turn her into stone with one wrong glance?

'Nowhere in all the seven mystic realms is as well protected as Monsters' Realm,' Hera said. 'No one could have gotten in and out of there without one of the monsters or creatures noticing. Honestly, I think you are panicking over nothing. You'll probably find it when you're searching for something else. That's how I always find my car keys.'

'We didn't lose it! It's been stolen,' Stheno yelled. 'Our sister's headless body is just lying around in her room, refusing to come out, refusing to engage with anyone – even us. This could be the death of her!'

In the front room Zeus stirred, snuffled, and the two gorgons froze.

'Don't worry,' Hera said. 'Like I said, nothing wakes him when he's drunk. And he's always drunk.'

As if to prove her point, a rumbling snore emanated from the parlour, punctuated by a loud and slightly squeaky sleep fart. The gorgons wrinkled their noses in distaste but quickly moved on.

'Hera, you've always been the one to ferret things out. Nothing gets past you once you decide to find the truth. How many of Zeus' affairs did you uncover, how many illegitimate kiddies did you track down? We need you–'

Hera held her hand up and shook her head, cutting Euryale off. 'The world has moved on, ladies. I am no longer the Queen of Olympus and you are no longer my subjects. If you need help, I'm not the one to come to any more. You should call the Entity Behavioural and Compliance Unit.'

'We can't call the EBCU!' Euryale protested. 'You know that. Medusa being out of Monsters' Realm is in direct contravention of the *Safety from Monsters Act*, even if it isn't her fault.'

'If the other gods and goddesses knew Medusa's mighty gaze was no longer in Monsters' Realm, they would hunt her head down like she was nothing more than some sort of dangerous animal,' Stheno growled. 'They would kill her and you know it.'

'I'm sure that wouldn't be the case,' Hera said. The EBCU were an officious group of bureaucrats who took an inordinate amount of pleasure in using their power to make their tiny little lives mean something, but they would never do anything as straightforward or humane as a simple monster killing.

No, if the EBCU got involved the chances were that even if they managed to prove it was stolen and track the head down, they would present Medusa with a heavy fine for not safeguarding it correctly, while letting whoever had actually stolen it off with nothing more than a sternly worded warning not to do it again. Then they would demand everyone involved fill out 15 pages of unnecessary paperwork, which would promptly be misplaced; along with Medusa's newly recovered head, not to be recovered for several centuries until some lowly shipping clerk accidently found it misfiled somewhere in what the EBCU euphemistically called their 'records room'. Complain as people might about wrathful gods, at least they just used to smite people and be done with it.

'Hera, we can't move freely through the other realms,' Euryale said. 'We could be killed on sight just for being here talking to you. We can't find her without help.'

Hera hesitated but shook her head again. Her days of creeping around and spying, searching for evidence against any who wronged her... sure, they had been fun in their way, but she was over that now. As she had told the sisters, the world had moved on. Her detective ways were behind her, and what lay ahead was endless hours watching reality television and reminiscing about the old days.

That reminded her – new episodes of *Judge Janus* were being released today; she would need to make sure she didn't miss that. There was nothing Hera found more entertaining than seeing the two-faced judge argue the verdict with himself.

'I'm sorry, ladies, but I can't help you.'

'I told you she would be useless,' Stheno growled. 'There was a time when everyone was terrified of you, Hera. You were one of the most powerful goddesses in the known world. Now what are you? A dowdy old suburban housewife.' Stheno stood up, disgusted.

'You want to be careful what you say,' Hera said. But she was rattled; the gorgon's words hurt, mostly because there was a ring of truth to them.

Euryale gestured for her sister to sit down. The air in the kitchen had become fizzy with supernatural power and indignation.

'We came to you because, despite the fact you are a cold-hearted old bitch, you have always been good at finding out things,' Stheno said. 'We need a good detective who won't take Medusa's head for themselves once they find it.'

'And what makes you think I wouldn't?' Hera countered.

The gorgons glanced at each other and then Euryale spoke, trying to soften her words, aware they had perhaps insulted the goddess quite enough for one day.

'Because as rotten as you sometimes were, you never did anything simply for power or glory. It was always about your pride.'

Hera softened slightly, mollified by the acknowledgement of her dignity.

'And just looking around here it's pretty obvious you could do with something to take pride in,' Stheno added as the teetering dirty plates lost their fight against gravity and smashed to the floor.

Hera's legendary anger rose in her throat as she glared at the dishes and then stood quickly, flung open the kitchen door and strode into the living room. Who did these gorgons think they were, insulting her in her own home? She deserved more respect than this!

The gorgons hesitated, but then reluctantly followed, standing at the front door as Hera indicated they were to leave. Euryale made to say something else but Hera shook her head, her irritation and anger preventing her from hearing any more from these two. The gorgons stepped outside and Hera stood on her threshold as Euryale turned to make a final comment. But before she could speak, Hera cut in icily.

'And before you suggest I'm slovenly – you should remember that I'm not the one who managed to lose my sister's head. Twice!'

And with that she slammed the door directly in Euryale's face and locked it securely before turning back to her parlour.

Hera sank down heavily on the faded settee and flicked the television back on. The *Oh My God!* episode was almost over and Dionysus was promoting the next show, which he promised would be the best yet.

'Next week: *Centaur Love – Bestiality or True Romance?* You don't want to miss it!'

Dionysus winked into the camera and then the credits came up, rolling over old footage of several catfights, shouting matches and confrontations.

Hera turned off the television, trying to ignore the little voice inside her which kept repeating the gorgons' words. Was she really so reluctant to help the gorgons because she knew she wasn't what she once was? That the glory of her past was behind her and, as a middle-aged former deity, she had, as they had suggested, simply gotten past it?

She ate the last Tim Tam in the packet, scrunched up the plastic and tossed it on the coffee table among the empty pizza boxes and half full cups of tea. She stood up, preparing to get herself another packet from the kitchen and caught a glimpse of herself in a large mirror on the wall opposite her. She stopped and, for the first time in a long while, really looked at her reflection. Her once striking mane of mahogany hair was grey, her goddess complexion dried and tired. She also noticed her housecoat was on inside out.

Over in the corner, Zeus awoke and glanced up at her, bleary eyed.

'Hey Hera, can you get me a beer?' he asked groggily before turning his attention to the TV. Realising it was silent he looked around for the TV remote, which Hera had left on the couch a few feet away from him. He reached for it but was unable to get anywhere near it without getting out of his chair, so he gave up and settled back in, pointedly looking at Hera and then at the remote. Hera ignored him and went into the bedroom to get dressed.

'There are chops in the freezer for dinner and you can defrost them if you want,' she called out.

'But I don't know how to use the oven!' Zeus called back, alarmed.

'Oh, for Olympus' sake, Zeus, you invented fire. I'm sure you can work it out. I'll be back soon.'

Hera emerged dressed in a fresh clean blouse, skirt and her favourite slightly scuffed boots.

'Where are you going?'

'I'm going out,' she said, pulling on her coat.

'Out?' said Zeus surprised. 'You don't go out. What do you want to go out for?'

Hera shrugged. As much as she hated to admit it, the gorgons' words had hit home and she felt a bit stung. Partly by the idea that she was past it, but mostly by their accusation that she was no longer seen as a great and powerful goddess. Hera didn't like that one bit. So maybe she would go throw a bit of weight around in the Divine Realm. Turn over some stones and ask a few questions. Medusa's head was probably just misplaced, but it wouldn't hurt to go and show the mystical realms that she was still someone to be reckoned with.

She would need a bit of a power-up first though.

'Don't you go spending our points on makeovers and shopping sprees—' Zeus began, but he was cut off by the sound of the front door slamming shut as Hera left the house.

Zeus shrugged and zapped some divine energy at the remote control, causing it to fly into his outstretched hand. He pressed play and reclined his armchair to a 45-degree angle. As he settled back into the soft cushions, he muttered under his breath, 'Least she could have done was got me a beer before she left.'

2

Trouble at the Trove

HERA WANDERED UP NORTON STREET, PAST THE ITALIAN CAFES AND expensive leather-shoe stores, onto Parramatta Road. She did like this area of the city, known locally as Little Italy, full of the descendants of her adopted people. Although Hera would always think of herself as Greek, she had a special fondness for the crazy Latins who had hijacked her and rechristened her Juno.

Zeus may have remained loyal in his heart to Greek Olympus, but Hera appreciated her role as the warrior queen to the Roman Empire. Without them her fame would not have spread as far or as strongly. And then where would they be?

She turned the corner and stepped into a small convenience store, where the man behind the counter nodded at her knowingly. She nodded back and walked to the long line of fridges that filled the rear wall. She selected the one containing fresh fruit and vegetables. Many people might think a fridge in a suburban convenience store was an odd place for an interdimensional portal, but it had proven a rather clever choice. Humans never thought to question why there were so many of these stores all over the world and why any of them would bother stocking healthy options when all they ever sold to their human customers were doughnuts and cheap coffees. As Hera pushed the shelves aside, the interior lit up with a golden light, and she stepped through the dimly glowing portal and took the left-hand turn into the Trove.

The Trove of Existence was an intimidating place. White-clad employees sat in a white room behind almost invisible glass desks, tapping information into state-of-the-art touch technology screens. The only thing that wasn't white or transparent were the flashing LED numbers that lined the walls in vivid green, red and yellow – calculating the current faith levels.

Hera knew her name would not be appearing on the main wall. That sacred space was dominated by the current gods – Johnnies-come-lately who had no need to use the Lore Courts to ensure they had enough existence credits to live a decent life.

Not that she, or any of the major Olympians, were that poor yet. Their fame was strong enough to give them enough credits to live comfortable lives. Only her brother Hades seemed to use the courts to help boost his income. But then, he had never been any good with money.

The lights flashed green and numbers increased as more people were born or converted into specific faiths. Christianity, Buddhism and Islam were still up, but it was clear their numbers were dropping from the peaks of years past.

The Hindu gods took up a wall all on their own and seemed to be trading quite well – Ganesha particularly seemed to have gained points overnight, but then, being the Hindu god of luck made him a popular choice, particularly with all the internet gambling that was going on nowadays.

Hera was greeted with a smile as she approached the teller. A tall elf stood at the window, looking at her serenely.

'Gondaline, is that you?' Hera asked.

'Sure is.'

'But you look so different? You've grown about six feet.'

The elven girl shrugged. 'Human fashion.'

Hera nodded, understanding. Some of the lower mythical creatures were much more at the mercy of changes in human imagination than the more ancient and higher-level gods and demigods. She remembered the vampire transformation of the 19th century when what were essentially ugly, lumbering blood-sucking corpses suddenly turned into tall Byronesque aristocrats overnight. Although they definitely smelt better, she found their romantic melancholy and newly inspired narcissism more distasteful than their previous ghoulish grave robbing.

'Are you here to make a deposit or a withdrawal?' Gondaline asked.

'Withdrawal,' Hera replied.

Gondaline tapped some numbers into a large computer in front of her and nodded admiringly. 'Would you need to break one of the bonds?'

'No, no,' Hera replied, 'just some of the floating credit will do. Say 2000.'

Gondaline nodded, tapped the computer a couple more times and then handed Hera a tablet for her to breathe into.

Identification had been one of the biggest issues when the credit system had been envisaged. Mythical creatures, gods and goddesses had so many possible incarnations, names or appearances, plus so many had chameleon and shape-shifting powers, that picture identification had proven impossible.

It had taken the Norse goddess Freya to work out that the living breath was the only sure way to determine who was who, as this was the source of all creation and the only distinction between the mythical creatures throughout the universe.

The tablet bleeped appreciatively and Gondaline smiled as Hera felt the power within her rise. The usual creaks and painful twinges that she had put up with over the past few years disappeared.

Hera focused the power within her and her stature rose, her face started to glow, the lobby around her crackled with power.

'Wow,' Gondaline breathed.

Hera smiled, rejuvenated. She really should remember that she was a goddess every now and then. She had forgotten what it felt like to be a deity.

'Would you like to sign up for our remote banking today, Queen Hera?' Gondaline asked as Hera handed back the tablet. 'It would save you from coming into the Trove.'

Hera shook her head. Why were these places always trying to force customers out of their premises? She liked coming in; it was one of the few outings she had now that the banshees had shut down their monthly bingo afternoons due to noise complaints.

But before Hera could voice her disinterest in the many so called benefits of the online existence banking system, the walls around the Trove started flashing wildly. Gondaline looked over at the Existence Point Indices with concern. The numbers were fluctuating quickly; belief points were starting to go off the charts.

'What's going on?' Hera asked.

'I don't know,' the elf responded as she furiously tapped at her computer. 'It's probably nothing, but human belief has suddenly jumped up. We don't usually see this level of awe and fear.'

Hera watched as existence points rose quickly across the boards.

Gondaline's lovely face creased into a mask of worry. 'Usually fluctuations like this are caused by one of the monsters leaving Monsters' Realm and kicking up their points with a sighting or two, but this – it's in the wrong region for a Nessie or Bigfoot event. It's in the middle of nowhere and, as far as we have been advised, the Nature Goddess Collective have no natural disasters planned anywhere near there for another few weeks.' Gondaline tapped more urgently into her computer. 'It looks like it could be an unscheduled foundational event – linking to instinctual pagan beliefs.'

She tapped again, even more worried.

'It has to be a monster attack,' she said, frowning, 'but they wouldn't break the treaty, surely.'

Hera noticed a number of the Trove employees were looking decidedly nervous as a centaur appeared from the back offices. He was wearing a pressed white shirt with a silk tie and an expensive Armani coat on his human torso, his horse body beneath glossy and shiny. A gold identity tag hanging around his neck identified him as Chiron, manager of the Trove.

'Right,' he said, 'we've identified the problem. It seems a number of migrant workers were turned to stone in a small field in remote Australia.'

A wave of trepidation moved through the room as the implications set in.

'We've issued a media release through our contacts, so no need to worry. Social media will be flooded with reports that it's simply a prank by a contemporary artist or television magician. Points should soon settle to normal levels.'

The centaur noticed Hera standing by the desk and made a beeline towards her. 'Queen Hera,' he said, bowing.

'Chiron,' Hera greeted her old friend 'It wasn't a contemporary art prank though, was it?'

The centaur shook his head and looked around cautiously. 'No, madam, it was not.'

He pulled Hera gently aside so his employees wouldn't overhear his next words. 'We'll have to investigate, of course, but it certainly looks like an old-fashioned petrification. I haven't seen anything like this since Medusa was, well, you know. Of course, that can't be it. She'd never leave Monsters' Realm; would she?'

Chiron's naturally ruddy complexion was turning a concerning shade of white. All the old gods and creatures remembered a time when heroes and monsters terrorised the human realm. Dragons flew the skies, incinerating armies of men, and many-faced demons tempted ignorant villagers into darkened caves to be killed, sacrificed and eaten. But none of that had really threatened the immortal realm – not the way Medusa and her gorgon glare did.

Chiron turned to Hera, 'You haven't heard anything, Ma'am, up in the higher orders?'

'Why would I know anything?' Hera snapped back. 'I'm a fallen goddess, not one of the decision makers these days.'

Chiron's body rippled as a shiver of fear raised across his back and hind legs.

'I'm sorry. I didn't mean any offence. It's just, well, it's a bad thing for us Greco-Roman creatures, isn't it, one of our ancient monsters out there terrorising the human realm. Odin and the Norse gods are always looking for an excuse to throw us off the Divine Governing Council, never mind the damage this could do to our standing in the mythological community.'

'Don't be silly. Medusa knows if she or either of her sisters left Monsters' Realm they would be killed on sight. It's part of the treaty. I'm sure it's something else entirely. Probably a man-made weapon or something.'

Chiron nodded curtly. 'Maybe, but we all know what happened the last time the power of Medusa got loose on the Mortal Realm. It didn't end well for anyone, particularly Atlas.'

'I'm sure everything will be fine. I've got to go.'

But as Hera bustled out onto the street, she knew everything wasn't going to be fine; it seemed the gorgon sisters had been right. And she hadn't acted fast enough. Medusa's name was already being mentioned and Chiron's suggestion that this might result in the Greek deities being removed from the divine governing bodies was, in Hera's opinion, the least of their worries.

3

The Courts of Lore

HERA STEPPED OFF THE BUS AND HEADED TOWARDS THE GREATER Sydney courts, but instead of making her way through the metal detectors and security guards, she turned down a maintenance corridor and walked up to a refreshment vending machine. She pushed the button for Healthy Juice and the machine sprang open slightly. She checked both ends of the corridor before pulling the door of the cleverly disguised portal, just big enough to slip through to her real destination – the ancient Court of Lore.

Once inside the mystical court building, she checked a nearby sign advertising the current cases and their corresponding court numbers and presiding judges. Finding what she wanted, she hurried down into the depths of the court.

She entered the large, rowan-wood chamber and saw her stepdaughter Athena, goddess of wisdom, justice and truth, sitting at the front of the impressive courtroom as two applicants aggressively argued their claims to some disputed credits.

Hera was not surprised to see Hades sitting in the defendant's chair as a forked-tongued Lucifer tried, without much effect, to claim, *for the hundredth time*, that Athena, as an Olympian goddess, was too biased to oversee a case involving her uncle.

Athena eyed him coldly and flicked a look at her watch in a gesture of annoyance, then turned back to Lucifer and smiled coldly.

'I have told you before, Lucifer, I am the Goddess of Justice – I cannot be unfair; I was not imagined that way. Much as you cannot be trustworthy nor kind-hearted based on your own human design. Now present your case or be gone – I have many other cases to hear today and I am not of a mind to put up with any more of your grandstanding.'

Lucifer stamped his cloven hoof and ruffled his papers, but he knew better than to keep pressing the issue.

'Fine,' he said, handing the chubby little dragon, who acted as court clerk, an old scroll he had fished out of his pile of paperwork. 'I refer you to case Satan v Hades 1109AD. The concept of Hell, although clearly derivative of the kingdom of Hades as an underworld, where the dead go in the afterlife, has some key conceptual differences to the creation of the Christian Hell. Namely, that Hades has never been a pure place of torment and torture.'

Lucifer smiled proudly at the distinction and then continued. 'Furthermore, the introduction of brimstone, sulphur and the substitution of the giant three-headed flame-breathing dog with demons and imps was further evidence of specific changes in the originating work to determine that Hell, and the new mythology inspired by it, was essentially a new work and therefore generated its own existence capital.'

Athena consulted the scroll handed to her by the dragon clerk and nodded solemnly.

Lucifer turned with a theatrical flourish. 'Not to mention Lucifer AKA Satan AKA Lord of the Flies AKA Beelzebub has a far more dynamic and interesting personality than boring old Hades.'

'Objection!' called Hades, standing up with dignified annoyance. 'There was no mention in that previous ruling that Lucifer was more dynamic or interesting.'

Athena waved her hand. 'Sustained. I would advise Lucifer to get to the point before I lose patience completely.'

'Of course, dear lady,' Lucifer replied simperingly, 'The basis of my case is that, as pursuant to the ruling in the case previously mentioned, the location of Hades and Hell are distinctly different territories and by association the person of Hades and myself are also neither connected nor required to pool existence points.'

'Yes, yes,' Athena replied, 'I know the ruling. In what way has it been broken?'

'It has come to my attention that my congregation of believers have been encouraged to utter the words "Go to Hades" instead of the traditional "Go to Hell" as was their usual curse. I believe Hades himself has purposely taken pains to encourage this practice in an effort to steal the existence points generated by such utterances.'

Hades spoke up again. 'I deny that claim!'

'Please wait your turn,' Athena told her uncle. 'You will have a chance to speak in a moment.'

She turned her attention back to Lucifer, who was again rifling through his pile of paperwork. 'As for this claim, how an entity chooses to create or increase belief in themselves is, as you know, Lucifer, outside the jurisdiction of this court. As long as they don't break the Great Lores, I can only make a judgement on whether the existence credits generated are going to the correct recipient.'

'That is my point,' Lucifer cried. 'Clearly "Go to Hades" is a variation of the term "Go to Hell". And as such its meaning is based traditionally in the Lore of Hell, not Hades. Hades is neither a place of torture nor torment specifically, so it would be meaningless for humans to curse each other to go there.'

'Perhaps they were wishing each other a nice trip,' Hades commented mildly.

Lucifer turned around sharply, flames sparking around his hooves.

'You know that's not what they meant. It's a curse and so it properly belongs to my lore.' He turned back to face Athena. 'I should be getting all the existence credits for it. Not him!'

Athena turned to Hades. 'And you want to dispute this claim?'

'Obviously,' Hades replied lethargically. 'They say Hades; my name and my underworld are Hades. Those points are clearly mine.'

Athena nodded. 'Very well. I will make a ruling based on the facts at hand. It is clear that the precedent specifically severed ties between Hades and Hell and as such no pooling of points is automatic without separate agreement between the parties. It is also clear that Hades, as a trademark, is being used in this situation. And the use of the word Hades is copyrighted to – Hades.'

Lucifer looked as though he might throw a fit but Athena cooled him with a warning glance and he sat, sullenly silent.

'However, it is also true that the lore states that Hell is a place of torment and torture exclusively, while Hades, although there are areas of unpleasantness, is not specifically branded as a place of suffering. It was simply the destination for souls after death where they can rest or be punished based on their life behaviours.

'Therefore, I conclude that when the intention behind the word "Hades" is used to imply suffering and damnation, those points will be accrued to Lucifer, but where the context of the statement is made in jest or does not imply a curse, then the points will be awarded to Hades. That is the ruling. That is the new Lore.'

Lucifer beamed, happy to have won his point if not the entire case. Hades, however, continued to sit, idly playing with his pen.

He cocked a single eyebrow towards Athena and asked casually, 'And when the word Hell is used in the context of a joke or a place that the originator does not believe in, such as when uttered by, let's say...' he paused for effect '...*atheists*, then does the same lore apply?'

Lucifer suddenly looked panic stricken. A large chunk of his existence points came directly from atheists, who loved talking about how they were happy to go to Hell if the Christian right-wingers weren't going to be there.

Athena nodded. 'I see your point. Yes, that would be a fair use of the ruling,' she said, making a note on the paper in front of her.

'But – but that's not fair!' Lucifer jumped up from his chair, scorching the table with his uncontrolled emotional display.

'I'm sorry, Lucifer, but you opened the door,' Athena replied, stamping the ruling with the Lore seal and shuffling the papers into the pile of completed hearings. 'You wanted to redefine the context and I have done so. You do not get any existence points from references to Hell made in jest. Case closed; court is adjourned.'

Lucifer twirled on his hooves and stamped out of the room, singeing Hera's clothes as he stormed past and slammed the door behind him.

Hades stood up and, seeing Hera, greeted her with a grin. 'When will that little upstart learn that all his tricks were mine first?'

Hera smiled back at him and nodded. No doubt the battle between Lucifer and Hades would continue into round two, but for now her brother could enjoy his victory.

Athena, seeing her stepmother, excused herself and stepped down onto the courtroom floor. She hugged Hera warmly. 'You seem well,' she said. 'Credit withdrawal?'

'Yes, I thought I should treat myself.'

Athena smiled but Hera could see the concern on her face.

'Something's wrong,' Athena stated.

'Why would you think there is something wrong just because I spend a few existence points on myself?'

Athena shook her head. 'It's not that. I can read your face. I rarely see you worried, but you're worried now.'

Hera considered assuring her stepdaughter that she was not upset in the least, but this was the Goddess of Truth she was talking to. Athena could spot any lie, so there really was no point in trying to pretend that she was not a tiny bit rattled.

'Have you heard about the incident on the Mortal Realm this morning?' Hera asked.

'No, I've been in court all day? What's happened?'

Hera glanced at Hades, who was trying to look like he wasn't eavesdropping.

'Can we go into your chambers? We need to talk privately.'

'Yes, of course,' Athena replied, her curiosity clearly sparked.

Hera smiled. One way to get Athena interested was to give her a potential problem to solve. There was nothing the Goddess of Wisdom liked better than to give advice and show off her remarkable reasoning skills. Skills that Hera had more than once found very helpful indeed.

Athena led her stepmother into the inner chambers as Hades watched them leave, his eyebrows raised quizzically, but there was no way Hera was going to let Hades anywhere near the information she had to share.

4

The Goddess of Wisdom

ONCE IN THE CHAMBERS, HERA CLOSED THE DOOR AND ATHENA GOT out two glasses and a bottle of organic nectar. Hera accepted her drink gratefully and sank into the overstuffed Chesterfield that stretched across the side of Athena's beautifully decorated office. Power-up or not, Hera was several thousand years old and her feet were starting to ache.

'So, spill it?' Athena said.

'It's probably nothing. But there was a mystical attack in the Mortal Realm this morning.'

'Oh dear,' Athena replied. 'Who was it? Are the lizard people making a play to become a proper religious entity again?'

Hera shook her head. 'It looks like it could have been a gorgon attack.'

Athena's face became a mask of worry and concern. Hera knew Athena's attachment to the monsters of the Greek pantheon, but the gorgons were of particular importance to her. They had a history, so to speak.

'Medusa's not aggressive. She has always acted only in defence of herself,' Athena said firmly.

Hera nodded. 'Maybe, but the gorgon's gift is pretty specific. There aren't many creatures given that power. I mean, a basilisk could be responsible I suppose, but they were declared extinct centuries ago. Long before you pushed through the PMCA.'

The Preservation of Mythical Creatures Act, or PMCA, had been Athena's pet project for centuries and she had been extremely proud when it finally got passed through the EBCU in 1876, although it didn't really stop most of the jackasses in the Divine Realm having monster-hunting parties and ordering phoenix under glass for their pantheon revival parties. The EBCU tried to enforce it, but when you can't prove a creature exists, it can be fairly tricky to try to protect it.

'Yes, the basilisks are long gone,' Athena replied sadly. 'But it couldn't be a gorgon; they never leave Monsters' Realm.'

'That's not completely true,' Hera said. 'The sisters were on the Mortal Realm today.'

'The sisters? You mean the gorgon sisters?' Athena frowned. 'They know they have to get special permission to leave their realm. They could have been smited on sight!'

Hera nodded, impatient that this was the part Athena had fixated on. 'It was hours ago, before the human attack, and anyway, I don't think it was them.'

Athena's frown deepened and Hera felt the tiny electric sparks in the frontal cortex of her brain that indicated the Goddess of Truth was beginning to root around in there.

'Why?'

Hera sharpened her defences against Athena's powers. Although she intended to tell the truth, she wasn't sure yet if she was going to tell all of it, so best not to make Athena too suspicious. In any case, it was damn rude of Athena to just assume that there was a possibility of dishonesty. Athena claimed she couldn't help it, that the power to pick up on lies was automatic and just as upsetting to her as the people she probed. Hera knew that was true: just as Athena could almost always pick up on a lie, she could also never effectively tell one.

'Because... well, they came to the Mortal Realm to ask for my help.'

'The gorgons were at your house, and you didn't think to report this?' Athena replied, her face clouding with righteous fury.

'Not all of them. Just Stheno and Euryale. They weren't there long,' Hera said, then noting Athena's expression, she added, 'I'm not going to go running to the EBCU over every little thing.'

Athena, still ruffled, calmed slightly. 'Okay, well, it's done now. What help did they need?'

Hera thought again about lying to her stepdaughter. It wouldn't look good to admit that she may have known that Medusa's head had gone missing a good few hours before the incident had happened. But even if Hera's defences hid the actual lie, Athena would know she was being deceived and the fact was, she needed Athena onside. There was nothing for it but to reveal the truth.

'They said someone had stolen Medusa's head and they wanted my help to find it.'

Athena's reaction was not what Hera had expected. Instead of shocked or angry, Athena looked hurt.

'Why didn't they come to me?' she asked.

Hera rolled her eyes. 'I think they might see you as part of the system, Athena.'

Athena started. 'How could they think such a thing? I have done everything for them!'

Of course Athena would think she would be the first point of call for any monster in trouble. After all, it was Athena who had campaigned for the Mythical Creature Preservation Acts, as well as being instrumental in creating the laws that allowed Monsters' Realm to be kept in monster hands and not turned into a supernatural theme park, which was what many of the other deities had lobbied for.

But the fact was, Athena was a part of the system that still actively discriminated against non-deity creatures. Maybe not as bad as the EBCU, or the Magic Suppression Bureau, or the old boys club that was the Divine Governing Council, but the Courts of Lore was still a place where those with divine heritage could find more justice and support than those without.

Indeed only moments ago Athena had been more worried that the gorgons had not filled in the required paperwork to get to the Mortal Realm, than about what may have prompted them to ignore those rules. The goddess may not be quite as bad as the paper pushers at the EBCU, but she did believe in and enforce a lot of the bureaucracy that made being a mythical creature or deity a lot more complicated than it had been in years past. Plus, she and the gorgon sisters did have a bit of a chequered history. Medusa may have asked to be turned into a hideous-faced monster, but, as far as Hera knew, the sisters had been given little choice in the matter as Athena had overzealously transformed the entire trio into serpent-haired gorgons.

Athena shook her head and regained her composure.

'So, what did you do when they told you?'

'Nothing. I told them to go away.'

Athena couldn't hide her genuine dismay as she slammed her fist down on her desk, startling the sleeping owl perched on the edge of the chair behind her. The bird screeched irritably and Athena immediately soothed it, stroking its golden feathers and offering it a small slice of beef that she pulled from a nearby drawer.

The bird settled and regarded both goddesses with wide, slightly creepy amber eyes.

'Look, I thought they were being dramatic,' Hera replied in an effort to get Athena back onside. 'You know what they're like. Medusa is always losing her head. The collar hasn't fit properly since she started Weight-Watchers and dropped all those pounds a few years ago.'

Athena pursed her lips. 'Except a group of petrified farm workers seems to suggest the sisters weren't making it up, don't they?'

'All right, maybe I made a misjudgement. Can't be helped. The point is, what do we do now?'

'We?'

Hera didn't reply and her stepdaughter sighed heavily and sat on her large leather desk chair. The owl hopped onto Athena's shoulder without taking its startling eyes off Hera.

'Monsters' Realm is the safest in all the divine worlds,' Athena said finally.

Hera pulled her eyes from the owl's gaze and looked at Athena, who was doodling on a yellow legal pad. A sure sign her mind was in problem-solving gear. Hera smiled quietly to herself. It seemed Athena was going to help after all.

'It would take someone with a lot of power to get in and out of there unseen – and uneaten. And why would someone risk it?' Athena continued, noting down the words *Monsters' Realm, security* and *risk* on her pad, followed with a trio of question marks. 'Especially if all they planned to do was zap a couple of innocent fruit pickers. It doesn't make any sense.'

Hera shrugged. 'Maybe the fruit pickers weren't the real target. There is nothing, in any realm, as powerful as a gorgon's glare if you wanted to go after a god.'

Athena looked up. 'You think that's the end game?'

'Possibly. There's a lot of bad blood in the Divine Realm, supernatural idiots jostling for power. Old and new gods could easily see Medusa's gift as a way to get rid of some of the competition.'

'So why go after humans?'

'Target practice. It's what I would do if I had just found a new weapon. Test it out, see what it could do.'

Athena frowned. 'You would have to be pretty stupid or desperate to go after a gorgon though. There are much easier options to start a holy war.'

'But any as effective?' Hera asked.

Athena thought for a moment. 'Could the sisters have petrified those humans? As a way to make you pay attention to their concerns? Punish you for ignoring them when they came for help?'

Hera shook her head. 'I can't see how it would benefit them. They need this to be secret. If the other deities discover that Medusa's power is loose or being used by someone, well, that's all that would be needed to exempt the gorgons from the Preservation Act and give the deities and the EBCU the excuse they want to hunt the sisters down and kill them as a divine menace. Euryale and Stheno would be signing their own death warrants, as well as Medusa's.'

'Poor monsters,' Athena said. 'Why can't everyone just leave them in peace?'

Athena got up and poured herself another long glass of Ouzo. 'Who am I to talk though, right? Everything bad that has happened to them is because of me.'

'Bad things were happening for Medusa long before you got involved and you know it. Without you she would have been a victim of Poseidon or any other male who wanted to victimise her for as long as she was deemed desirable. We all know beauty can be a curse for a human woman. You did what you did to save her.'

At the sound of Poseidon's name, Athena winced, and then slumped down on the sofa next to Hera. The rivalry between Poseidon and Athena, created when Zeus had awarded the patronage of the state of Athens to his newly-discovered daughter rather than, as he had promised, to the god of the sea, had always saddened Athena. It was not her fault and Hera knew how hard she had tried in those first few centuries to mend fences between herself and Poseidon.

But the sea god's animosity had only grown stronger as the Athenians openly embraced their new female patron over the increasingly jealous

Poseidon, giving the impressive young goddess power over justice, war, peace, truth and wisdom. Soon this goddess, who had started as nothing more than a pain in Zeus' temple, was a more powerful deity than Poseidon had ever been, which was why he took every opportunity to attack her temples and followers, and why he had singled out Medusa for his brutality and viciousness, as no one else was so devoted to Athena.

It was Poseidon's envy that had forced Athena to do what she did to protect her devout priestess, but Hera knew Athena still felt guilt over Medusa's treatment. Which was why she had moulded the Gorgon's face into her shield, a promise to protect the gorgons, and other monsters, against the injustice of the mystical and mortal realms.

'You and I both know Poseidon wouldn't have let her alone. If you hadn't saved her, he would have attacked her again and again.' Hera reassured her stepdaughter. 'You made the best decision you could.'

Athena nodded and downed the rest of her drink as Hera stroked her arm soothingly, unsettling the owl, who flew off Athena's shoulder and settled again on the chair.

'She was just an innocent girl who loved me so much she dedicated her life to my service. He treated her like nothing but a tool to use against me,' Athena said. 'And I let him do it.'

'Maybe. Or maybe he targeted her because he is a god and that is what they do. Women are merely playthings to them. We both know that. The only real protection for a human female is to become a monster.'

Athena nodded. 'Yes, well, Medusa isn't just a plaything now. Or even just a monster. She's a weapon. So, while I may have saved her in the short term, I didn't do much to take the target off her back.'

Athena looked at her empty glass and grimaced, tossing it onto the floor where it shattered, but both goddesses, focused on the task at hand, ignored the glass explosion.

'I can't let her be victimised all over again,' Athena said. 'First Poseidon, then Perseus and now, well, whomever this is. We have to help her.'

Hera smiled, just as she had hoped, the Goddess of Justice was fully onboard.

'Okay, so who would know how to take Medusa from Monsters' Realm, and have a reason to do so?' Hera asked. 'Perseus?'

'Percy couldn't get near Monsters' Realm. There's an *Eat on Sight* order against him across the whole area.'

Hera considered this and nodded,

Athena went to her computer and tapped it into life.

'Although,' she said, looking at the screen, 'I've noticed some of the deity stats over the past few weeks and Percy has had a bit of a power surge recently. Those books and movies about him, they may have given him enough to think he could attempt it. Maybe make a move up the ladder?'

'He would have a long way to go. Perseus is basically two steps up from an imbecile. He only got her head last time because she was unprotected, in an isolated cave and asleep when he attacked.'

Athena frowned. 'You know, when I found Medusa's head the first time, he had it on a lazy Susan in the middle of his dining table as a conversation piece for guests. Blindfolded, but still! So, you're right: the man is a moron – but a lucky moron who loves to court danger.'

'Maybe it isn't an Olympian at all,' Hera said.

'Oh, it's an Olympian,' Athena replied. 'Who else would think of it?'

Hera voiced the thought that had been niggling at the back of her mind since her visit to the Trove. 'You don't think the head could be used against the reigning gods, do you?'

Hera could tell by Athena's expression that the idea had also occurred to her as well.

'The Great Lores have been working well for centuries. Why make a stupid ploy like that now?' Athena said, 'I mean, yeah, the reigning gods' powers are slightly waning, but they still have more than all of the pagan gods combined.'

Hera nodded again, lost in thought. It didn't really make logical sense, but then a lot of deities were completely illogical. Everyone knew the Divine Realm was full of grudges and petty squabbles that had more than once manifested horrible outcomes in the mortal realm.

Few of the gods were above vying with the others to maintain or wrestle power or settle a score. Those disagreements, conflicts and, in the worst cases, holy wars, not only had the potential to change divine regimes in the higher realms but usually had devastating effects on the unsuspecting humans who stubbornly believed these disasters were some sort of punishment for their own misdemeanours.

This continuing belief by humans that the Divine Realm had any interest in them at all was inexplicable to Hera, since most gods or goddesses had rarely, if ever, shown the least bit of concern for the welfare or point of view of their human creators. Gaia was the only one trying to look out for the creatures on Planet Earth, and look how they treated her – ignoring her repeated warnings that their general disregard for their natural environment, and the goddess who oversaw it, would result not in its death but their own.

To be fair, the disparaging view humans felt for the Earth Goddess was echoed by many of the deities as well. Most had stopped inviting her to any kind of social occasion, finding her veganism and consistent warnings about imminent environmental destruction not very conducive to successful dinner parties.

Also, unlike Gaia, most of the new gods agreed that increasing human populations was a good thing, as it helped cement their own existence. Each new human child could decide which of the competing gods to believe in and the more people who believed in you, the better your existence point balance became. It was simple economics really.

Many of the newer gods had doubled down on this, not just refusing to support a more sustainable human population but actually promoting unfettered procreation as part of their religious tenets. They may not actually care about the welfare of the citizens of the Mortal Realm, but most of the gods agreed that having a lot of them around was generally a good thing.

That was why, after several holy wars and clashes between deities resulted in massive human casualties, it was decided the gods needed a better way to deal with these conflicts, which would keep at least a reasonable number of their human creators alive. The Lore Courts were established by the wisest of the goddesses – Freya and Athena – and all deities agreed to use the courts as the first point of reconciliation for any personal conflict or existence point debate.

The goddesses had also decreed the Three Great Lores, which were ratified by the courts and garnered large penalties for trespass.

These lores were:

One: No deity or creature could harm or kill a classified god or goddess unless prescribed in a mortal scripture or mythology. Lower entities – such a monsters, heroes, demigods, fairies and mythical creatures – were forbidden to kill *any* deity under *any* circumstances and no more than two mortals per hundred years. Reigning gods could smite as many mortals as they liked, but only those who believed in them specifically and could not smite the believers of another religious deity.

Two: To stop any god or deity having too much undue influence in creating their own existence points, any communication from or appearances of current, past and emerging deities to humans must be enigmatic to the point of incomprehension and completely open to any and all kinds of interpretation.

Three: No divine entity could instigate a holy war or attack upon any existing deity who currently or previously was worshipped as a divine being by humankind. The only way a deity could take on primary power was through a majority of existence points generated by genuine human faith, and the only way one could be dethroned was through the rejection of the mortal fan-base in favour of a new entity.

Of course as time passed other rules started to become necessary, and a flourishing bureaucracy was born, which most deities and monsters found tiresome – but overall these three great lores had worked quite well for the past several hundred years. Sure there was the occasional infraction, including a recent tsunami that had been sparked by nothing more than a quarrel by two sea deities over an unpaid gambling debt, but overall mostly the Divine realms just got on with the business of being divine and monsters got on with being monsters and everything more or less went along quite well.

Not that the Lores had been warmly welcomed by all when they were first introduced. Unsurprisingly those who had at first opposed these rules were mainly gods of war and conflict, but they were mollified quite quickly on the discovery that humans were more than capable of instigating violence and genocide without any specific divine instruction. The fact they often then ascribed holy motivations to these acts of evil made the existence points for these deities all the more potent.

Surely it was unlikely therefore that any deity, old or new, would risk upsetting a balance of power that had worked well for thousands of years.

Athena also didn't seem convinced they were on the brink of a divine uprising. 'If it is an opening gambit in a new deity war, again I have to question, why attack humans? They must have known it would result in instant scrutiny.'

Hera waved her hand dismissively. She had never had much time for the disgusting flesh-and-blood creatures who crawled across every inch of the Mortal Realm. They were so fickle and ungrateful, picking up and dropping gods and goddesses at a whim. The minute they stopped revering her as the Queen of Olympus she stopped taking even the small amount of interest she had previously shown, and when they had opted to remove goddesses almost entirely from their religious beliefs, her disinterest turned into active dislike.

'I know you have a soft spot for them, Athena, but honestly if the objective is to break the third rule and start a full-on Holy war, then I doubt very much the perpetrator will care that about a few humans being turned to stone. It's already being covered up quite nicely by the EBCU as some art project or something. Those on the higher realms may claim they care about mortals but truly, they've always been more trouble than they're worth.'

Athena looked like she may have been about to argue, but Hera pushed her point home.

'Remember how they rewarded you and Prometheus for giving them fire? Dobbed you in to Zeus the first chance they got. You were lucky not to be on a mountain next to Prometheus getting your liver ripped out every day, too.'

'Yes, I always wondered why Zeus never punished me for that and made Prometheus pay so dearly.'

'Because Zeus knows how powerful you are, even now, and is terrified of you. Which is more than can be said for those humans you sacrificed everything for. Most of them don't even acknowledge you in that story at all any more, let alone appreciate how you still look out for them. Honestly, no other deity gives a toss about those irritating little mortals; not even the reigning gods bother with them that much, now that their religions have been established. Much as the humans insist on believing differently.'

'They can't help it, Hera; they are imperfect beings.'

'And they created imperfect gods, so they have to live with it,' Hera retorted, and Athena had to laugh.

'So, what do you want to do?' Athena asked.

'I want to just go home and put my feet up and binge *The Only Way Is Asgard* on Mystic TV,' Hera said. 'That's why I'm telling you. The gorgons should have come to you first, we both know it. It's you, not me who is the most capable goddess in all the realms. I'm sure you'll work something out.'

'Oh no you don't, Hera,' Athena said. 'Whatever their reasons the gorgons came to you, not me. So you are not dumping this. I'm happy to help you, but it's your responsibility. You didn't act quickly enough, so you are the one to help fix it.'

Hera had expected as much. She wished she had just ignored her conscience and gone home after the incident at the Trove. She wasn't going to get to see the season finale of *The Only Way Is Asgard* before it was spoiled on Facebook now.

'Okay, okay, we'll go to Monsters' Realm, ask a few questions. Maybe we'll get it sorted by dinner time.'

'Good,' Athena said. 'But just to be on the safe side, I'll reschedule my cases for the next week.'

Athena pulled over her huge diary and opened it to the current date.

'Four more hearings today, but nothing that requires me particularly,' she said, running her finger down the lines of court appointments. 'The leprechauns are still trying to claim existence credit for every Pride rainbow flag. They have an argument, it has been a literal pot of gold for a lot of companies who have adopted it. But I think Ma'at would be a better judge for that anyway.' She paused. 'I should probably be here when the "God is dead" case finally moves forward, though.'

Hera had heard about this case. The Christian god had been subpoenaed again after failing to turn up the last 12 times the case had been scheduled.

'Is it likely he'll show?'

Athena shook her head. 'No, not really. We've already issued a number of bench warrants. But without a *habeas corpus* we can't officially determine if he is deceased or just moving in very mysterious ways. Normally we would dismiss it, but the atheist delegates bringing the case are very persistent.'

Athena closed her appointment diary and smiled up at Hera. 'Ha, Atheists!'

The two women laughed.

The idea that these people, who believed in nothing, would have the gall to use agents within the divine lore courts to settle their dispute was both amusing and ironic. The newer gods sometimes worried about the existence of these disbelieving humans. It was true that if they really did manage to bring the others to their way of thinking they could destroy the Divine Realm and all who lived in it. But the savvier goddesses, who oversaw the Courts of Lore, knew that every single atheist at some point in their lives made reference to or pleaded with some god or another. They were in fact a valuable source of existence credit, if properly managed, as Hades' previous case had just so aptly demonstrated.

Athena picked up the crystal phone on her desk. 'Let me contact Ma'at to take over my cases and we can get going.'

5

The Realm of Monsters

As Hera and Athena stepped through the portal and onto the Monster's beach, a warm summer breeze drifted from the tranquil waters, which belied the razor-toothed creatures that swam in its depths. Neat, pastel-coloured houses lined the shore, many with cane garden sets turned towards the ocean, where reptilian-like sunbathers caught the last warm rays of the perpetually summer sun. One might expect Monsters' Realm to be chaotic, barren and violent, but actually it had won the Supernatural Tidy Realm Award the past two centuries running, something of which the citizenry was inordinately proud. Hera had always thought that, were it not for the small problem that most visitors would possibly be eaten, the realm could enjoy quite a thriving tourism industry. It certainly was one of the more pleasant environments in Hera's experience.

The monsters had worked out long ago that their best chance of survival was to stick together, so they pooled all their existence points and created their own island realm. Humans may be fickle in their gods, but their belief in monsters seemed to be surprisingly resilient, so Monsters' Realm became one of the most beautiful and well-resourced realms in all the dimensions. It helped that if there was ever a belief deficit, they need only send Nessie out for a swim in the loch during tourist season or have Bigfoot appear in a particularly grainy photograph to spike them back up to lucrative levels.

The older monsters rarely had to bother themselves with appearing to humans anymore – happily retired, they could focus their attention on their baking and gardens.

The many-headed Hydra, watering her peonies, turned one of her heads towards Athena and Hera and, after squinting for a moment, waved to them both in recognition. Unlike many of the other worlds, Monsters' Realm felt no need for guardians or custom officers at their portal entrances. They had much more effective ways of ensuring unwelcome visitors regretted their intrusion upon the isle.

'Why, Madam Hera and young Athena,' Hydra's first head addressed them directly cheerily.

'How lovely to see you.' Hydra's second head added.

'Are you here for the Tidy Realm presentation?' a third enquired.

'Oh congratulations, we heard about that,' Athena replied, expertly acknowledging all six heads with her gaze. 'But actually, we are here to see the gorgon sisters.'

A cloud passed over Hydra's faces and several of her heads shook at once. 'Terrible business that. I have offered her one of mine, you know, but the sisters say Medusa only wants her own head. It must be hard, having just the one.'

'The monsters here know the head has gone missing?' Hera asked, surprised. So much for the gorgons keeping it a secret.

'Oh yes, dear. Not much stays a secret in Monsters' Realm.'

'When did you find out?' Hera enquired.

'Oh, I helped the sisters look for it when they first realised it was missing. Yesterday, I think. Thought it might have been misplaced, you know; she does that sometimes.'

'Yes,' Hera agreed.

'But that business with the humans, well, that kind of indicates otherwise, doesn't it?' Hydra's fifth head remarked shrewdly, eyeing Athena and Hera.

Hera grunted noncommittally but Athena's interest was obviously piqued.

'What do you think happened?'

The Hydra considered this for a moment, the six heads looking at each other a little nervously, as if deciding which should speak first. It was finally Head Number Six that broke the silence.

'Hate to say it, but we think someone stole it.'

'Definitely,' agreed Head Number Four.

Hera noticed a look of disagreement on Head Number Three and addressed that head directly.

'But you don't think so?'

'Oh, yes,' Hydra's third head responded, startled. 'Must have been, of course. But security here is tight. The werewolves alone can sniff out any intruder from 1000 feet away. I can't see how they could have got on and off our island without tripping some kind of alarm. And we aren't slack here at the portal gates; one of us would have seen someone sneaking in, no one gets past us.'

'But it was definitely stolen,' the fourth head repeated in a determined way.

'Oh yes,' the third said quickly. 'Yes, no doubt, but *how* is the tricky thing.'

The other heads nodded in agreement, all looking slightly uneasy at the implications of their home being breached by outsiders who had somehow managed to escape with their lives.

'Are you here to help the gorgons find it?' Hydra's first head asked, expertly changing the direction of the conversation.

'We just have a few questions,' Athena answered smoothly.

'You do know none of us had anything to do with it. There's no reason for you or the other deities to come down here with torches and lightning strikes.'

'Of course not,' Athena said quickly. 'No one in the Divine Realm is even thinking of doing such a thing, I assure you.'

The Hydra's heads still seemed somewhat suspicious, but a few of them smiled tightly before turning back to the garden. The third head, however, continued to look at the goddesses and once the others turned away, she extended herself towards Hera.

'No one here had anything to do with it. No one,' she snarled, urgently.

Athena and Hera nodded. 'We only want to help. You have nothing to fear from us,' Hera reassured her.

'If you really do want to help, then find it quickly. The sooner Medusa's head is back here the better it is for everyone.'

'We will,' Athena said. 'You have my word.'

The third head relaxed and nodded. Athena's word meant something, even in this realm. 'Okay, that's good enough for me. And on your way up to the gorgon cave, mind you avoid the yeti; he's in a filthy mood at the moment. Thinks the werewolves have given him fleas.'

'Thanks for the heads-up,' Athena replied and was rewarded with a disgusted look from two of the heads, although Number Three seemed to enjoy the pun.

As the two goddesses walked up the main street, Athena shook her head. 'I've never seen the Hydra scared, but she definitely looked and sounded nervous.'

Hera shrugged. 'Can you blame her? She's the main gatekeeper of the portal and someone got past all of her eyes. Whatever way this plays out, it's bad publicity for Monsters' Realm. Either someone here is responsible – which is bad; or someone from one of the other realms, possibly a mortal, breached their security and got away with attacking one of the most powerful creatures here – which is worse.'

Athena nodded. 'Whatever the truth, it doesn't take much to get a paranoid group of entitled beings to scapegoat those who are different. These creatures may be powerful, but we both know they couldn't withstand the might of the whole Divine Realm if the gods did decide to try and eradicate them.'

'That's the only reason I am helping out on this damn fool errand,' Hera remarked.

'What, the stone farmers weren't enough of a reason?' Athena asked.

Hera gave her a withering look. 'They're just humans, but monsters, they deserve a bit of justice.'

The gorgons' cave was a way up Yeti Mountain and required a bit of extreme mountaineering to reach. Yet again Hera cursed the old Greeks for not giving her the specific power of flight. It would come in handy so very often. She struggled up the hillside, catching her hem on some brambles on the way up.

Maybe she should mount a case in the Court of Lore that the humans hadn't specifically said that she couldn't fly, because really, she was way too old for all this tramping about. But even if she won such a case, the angels got quite stroppy if non-winged creatures came into their airspace. The *Superman versus Archangel Gabriel* court case had ended with both sides being quite literally battered and bruised, and even now the predetermined flight paths were routinely breached by both parties. A few bramble scratches and some shortness of breath probably wasn't such a bad thing compared to going up against that kind of legal bunfight.

Once she caught her breath, she realised how out of shape she was, even with her recent power-up. She hadn't been like this when they all lived on Mount Olympus. She had been able to ascend and descend that peak without a qualm.

Athena, tall and lithe with the classic ancient Greek athletic body type, seemed to have no trouble at all navigating the steep slopes. She barely paused for breath and left Hera several lengths behind as she power walked up the steep slope, stopping at the first crest to check the read-out on her Fitbit.

As Hera struggled up a particularly rocky ledge, she almost lost her footing in surprise as a tremendous yell of fury resounded up and down the mountainside.

Hera instinctively held up her hands in a defensive pose, ready to smite anything that may fly out at her. Athena, a little more monster wise, simply scrambled up to the ledge and placed her hands over her ears as the noise steadily increased in pitch and volume. Hera, almost deafened, followed her stepdaughter's lead and managed to drown out a little of the roar.

'What is that?' she yelled to Athena, who shook her head, indicating that there was no use talking just yet. Then, as suddenly as it had started, the noise stopped. Hera gingerly removed her fingers from her ears and looked around, still trying to work out where the noise had come from.

Athena, seemingly unfazed, simply picked up her skirts and continued to power walk up the mountainside.

'What was that?' Hera asked again, jogging to keep up with her.

Athena shrugged. 'A new monster has just been created,' she said. Then she stopped and gave Hera a wry smile. 'Just be thankful it wasn't a new god – that can be extremely uncomfortable.'

Athena picked up her skirts again and continued on, Hera following cautiously behind, checking the shadows around her.

6

The Men Get Involved

IT HAD BEEN FIVE HOURS SINCE HERA HAD GONE OFF ON HER DAMN fool adventure and Zeus was getting grumpy. The microwave completely baffled him and the freezer had frosted over his pork chops, making them almost impossible to get out of the bloody thing.

He had tried using his lightning bolt to defrost the meat while still in the freezer and had almost electrocuted himself, so he resorted to chipping the meat out with a screwdriver, leaving his arm aching from the effort. Once freed the meat presented another problem. How was it to be cooked? Hera was the one who did the meals. The oven was a complete mystery to him, as were most of the machines and inventions of humankind.

He had always known how lucky he was to have Hera, even during all his infidelities and carry-on back when being a god of Olympus meant something. But since they had been down on the human plane, Hera's value to him had increased tenfold. Not only could she seemingly use these inexplicable human contraptions with ease, she was also perfectly able to navigate a shopping trolley down a crowded grocery aisle, patiently wait through the phone tree when they phoned the gas company without exploding the handset in frustration, and, best of all, she could cook this human drudge so that it tasted almost like ambrosia.

He had learnt to do none of these things.

Being immortal was a great thing when you were all powerful, living it large on the belief of all the civilised world, but when you suddenly had to survive on the existence points afforded by some dusty artworks, a few History Channel documentaries and the infrequent rise of a Greek or Roman-themed superhero movie, then eternal life could drag.

He knew he could use a bit more power than he did; they certainly weren't badly off, but he agreed with Hera that they had better learn to live on a fixed income now as their existence points were never going to rise to the dizzying heights they had once enjoyed. They would be wise to put aside enough each year, while there were still points coming in, to cover for the inevitable time when those existence points would, well, cease to exist.

Still, it was humiliating, living like this. Gradually he had stopped calling his old buddies, depressed at how far they had all fallen. Only Hades seemed to be living the good life now.

Oh yes, he and Hera were doing well enough, they had points in the bank and enough coming in every day. In fact, most of the family still had high profiles in the human world, thanks to the statues and mythologies littered across the globe. Enshrined now as artefacts and stories rather than conduits of divine wisdom and communication, sure, but points were points and he was grateful to have them at all.

Still, he ached for his old power back, wanted to feel what it was like to hold human life in his hands, able to destroy or create on a whim. And, of course, he missed the ladies.

Gone were the days when he could run off with any pretty young maiden that took his fancy, willing or otherwise, able to have his way with her until Hera inevitability found out and wrenched him back into their marital bonds. Oh, how good it had been then – no woman had the option to turn him down, even in the unlikely event they wanted to. Unlimited had been his power and now... now he couldn't remember the last time a member of the fair sex had even given him the time of day.

Okay, he could remember – it was last Tuesday, and a particularly delectable young woman had approached him at the bus stop, asking if he needed any help getting home. She had thought him a befuddled old man simply because he could not remember, for the life of him, which bus ran into Marrickville from Parramatta Road.

Humiliated, he had tried to feel up her skirt, to prove to her that he was a virile, sexy man, only to be beaten roundly about the head with her computer satchel as she yelled something about 'Me Too'!

A number of passers-by came to assist her and he soon found himself in a police cell charged with indecent conduct. Indecent conduct? How could anything a god wanted to do be indecent?

He had sat in that sterile, featureless cell for seven hours before a tight-mouthed Hera had finally appeared to bail him out. He had tried to explain that he hadn't really done anything, as he had been interrupted before he could really get any, but she refused to listen and was still not speaking to him. Boy, could that woman hold a grudge.

The memory was almost worse than the event itself and he decided to ignore the stupid divine lores about not using magical or divine energy on the mortal realm, and threw the chops into the oven, lighting it up with a few directed zaps of his divine lightning. The meat set alight and he slammed the oven door closed and listened smugly as the fire blazed within.

The telephone chirped in the living room and he wandered out and picked it up without checking the caller ID. It didn't really matter who it was; Zeus was bored and he would happily talk to anyone, even a telemarketer, if given half the chance.

It wasn't a telemarketer, though; it was worse. It was Hades.

'Hello, brother,' Hades' velvety voice purred. 'How are you doing?'

'Fine,' Zeus replied, immediately suspicious. Hades never called unless he wanted something, and these days Zeus had very little to spare.

'Good, good,' Hades responded, his purr turning into almost a coo.

Zeus' wariness raised a level. 'Listen, Hades, I don't have any time right now. I'm making dinner.'

'Oh, sorry to interrupt you, brother. I know how you like your food.'

Zeus could feel Hades' ridicule and couldn't help glancing down at his overhanging belly, which was squeezing out like fleshy toothpaste above his waistband. Hades himself was in perfect shape, toned and sun-washed like an Olympian god should be.

Now that Hades was no longer technically required to rule the Underworld, he was free to spend his days wherever he wished, and Hades showed a distinct preference for tropical islands, where he spent his days hanging out with the young, hip and trendy. He and his wife, Persephone, were part of the jet set now, enjoying all that came with it. Indeed, Hades bore virtually no resemblance to the pale, thin, cricket-like creature he had been back when the Olympians had ruled the known world.

How his existence points afforded such a lavish lifestyle, Zeus did not know. No doubt Hades was living on divine credit and at some point a troll would turn up at his door with a baseball bat and a demand for payment.

'Just wondering if you know why Hera was at the Lore Court today. She was talking to Athena about something?' Hades continued.

'No idea,' Zeus replied, noticing a burning smell coming from the kitchen.

'I thought I might have overheard something about Monsters' Realm,' Hades said.

Zeus, distracted by the smell, was barely listening. 'Yeah, yeah, probably. The gorgons were here earlier,' he said.

'Really?' Hades replied.

Zeus noticed the sudden change in Hades' tone. Something was brewing in that smart but amoral head of his brother's, and that usually meant trouble. Suddenly Zeus realised how odd it was that the gorgons should be in his house at all. He had been almost asleep, but he was sure it had been them. The hissing of those infernal snakes had awoken him from a nice dream. Hades' belief that Hera was interested in the Monsters' Realm and the visit of those snakey sisters had to be connected, although he wasn't sure how.

The smoke coming from the kitchen was getting denser now and the house was filling with the smell of burning meat, and melting plastic, but Zeus ignored it, focused on what scheme his brother may be getting into and how he could benefit from it.

'Why do you care where Hera goes?'

'I don't,' Hades answered quickly. 'It's just, well, there's been a few rumours about in the Lore Court today. One of the monsters mentioned that the gorgons were in a bit of bother again.'

Zeus wished he had paid attention when Hera and the gorgons had been talking. Now he would have to get the information out of Hades. The trick, he knew, was to ensure Hades didn't think Zeus wanted to know.

'Ah, well, you know Athena and Hera, thick as thieves, those two.'

'Hmm.' Hades paused for a moment. 'So Hera didn't say anything to you? Didn't mention what she might be doing in Monsters' Realm?'

Zeus slapped his head. Why hadn't he listened to her when she headed out this morning? He couldn't even remember what she had said. Did she mention Monsters' Realm? At the time he had been more worried about who was going to cook him dinner than where Hera was going to be instead of here, preparing it.

'You know communication between a husband and wife is sacrosact, Hades,' Zeus replied. 'I can't see why it matters to you anyway.'

'Don't be obtuse, brother, you know exactly why it matters to me; why it should matter to all of us. We both know the gorgon's glare is the only thing, on any plane, that can affect a deity. If Medusa is running around loose, we should all be pretty concerned.'

'Who told you she's loose?' Zeus asked suspiciously.

'Don't you pay attention to the Mystic News Channel?' Hades asked, exasperated. 'Humans were petrified this morning. Honestly, Zeus, I know you have very little interest in the world, but something must occasionally penetrate your beer haze!'

Zeus ignored the insult, pleased that his brother was getting rattled. A rattled Hades was easier to manipulate.

'That is concerning,' he said. 'But I'm sure it's just a contemporary art project or something. Nothing to be concerned about. Medusa would never leave Monsters' Realm. She knows the rules.'

'Maybe she didn't leave,' Hades said. 'Maybe someone took her.'

Zeus frowned. Now that was concerning. 'You think so?'

'I heard that the reigning gods have gone into hiding just in case,' Hades replied.

'Oh, don't be ridiculous, the new reigning gods have never come out of hiding to begin with. They aren't like we used to be,' Zeus snapped. 'We used to walk among our believers.'

'Yes, well, the older reigning gods are definitely worried. Shiva is ranting around like nobody's business. He wants the head destroyed once and for all and he's put a 500 million existence point bounty on it. Whoever finds it and destroys it, collects.'

Zeus frowned. Five hundred million existence points? That would be enough for any deity to live comfortably for centuries, even splurge a little – like on a new lightning bolt upgrade, for example. Zeus' mind started to tick over. Hades wouldn't have told him about the reward if he thought he could get it himself. His brother clearly felt he needed Zeus' help, and that help could be very, very expensive, if he played his cards right.

'So why are you calling me?'

'Because Hera obviously knows something. Listen, brother, if we pool our resources, we can have a pretty good shot at those points. You know Hera won't agree with any of this. She'll just cover for Medusa. Those lousy women always stick together. Do you want to spend the next thousand years in that crummy little semi because your wife is too soft hearted to do the smart thing?'

Zeus thought about it. Hera wasn't known for standing up for other women. If anything, he found it incredibly easy to redirect her justifiable rage against him and his infidelities into often unjustifiable rage against those who he had cheated on her with. She never seemed to care whether the women were willing participants or not. So, no doubt he could once again convince his wife to stop working for the gorgons' benefit and, as a faithful wife and mother, put all her energies into turning this situation to their, or more rightly, his advantage.

'I'll get back to you,' he said, hanging up the phone and punching in Hera's number. It was time to find out exactly where his wife was and what she was up to.

Behind him, the lightning fire, far too hot for any human appliance, continued to burn through the stove top and licked up towards the kitchen drapes and wooden cabinets.

7

Interview with a Monster

'YOU COULDN'T POSSIBLY SUSPECT US,' STHENO CRIED.

'Why wouldn't we?' Hera asked. 'The most obvious suspects are always family.'

Stheno hissed angrily and Athena smiled at her, apparently trying to diffuse the situation. 'What my stepmother means is that you asked us to investigate and that means leaving no stone unturned. Even if that means having to ask some uncomfortable questions.'

Stheno scrunched up her nose but settled back into her plush Chesterfield lounge chair and glared sullenly but silently through her dark sunglasses at the two goddesses sitting across from her. Athena and Hera perched on a less comfortable, but highly decorative, Italian gothic chaise, while Euryale, sporting more fashionable Dior sunglasses, stood behind her sister, gently massaging Stheno's tense shoulders with strong, taloned fingers.

'We didn't ask you to investigate,' Stheno said pointedly. 'We asked Hera. You shouldn't even be here.'

There was no love lost between Athena and Stheno, which, Hera thought, was why her stepdaughter was probably being way too nice in the face of some pretty blatant rudeness from the gorgon. She could understand the animosity, in a way, because it had been Athena who had turned Stheno and Euryale into gorgons. At Medusa's request, sure, but still without the two older sisters' specific permission. So it was unsurprising that Stheno still held a bit of a grudge about it.

Euryale, however seemed determined to keep the peace, calming her sister and serving them all Earl Grey tea in delicate, English teacups.

'Of course we want to do everything we can to help our sister,' she said, passing Hera an iced vovo.

Stheno threw Euryale a filthy glance but said nothing, shoving her own biscuits into her mouth and crunching on them noisily as her way to continue to show her displeasure.

Athena smiled again, balancing her cup of tea on her knees. Hera's cup was sitting on a lace doily on the back of a particularly well-placed petrified man who functioned as an effective coffee table.

'So, what can you tell us?' Athena prompted.

Euryale shrugged. 'We don't really know anything.'

'Oh for goodness sake!' Hera said impatiently. 'When did the head go missing, exactly?'

'Um, well, we noticed it gone yesterday,' Euryale said, sipping her tea gracefully. 'But Medusa may have been trying to find it by herself for a while, so I would say it may have actually disappeared on Monday.'

'Neither of us saw Medusa on Monday or Sunday,' Stheno said through a mouthful of biscuits. 'The Tidy Realm judging committee were doing a garden inspection and both Euryale and I had volunteered to help protect them from some of the less civilised monsters.'

'Okay,' Athena said, jotting down notes on her yellow legal pad. 'So the head could have gone missing as early as Sunday?'

'Yes, it could have,' Euryale replied. 'It was a very busy day. Creatures from all over Monsters' and other realms were running around the city causing all kinds of problems. There was a bit of a fuss when one of the committee members accidently got eaten by an Ogre.'

'We thought we would lose our Tidy Realm award for sure.' Stheno added. 'Luckily our recycling campaign is the best in the seven realms, so even though we lost some valuable votes, we won in the end.'

'So, there were a lot of strangers wandering about?' Hera asked.

'Oh yes, the committee members come from all over the place, plus there are quite a few in their entourage. And because of all the added security and the "no eating others" policy on the day, we had a number of tourists take advantage of the opportunity to see Monsters' Realm and probably get out alive.'

'There were even some humans here,' Stheno added.

'Were there?' Euryale asked, surprised.

'Oh yes, I specifically remember seeing them. I thought maybe they were a food delivery, but they all left on a big yellow tour bus, limbs intact.'

'Is that very unusual?' Athena asked. 'For humans to come onto this plane?'

'Well, it's unusual for them to leave afterwards,' Stheno replied.

Euryale gave her a warning look. 'Sometimes the vampires smuggle some in for a party or whatever and let a few go. We usually turn a blind eye, as long as they glamour the surviving guests into forgetting the portal address. But it's unusual for humans to find their way in and out on their own.'

Athena screwed up her nose, but Hera thought it fair enough. The humans had imagined these monsters with a taste for human blood; it was too late now to complain if it meant a few of them got turned into a human version of home-delivered pizza.

'You say you were both in the village with the Tidy Realm people?' Athena questioned.

'Yes, that's right, both of us,' Euryale said. 'We stayed down overnight because they were having a dinner dance. We so rarely get into town these days. We thought it would be rather fun.'

'Can anyone verify this?' Hera asked, watching Athena to see if she was detecting any deception.

'Stheno's boyfriend can verify her for the whole night and most of the next morning!' Euryale said cheekily.

Stheno reddened and shook her head. 'Shut up!'

'We should talk to this boyfriend,' Hera said.

'Is that really necessary?' Stheno replied, blushing furiously.

Hera thought it was. Not only could this mystery man verify what Stheno was saying, but he was another contact she could potentially get information from.

'Okay,' Stheno relented. 'His name is Jacko. He lives in the A-frame on Shelley Avenue.'

Athena noted this down. Then she looked at Euryale directly.

'Can we see Medusa now?'

Euryale's hands shook slightly, causing her to spill her tea into her saucer.

'Why do you need to do that?'

'Because,' Athena said, 'we need to verify that she is still here and that her head, well, isn't.'

Euryale and Stheno exchanged glances and Athena narrowed her eyes, no doubt trying to sense if the sisters were trying to hide anything.

'Medusa doesn't like people seeing her like this. She's very... well, she gets very upset,' Euryale said slowly.

'We need to see her,' Hera insisted.

Euryale stood up and straightened her dress carefully before indicating that Stheno should get up also.

'Okay, but please don't disturb her. She has been sleeping for the last few days. It's better when she's sleeping. When she's awake her body wanders off and it's pretty disturbing.'

'Not to mention how hard it is to locate when she can neither see nor hear you calling for her,' Stheno grumbled. 'Last time she wandered off, she was missing for hours.'

'We just want to look in on her,' Athena assured them.

Euryale led the goddesses down a dimly lit hallway, illuminated by petrified men holding torches, and led them through a heavy wooden door, decoratively carved with curling snakes and writhing serpents. She knocked quietly, 'Medusa, are you awake, dear?'

There was no answer and Hera gave Athena a puzzled look.

'How can she hear you if her head is missing?' Hera asked.

Euryale looked embarrassed.

'Just force of habit,' she said as she pushed the door open and peered in. Satisfied, she opened the door wider and allowed the goddesses inside.

They stepped into a stone-walled room, tastefully decorated in soft greens and purple hanging tapestries. A large wooden chair nestled in the corner under a softly glowing reading lamp. Dominating the centre of the room was a large four-poster bed.

Lying in the bed, only partially obscured by gauze curtains, was Medusa, curled up in a sleeping pose. The gorgon shifted slightly as the women entered the room, although Hera decided that action must have been coincidental as it was clear, looking at her headless body, that there was no way Medusa could have heard them come in.

'Satisfied?' Stheno hissed.

Hera tore her gaze away from the headless gorgon and nodded. 'Yes. Thank you."

She took Athena's arm and guided her as they backed out of the room into the hallway. Stheno and Euryale followed, softly closing the door behind them.

'Is that all you need?' Euryale asked as they walked back down the hall.

'One last thing,' Hera replied. 'Have you seen anyone suspicious hanging around the mountain, or visiting Medusa in the last few months?'

'No, not really. Medusa doesn't really get visitors. Even in Monsters' Realm she's pretty terrifying.'

Athena raised her eyebrows. 'But you and Stheno seem to be quite involved with the other citizens. Why are they so afraid of Medusa and not you? Couldn't any one of you freeze them with a glance?'

Euryale and Stheno glanced at each other and Athena frowned. 'Don't lie if you want our help,' she warned.

The two gorgons gave each other a quick look and then, without any warning, they both pulled off their sunglasses.

Athena, knowing a moment in advance what was to happen, pushed Hera backwards and over a petrified man that was serving as an umbrella stand at the mouth of the hallway. Hera landed awkwardly on her hip and cried out in pain as Athena dived on top of her, covering her eyes. Hera closed hers but it was too late – even with the warning, both goddesses had caught an unexpected glimpse into the large multi-coloured eyes of the gorgons!

Hera opened her eyes slowly, not sure why being petrified felt no different than being flesh and blood. She certainly hadn't expected her hip to still throb with pain if she had been turned to stone.

But, she realised, neither she nor Athena had been added to the gorgons' impressive human statue collection.

'What the Hades?' Hera said, glaring at the smirking sisters. 'I thought you lot turned people who looked at you to stone. I mean, it's kind of your thing, isn't it?'

'Does it not work on divine beings?' Athena asked, clearly as confused as Hera.

'No. I mean, yes, well–' Euryale started.

'We've never had that power,' Stheno said impatiently. 'Only Medusa has it. If she looked at you, then yeah, you'd be stone cold dead.'

Athena looked at the sisters in amazement. 'So you aren't gorgons?'

Stheno growled. 'We *are* gorgons! Just not the original gorgon.'

Euryale soothed Stheno by rubbing her shoulder.

'It would seem that only the first true gorgon has that particular gift,' Euryale said. She turned to Athena. 'When you and Medusa decided to share her curse with us, her sisters, you didn't really give it as much oomph as you did with her.'

'She always was your favourite,' Stheno muttered.

Athena shook her head uncertainly. 'No, that's not right.' She stopped for a moment, considering. 'Well, I suppose I might not have; I mean, I was a bit rushed at the time.' She suddenly turned back to look the sisters in the eye. 'But why didn't you ever tell anyone?'

'Medusa said it was safer for all of us if everyone thought we all had the gorgon's gift.'

Hera considered this. It was true that she had never heard of the sisters actually freezing anyone. Everyone had just assumed. Although it did explain how Perseus had managed to escape the Gorgons Lair so effectively after beheading the sleeping Medusa.

'Euryale and I have very little power at all,' Stheno said quietly.

'Aside from our charming visage, razor-sharp teeth and claws and inhuman strength, of course,' Euryale said with a smile.

Stheno's mood didn't lighten. 'Yeah, sure. But nowhere near enough to cause any real damage.'

'But you are still impervious to the gaze,' Hera said. 'You obviously don't turn to stone if Medusa looks at you.'

'Yes, that's right,' Euryale said. 'We're immune.'

'That gives you a good motive for taking Medusa's head then,' Hera said.

Athena and the sisters looked startled; the gorgons' serpentine hair hissing with displeasure.

'What motive?' Euryale responded. It was the first time Hera had seen her so rattled, and glancing at Athena she noticed that her stepdaughter had noticed this too.

'You were jealous that Medusa had all the power,' Hera said. 'Maybe you wanted to use her power yourselves, like people thought you could.

You are perfectly placed to take the head and leave her sitting in there, defenceless.'

Stheno shook her head forcefully, her serpent hair writhing with anger at the accusation.

'You seem to think the gorgon power is something worth having! A glare that petrifies all that gaze upon you – what kind of power is that? Medusa liked it, kept telling us it was a gift, but then, she always hated being looked at.'

'She's an introvert,' Euryale added, grimacing.

'Yes, indeed, never liked how much attention people paid her. Used to complain about being beautiful. Complain! I wish I had her problems,' Stheno muttered.

'Oh Stheno, you were quite pretty, in your own way,' Euryale said.

Stheno turned away, what looked like tears glistening unshed in her eyes.

'Shut up,' she said. 'We both know that this transformation was probably an improvement for me as far as looks are concerned. But it doesn't matter. At least back then I could party, get out a bit. Not like now, stuck in this cave.'

'But, if you don't have to avoid people, why live here?' Athena asked. 'Why not move into town? Have more of a social life?'

'Leave Medusa here alone?' Stheno cried. 'Abandoned, unprotected! I know you all think she's the most powerful monster in the seven realms, but she's fragile. Never been right since that bastard Perseus hacked off her head the first time, has she, Euri?'

Euryale nodded. 'Nightmares, agoraphobia, flashbacks – you name it, she suffers with it. Stheno may hate to admit it, but you were right to transform us when you changed Medusa. As powerful as she is, she would never have coped all on her own. Especially after what Perseus did to her. '

Hera considered this. The crimes of that so-called hero continued to resonate, even now, and he has never once paid any price for it.

'I'm sorry if it looked like we were accusing you of anything,' Athena said, placing her hand on Euryale's shoulder. 'We just needed to make sure we had all the facts before we go looking into this. But I believe you, and we will do what we can.'

Euryale brushed the tears from her incredible multi-coloured eyes and shrugged off Athena's hand, ignoring the goddess of wisdom and justice and looking at Hera instead.

'So you will help us?'

'Yes, we'll help you,' she said gruffly.

'How can you be so sure you'll even be able to find her?' Stheno challenged.

'Finding her won't be the problem, ' Hera replied. 'Whoever took her has already started using the gaze, and they are not being particularly discreet. No, the hard part will be getting her away from them without getting ourselves or anyone else stoned to death. But if it's possible to do, we'll do it.'

'Why have you changed your mind? This morning you couldn't get rid of us quick enough.' Euryale asked, quietly.

'Because I'm tired of women constantly being demonised and treated like objects I suppose.' Hera replied. Hera hadn't even realised she felt that way until she had articulated it, but it was true. Women, whether goddesses or monsters got a pretty raw deal overall and she was sick of it. And, honestly if there was anyone in the seven realms Hera felt didn't deserve more punishment for existing, it was Medusa.

'Thank you, Queen Hera,' Euryale said, bowing to Hera. 'Medusa told us we could count on you.'

Hera nodded. She was faintly surprised that Medusa would have mentioned her at all. Athena had always been Medusa's champion and, although she hated to admit it, Hera's reputation for helping her fellow women wasn't the best. Still, Hera thought, she was the Queen of the Gods so why wouldn't they come to her for help in their time of crisis?

8

The First Real Suspect

'What did Zeus have to say?' Persephone asked, glancing up from her gossip magazine as Hades pocketed his mobile phone.

Hades shook his head. 'Decidedly unhelpful.'

Persephone smiled her amazing, earth-shattering smile and he couldn't stay dour.

'No matter. I'll get there in the end. You know me.' He bent down and kissed his wife on her full, luscious lips.

Even after all these years, it never failed to send a tingle down his spine. It always reminded him of the first time he had ever laid eyes on her, this golden goddess of spring, as she walked through the world, painting the land with blossoms and sunlight and the music of nature. She was everything he was not. The warmth to his cold heart, the light which could brighten his dour dark demeanour, and the loveliness of spring in the cold winter of Hades' underworld.

She was so beautiful, so far beyond his league that when the Greek gods lost their divinity, he had expected their bargain too would be dissolved and that this extraordinary goddess would finally leave him for good. After all he had no way to stop her from doing so.

Inexplicably she had stayed, and this made him love her even more than he already did. Now, as always, there was nothing he would not do for her to keep her by her side. Finally unchained from their underworld duties, he promised her a life full of everything she had missed in dark, dank caverns of their underground home.

'Persephone, I shall make you so happy,' he had cried, hugging her as she revealed her intention to stay by his side. 'We can go anywhere you want to go. Do anything you want to do.'

And oh, she had smiled her perfect smile and told him of her plans: ski fields and winery tours, access to the great literary salons and Roman parties. His smile didn't falter nor his embrace loosen as she spoke, although nothing she said filled him with excitement. He was, at heart, a quiet, solitary figure, a creature of the shadows and of the darkness. Snow fields and noisy orgies filled with Eurotrash was not really his scene. But still he promised and she kissed him and told him she knew he would look out for her, just as he always had. And he fully intended to.

So up into the Mortal Realm they had gone. Hades hadn't acclimatised well at first. His pasty skin burnt to a crisp within hours in the sun and he developed persistent tinnitus from all the shrieking, dancing people who mobbed around them at impossibly loud parties. As the decades passed he watched in alarm as his nest egg of existence points started to disappear on luxuries and travel. But he never complained. This was what made Persephone happy, and her happiness was worth these sacrifices and more.

After a few hundred years he was able to access 50+ sun screen and industrial-strength earplugs so was more able to enjoy her world, which by this time consisted of midnight raves in Ibiza and impossibly expensive shopping sprees at Milan, Paris and New York Fashion weeks. And while his financial situation continued to deteriorate, he found himself actually able to enjoy this world of earthly delights, as he took up surfing and adventure sports, joined the right clubs and cashed in his existence credits on fine homes, luxury cars, expensive clothes, solariums and the best things that his divine fame could buy. Over time Hades became erudite and elegant – almost unrecognisable from the pale, humourless god he had once been.

Now he was a sun-kissed, muscular Adonis, almost as handsome as the original youth who Persephone had engaged in a number of affairs with. He never begrudged her these infidelities, never felt he had a right to stop her cheating on him, considering all she had given up during their days in the dark kingdom. But he would never cheat on her. Never give her even one moment's doubt that he loved her absolutely and without equal. He was a rarity in the divine world: a faithful god.

But this lifestyle wasn't cheap and he was running out of existence points fast. To keep up, Hades had started to borrow heavily, and although so far managing to keep one step ahead of his creditors, he knew he couldn't keep them hanging for much longer. It wasn't just a troll beating he feared, should his house of cards fall; a God with no existence credits, unable to keep up repayments on his debts, would find himself fading away altogether, lost in the ether with all the other lost and unloved gods who had simply ceased to exist. He may have once been one of the most powerful of the old Olympians, but he was not one of the more popular or celebrated of the Greek gods in modern times. His opportunities to earn existence points were far more limited than those of his siblings, nephews and nieces, all of whom still enjoyed an enduring popularity he never understood.

No, if Hades fell into poverty there was no way to quickly generate credit and that meant Persephone would leave him, she would have too, just to ensure her own survival. As much as he liked to tell himself differently, he knew that his existence credits were a large part of the reason such a beautiful and wondrous creature stayed in their marriage.

Persephone had almost no savings of her own. She had never been one of the most popular goddesses in the Greek or Roman pantheon, always relying on him or her mother for the existence points necessary to keep up her preferred lifestyle. But in these modern times her situation was even more dire. Current humans had little regard for a nature goddess and so her income of existence credits was unreliable – buoyed only by the occasional hippy giving their squawking home-birthed infant her name, which the child would almost invariably change as soon as she was old enough to legally do so.

Hades had to take care of her, and take care of her he would. He just had to solve this small credit problem first.

Yesterday, as they flew in his private jet above the sun-drenched Amalfi Coast, checking his stock options and calculating his expected existence point revenue for the year, he had begun to despair. But today it seemed a possible solution had raised its ugly gorgon head, and he was not about to miss out on the opportunity.

'I think we should take Cerberus on an outing,' Hades remarked.

'Oh, I do miss Puppy!' Persephone exclaimed, instantly excited at the prospect of seeing her beloved pet. Although she had agreed that a three-headed, six-foot-high dog, who shot blue flames out of his mouth, was a difficult animal to keep in their penthouse apartment in New York, she often openly lamented that they could not find a way to bring Cerbie onto the human realm.

Hades, pleased by her happiness and the idea that was now forming in his head, picked up the phone and directed the captain to steer towards the Bermuda Triangle.

'Right away, sir,' the captain replied, not quite managing to keep the concerned quiver from his voice.

Hera glanced down at her buzzing phone and pressed the decline button, noticing that there were 12 other missed calls from Zeus. She dismissed them, irritated. He probably couldn't find the chops. Honestly, couldn't she leave the house for a few hours without her husband becoming completely incapable of feeding himself?

Athena shot her a questioning look but Hera shrugged it away and indicated that they should resume their conversation with the huge cyclops who currently sat, towering over both of them, on the bench in his massive house.

Despite his size, Jacko seemed, to all intents and purposes, a fairly kind-hearted and generally quite harmless creature. What he saw in the fiery, cruel-minded Stheno was a mystery, but logic rarely mattered in affairs of the heart; she, above all, knew that.

'Oh yes, Henny was here with me,' Jacko confirmed, using a pet name for Stheno that Hera found both odd and strangely appropriate at the same time.

'Do you ever visit the cave where she lives with her sisters?' Athena asked.

Jacko scratched his head, blinked his one massive eye and then nodded. 'Yeah, once or twice, but not often. Henny usually comes down here to meet me, because, well, because of Medusa. She might look at me the wrong way, if you know what I mean.'

'Did you ever see Medusa?'

Jacko paused for a long time, his eye blinking slowly. 'No, she usually stayed in her room. And if she was about, well Henny made sure I was kept out of her way. Very few people have seen her at all you know, not safe, is it. It's not that hard though, Medusa mainly keeps to herself, you know; never comes into town. Henny or Euri do the shopping and run the errands. And if I'm there, well, Henny's always worried I might catch a glimpse at the wrong time and, you know, *turn to stone*.' He said the last part as though it was a dirty comment uttered in front of a nun.

Athena considered this for a moment. 'When was the last time anyone saw Medusa?'

'Oh, Henny and Euri see her all the time.'

Athena nodded slowly but Hera was already moving on to the next question.

'And you were out in the town with Stheno – Henny – when the judging was happening for the awards, right?'

Jacko nodded slowly.

'Was there anything unusual you can remember about that day? Anyone out of place or perhaps heading up to the caves?'

Hera tried to hide her annoyance as Jacko again contemplated his answer. The clock on the wall ticked off five long, excruciating minutes before the giant nodded, although this time with a little more uncertainty.

'There was something. I don't know if it was unusual exactly. I mean, unusual in Monsters' Realm is, well, usual, but I did see something.'

Hera and Athena waited for Jacko to continue, but he just stared at them, a satisfied smile on his face for remembering something that may be of use.

'For Olympus' sake! What did you see?' Hera cried, her patience running out.

'What? Oh right, yeah. Well, it wasn't that unusual, really. I mean I had seen him before. But usually at night, and only once or twice. This was the first time he came in the daytime, you see.'

'Who?' Hera could feel her anger at this oaf rising by the second. She glanced over at her stepdaughter, but Athena seemed to be perfectly calm and relaxed, not at all perturbed by the giant's excruciating slowness. This just infuriated Hera all the more.

'Poseidon,' Jacko replied. 'He was heading up to the gorgons' cave, with a bunch of flowers.'

9

A Nice Outing for Cerberus

THE TWO GODDESSES LOOKED AT EACH OTHER IN SURPRISE. WHAT
in all the heavens was the God of the Sea doing visiting the woman who
had chosen to be turned into a hideous monster for the express purpose
of avoiding him?

After a few more questions it was clear Jacko had little more of value
to add, and quite honestly Hera was starting to get very annoyed with
the interminable slowness of the giant's answers. There was little point in
hanging around here, they had enough now to follow at least one obvious
line of enquiry.

'Thank you Jacko,' Athena said as the goddesses got up to leave, 'you
have been very helpful.'

Jacko beamed at them 'I'm always happy to help and Stheno has been
so upset. I hope you ladies can find her sister. She does love her so.'

Hera blinked in surprise. Jacko was clearly afraid of Medusa, but he
loved Stheno enough to hope she was returned to her. Hera had rarely
seen such selfless love in a man, and suddenly all her irritation towards
him disappeared. She gave him a genuine smile as he held open the huge
wooden door for them and courteously wished them well. For all his
lumbering slowness, Jacko was a real gentleman, and as unlikely a couple
as he and Stheno seemed, she felt they may have found that truly rare
thing, a happy partnership.

Hera and Athena emerged from Jacko's A-Frame and headed towards the exit portal. A small blue alien stepped in their path and offered them a flyer for an 'all you can eat' buffet. Hera shook her head resolutely, shuddering to think what might be on the menu at such a feast.

'Do you think Poseidon was trying to see Medusa?' Athena asked as the alien wandered off to deliver his pamphlets into the letterboxes of nearby dwellings.

Hera shook her head. 'There's no way she would want to see him, is there? Except maybe to turn him to stone.'

'Well, it has been a long time. Maybe she's forgiven him.'

Hera shook her head again. 'Women don't usually forgive the things he has done.'

Athena shrugged. 'Not every woman is like you, Hera.'

'What's that supposed to mean?'

Athena's serene expression didn't change. 'Well, you were never the forgiving type.'

Hera scowled. She couldn't really disagree, but to be fair she was expected to forgive an awful lot!

'Maybe so, but it's also true that Poseidon isn't really the flowers-and-chocolate type. More of the rapey, creepy, sneaky type. I very much doubt he was here to ask for forgiveness.'

'So, you think he took her head?' Athena asked, her brow arched.

'I wouldn't put it past him. After all, with her head gone, she's pretty much defenceless.'

Athena grimaced, no doubt thinking of Poseidon taking advantage of a headless Medusa. Hera tried to banish the thought as well.

'We'll have to speak to Poseidon,' Athena stated firmly.

Hera frowned. She had made a point of avoiding contact with her unpleasant brother as much as possible, and was frankly surprised that Athena seemed so keen to engage with the watery old mongrel either. But she had to admit, this was the first real lead they had uncovered, so, as much as they may want to avoid the god's damp company, they couldn't just ignore it.

Hera nodded reluctantly. 'The more we get into this, the more likely it seems that our family are involved in some way,' she said. 'I don't like it. I thought we were over with this kind of nonsense millennia ago.'

Athena frowned, and Hera realised that being a judge on the lore court probably gave her stepdaughter a different impression. But before Hera could admit her comment may have been a bit optimistic, a glowing light lit up the side of Athena's face. The scent of sweet honeysuckle and freshly mowed grass drifted through the air and, even before she turned, Hera knew who was responsible for this touch of spring.

Standing in the park was Persephone, haloed by a golden radiance, her hair expensively coiffed, wearing designer clothes and Jimmy Choo heels. A vision of loveliness that seemed so out of place on Monsters' Realm.

Persephone was daintily throwing a large, metal-studded cannon ball out onto the field while the black three-headed hound sitting beside her salivated wildly. The dog was about the height of a small elephant, and lightning fast as he galloped off to fetch the ball.

'Persephone,' Hera called, slightly blinded by rays of light as her sister-in-law turned towards her.

'Oh hello, Hera. A lovely day, isn't it?'

Cerberus returned with the ball and placed it, glowing hot from his flaming breath, at Persephone's feet. Unperturbed, the goddess picked it up carefully and expertly threw it again towards the other end of the field. Cerberus yelped in joy and tore off after it.

'We just brought Cerbie up to have a bit of a run. We haven't taken him out for ages.'

Hearing his name, the three-headed hound abandoned the ball chase and ran back to his mistress. 'We've missed you so much, haven't we?' she said to him in a baby voice. Persephone reached up on tiptoes and patted her beloved dog fondly on each of his giant black heads, while one of his blue forked tongues flicked out to lick her hand submissively. 'He's one of the main things I miss about not living in the Underworld any more.' she commented thoughtfully.

Hera put out her hand to pet one of Cerberus' heads too, only to be greeted by a low, menacing growl that reverberated around the shoreline. Hera smiled tightly but pulled her hand back to safety.

'Is Hades with you?' she asked.

'Of course. He's off at the shop getting Cerbie some severed fingers and a bottle of double-distilled virgin blood.' She patted the dog again. 'That's your favourite, isn't it, baby, huh?'

The dog wagged his reptilian tail, then bounded away, almost knocking down Hera and Athena as he rushed past.

'Calm down, boy,' Hades cried, looking a little worried as the huge dog came careening towards him. Panicked he tried to open the packet of severed fingers he was carrying before Cerberus reached him. But Cerbie wasn't listening and wouldn't be calmed as he ran directly at Hades, tackling him to the ground and snapping at the box. Hades tried, without success, to keep it from the dog's slobbering jaws.

'Argh, wait, I'll get them out,' Hades protested, struggling to reclaim the box as the monstrous dog stood, one paw pinning Hades down as all three heads tossed the box of snacks between them.

'Cerbie,' Persephone cried as she helped Hera wipe the dog drool off her dress. 'Settle down!'

Hearing his mistress, the dog stepped off Hades' chest and sat back on his haunches, dropping the box of snacks at Hades' feet. Hades got up and picked up the half-chewed box and shook a few of the fingers out before tossing one into each of Cerberus' slobbering mouths. They disappeared immediately.

'Sit, Cerberus,' Hades commanded.

The dog shook all his three heads and suddenly his third head snapped forward and snatched the box from Hades' hand, almost taking some of Hades' own fingers with it.

'Cerbie!' Persephone shouted. 'Bad dog!'

The hellhound turned, fixed all six eyes on his beloved mistress and whined softly.

She shook her head firmly as the hound beseeched her with three mournful expressions.

'No. Bad dog. No more snacks for you. Come here and sit down!'

The huge dog crawled over to Persephone, his serpent-headed tail tucked between his back legs, his faces contorted in misery. He cowered next to her and she patted his head lightly.

'It's all right,' she said soothingly. 'But Mama doesn't like you to snatch.' She scratched Cerberus' ear and he relaxed next to her.

Persephone's mobile phone rang. She dug it out of her Louis Vuitton handbag and pressed the receive button with a perfectly manicured nail.

'Hello? Oh, hello, Mother, how lovely to hear from you. I'm just in Monsters' Realm with Hades. Yes, Mother, I am still with him. I told you. Yes, I know.' Persephone covered the mouthpiece and gave Hades an apologetic smile. 'I'm going to talk to her over by the park bench. You catch up with Hera.' She glided to the other end of the park, her ever-loyal canine trotting bedside her.

Hades rolled his eyes, and Hera could imagine the kind of

conversation Persephone was having with her mother. Hades' mother-in-law had never liked him, but now that Persephone seemed to be staying with her abductor of her own volition, Hera was pretty sure Demeter would be putting all sorts of pressure on her daughter to date some of the more eligible new gods. Poor in existence points as she may be, Persephone certainly didn't lack charm and allure and more than a few gods had tried to gain her affection since the fall of the Greek pantheon.

It was not just Hera and Demeter who must wonder why such a beautiful and coveted goddess had stayed with a nasty old has-been like Hades. Hera suspected Hades must wonder too. Still Hera couldn't comment; after all, she had stayed with Zeus after their fall from Olympus. She supposed you just got used to someone over several thousand years, however much they may annoy you.

Hera shook her head, irritated with herself for thinking about her stupid husband when there were more pressing matters to deal with.

'Why are you here?' Hera asked, her eyes narrowing at Hades.

'Steph wanted to visit her dog,' he replied smoothly. Now that Cerberus was safely at the other end of the park, Hades had managed to reclaim his usual calm, cool demeanour.

'Are you following me?'

Hades half smiled at her. 'Why would I do that?'

'Don't play dumb, Hades; I know you hate that dog.'

'Well, Zeus mentioned you may need some help,' Hades replied.

Hera scowled. Damnit. She should've picked up her husband's calls. Though why Hades thought she would ever need his help was beyond her.

Athena stepped in between them and smiled graciously. 'We are just doing a little sightseeing; it's nothing you need to be concerned with, uncle.'

'You being here has nothing to do with Medusa – or her missing head, then?' Hades replied.

'How did you know about that?' Hera asked.

Hades smirked. 'I keep my ear to the ground, dear sister.'

'And your nose in everyone's business,' Hera replied.

She threw a look at Athena and then strode away, unwilling to dally with Hades any longer. Athena made to follow her to the portal but then Hera stopped and turned to her brother.

'Don't get messed up in this, Hades. I'm warning you. This isn't a time for your little schemes.'

'Dear sister,' Hades replied, 'It is always the time for my little schemes, now more than ever.' He smiled smugly and Hera turned on her heel, angrily dismissing him.

10

Journey to Atlantis

HERA HATED GOING TO ATLANTIS.

Although famed as a wondrous submerged city, it was in point of fact little more than a craggy outgrowth of rocks that sat soggily in the middle of the Alantic ocean. The Island was surrounded on all sides by sheer cliff faces and rocky shores teeming with the debris of hundreds of years of shipwrecks.

The island had little to recommend it, basically no more than a series of watery caverns and part-submerged tunnels and grottos so damp that just stepping inside made Hera's hair frizz up.

Hera also hated how Poseidon had refused to put the portal entrance on Atlantis itself, instead forcing every visitor to apparate metres out in the ocean and swim up onto the beach, often narrowly avoiding being stung by jellyfish, or chased by the occasional shark. It may have been an effective way to put off unwelcome visitors, but her sopping clothes would require several dry cleans to remove the stench of seawater and algae from them when she finally got home.

Hera held out her hand as Athena emerged from the water and her stepdaughter took it gratefully, balancing herself on the slippery rocks that formed the basis of Atlantis' dry dock.

Three large men with absurdly small tridents approached them. They were initially quite aggressive, but once they recognised Hera they bowed respectfully.

'Where is Poseidon?' Hera asked the Atlanteans.

'He's in his grotto,' the nearest one answered. 'Is he expecting you, Queen Hera?'

Hera pushed past them. She didn't need the men to take her to the grotto; she knew well the dank and damp throne room where the King of the Sea would sit for hours and complain. She had spent a number of miserable hours down there while the awful old man had tried to court her, thinking that a dripping, smelly undersea cave was a romantic setting for a meal of raw fish and whale stew.

It hadn't changed much. Long stalactites hung from the roof of the cave, dripping into large, green, murky puddles, beside the coral throne – that was so incredibly uncomfortable that no one could sit in it for more than a few minutes without feeling like it was some sort of torture implement. As Poseidon insisted on sitting on it, she supposed it was part of the reason he was always so irritable.

The God of the Sea looked up as Hera approached and his smile could easily have been mistaken for a grimace as he greeted her.

'Hera, how nice to see you.' His gaze moved to Athena and managed to become even less welcoming. 'And Athena, a rare honour.'

'Hello, brother,' Hera replied, politely bussing him on the cheek and trying to ignore the stench of sour oysters that emanated from his skin.

'Can I offer you some refreshments, or are you here to see the mermaid show? It doesn't start till six, but tickets sell out fast.'

Hera was in no mood for pleasantries. Her hair was already starting to frizz, and if she didn't make this quick her head would be an unmanageable afro that no human or divine conditioner could tame. Time to get straight to the point.

'Why have you been visiting Medusa?'

Poseidon looked startled before quickly regaining his composure. 'I haven't.'

'Don't lie, uncle; you were seen,' Athena said.

'I just take her some flowers once in a while.'

'Why?'

'It's what people do when they are courting.'

'You never brought me flowers,' Hera replied drily.

'Well, maybe if I had, things would have worked out better?'

Hera's expression said differently and Poseidon shook it off. 'Anyway, our marriage would have been political, not a love match, unlike with my dearest Medusa.'

'You and Medusa aren't a love match!' Athena responded.

Poseidon glared. 'Yes, we are, Athena. We would have been happily together if you hadn't interfered. But I am not going to let you stop me again.'

Hera noted the confidence in Poseidon's words. Was the man mad? The gorgon not only hated him with a passion, but she was one of the few women in the known dimensions who could quite literally freeze him in his tracks.

Athena, however, refused to be swayed. 'You need to give her head back, Poseidon. You might think it's a good tactic, but her sisters will kill you if you lay a hand on Medusa. Head or no head.'

Poseidon recoiled in mock horror. 'Why must you think so poorly of me?'

'Come off it, Poe,' Hera answered impatiently. 'You were seen on Monsters' Realm, stalking Medusa. We know. Just hand it over.'

'I wasn't stalking her. I told you: we're courting.'

Athena and Hera shook their heads. No one in that dripping, damp, hair-frizzing room believed a word Poseidon was saying.

'You two think you are so much better than me, don't you,' Poseidon said, his whole demeanour changing as suddenly as the weather at sea. 'Think no one could love me. Just because you didn't? Well, I can make Medusa love me. Make her.'

He leapt to his feet. 'And even you won't stop me this time.' He snarled at Athena, so violently that his thick white spittle flew across the cavern and landed on Athena's cheek. 'Medusa will be my bride.'

Athena calmly wiped Poseidon's spit from her face with a corner of her stola. When she spoke, her words were steady and calm. 'Having her head doesn't make her your bride; it makes her your prisoner.'

'Shut up, you bitch,' Poseidon shrieked, but Athena refused to give an inch, staring him down as he tried to intimidate her.

'Yeah, big man, what are you going to do? Huh? Attack me? Prove you're a big, powerful god by hitting a goddess? Is that who you are?'

Poseidon stopped his fist inches from her face, shaking in anger. Then, again, a sudden mood change.

His anger vanished, and a calm expression settled on his ragged, weathered face, erasing any evidence of the previous squall.

'I don't have Medusa's head. I'm as upset about her tragedy as you are. I even asked Perseus about it and he has no idea what happened either. I want nothing more than my beautiful Medusa returned to me. Whole and intact.'

'She turned herself into a monster to avoid you, Poseidon. Take a damn hint,' Hera replied, and suddenly the calm was gone again, but this time Poseidon's face crumpled inward, like a small boy having a tantrum.

'She turned her into a monster! *Her!*' Poseidon pointed angrily at Athena, more spittle running from his mouth. He moved towards Hera, his face beseeching, his tone wheedling. 'She was mine; I had her. And that bitch turned her against me. *She* turned her into a monster.' Tears of anger and frustration spilled down Poseidon's cheeks.

'You turned her against you all by yourself. I just helped make sure you could never violate her like that again,' Athena stated evenly, her serenity and quiet authority a stark contrast to Poseidon's emotional ravings.

'I loved her,' he screamed, running at Athena, his fists raised once again.

'You raped her,' Hera replied, apparating quickly between her stepdaughter and this mad god. Poseidon skidded to a halt, realising he now had two powerful goddesses against him, not just one. He glared at them for a moment, then, as suddenly as it had come, all of his anger left him and he was again calm and deflated. Just a greying, sad old man who slumped back into his coral throne.

'It's of no matter,' he said, adopting a regal disinterest, only slightly undermined by the wet marks of the tears he had been crying only a few moments earlier. 'The past is the past. My Atlantean guards are searching as we speak. They will find my beloved's head and I'll make my dear Medusa whole again. And when I do, everything will be as it should be.'

Hera was barely listening, thinking of something Poseidon had mentioned before his crazy outburst.

'Why did you contact Perseus? Do you think he has her?'

Everyone knew Perseus had taken Medusa's head the first time, so it was hardly surprising that Poseidon had suspected the half-son of Zeus. But it was too much of a coincidence not to follow up on. After all, Hera knew there was no such thing as coincidences.

Perseus was a likely suspect, when she thought about it. He may well have wanted back the power he had enjoyed when he had last held

Medusa's head and the whole mortal and immortal realm had been made to bow beneath him. Pretty intoxicating stuff for a moronic half god who had few friends in the divine world. In fact, if Hera recalled correctly most of her relatives had, at one time or another, wanted Perseus dead. Not that she could blame them. She herself had toyed with Perseus' demise a few times.

But Poseidon had done more than toy with the idea, the Sea God had been perhaps Perseus' most ardent enemy, trying to murder Perseus on at least four different occasions that Hera knew of. The boy had only survived because Zeus intervened. Not because he particularly cared for Perseus, who was, everyone agreed, a complete little shit, but because having his brother murder his children, even the illegitimate ones, tended to make Zeus look bad.

It never ceased to amaze Hera how incapable her brothers were at getting on with each other. Even when they had been powerful deities in one of the most powerful pantheons in the world, they were always throwing tantrums about something and trying to kill each other or their progeny. But now that both Zeus and Poseidon were little more than mythological has-beens, the two had become more than rivals; Hera would even go as far as to say they might be described as immortal enemies.

So why would Poseidon be chatting with Zeus' half-mortal son, the same guy who had successfully removed Medusa's head once before and refused to give her to Poseidon then either?

It didn't take a genius to work out something was going on between the two of them. Had some sort of deal been struck?

Poseidon looked away, reddening. He had clearly not meant to mention Perseus.

'I have no idea. I don't even know where he is. Now, I think it's time for you ladies to leave.'

Athena glanced over at Hera, alerting her that Poseidon was being deceptive, but before Hera could call him on it, the Atlantean guards stepped in and took Hera and Athena by the shoulders, attempting to force them towards the door. Hera glared at them and they quickly released the women. Poseidon shot the guards an angry look but didn't command them to re-engage.

'You say you love Medusa, but if you have removed any part of her from Monsters' Realm you know the EBCU won't stand for it. They will kill her, and maybe you as well,' Hera said. 'If you love Medusa as you say you do, I would advise you to return her head to Monsters' Realm immediately.'

Hera and Athena walked out of the throne room, followed by the cowed guards, who tried to act like they were in charge even though they knew they weren't.

Before they plunged into the ocean towards the portal, Hera pulled Athena aside. 'So, does he have her?'

Athena shook her head, 'I don't know. There was a lot of deception in what he was saying. He was telling the truth when he said he didn't know where Perseus was and seemed angry about that. But he has definitely been talking to Perseus about something, it felt important but I'm not sure what it was."

'We have to be careful. He's unpredictable and you know how he can hold a grudge.'

Athena nodded, but something else was on her mind. 'The one thing he was completely truthful about – he really does believe he and Medusa are getting back together.'

'He's unhinged. Always has been. Drinking seawater turns you mad, you know. I'm more worried about the fact that whatever we may suspect about him, there's very little we can do to prove it.'

'One thing I learnt at the lore courts: whenever you hit a dead end, just follow the existence credit,' Athena replied. 'Never fails to turn up something.'

Hades watched as his sister and niece plunged into the ocean and disappeared from sight. He agreed with much of what he had overheard. Poseidon knew something about this business. What Hera had failed to recognise was Poseidon's deep-seated hatred for her and Athena meant she was never going to get him to confess anything to her.

Hades couldn't think of two less likely interrogators for the God of the Sea, except maybe Zeus himself, but that lazy old bastard wasn't going to get involved in this; that much was clear from his quite disappointing conversation with the sky god earlier.

But maybe he could get a bit more out of the old seaweed bag; after all Poseidon and Hades only slightly despised each other, and in Olympian terms that was almost as close as two brothers could be.

He walked towards the grotto and into the cavern, none of the Tritons or Atlanteans daring to even look him in the eye, never mind confront him. The God of the Dead wasn't someone most wanted to mess with. He searched the caverns for Poseidon, carefully avoiding the larger puddles, although his Italian leather shoes were already ruined by seawater long before he found Poseidon – using his other throne room.

Poseidon zipped up, flushed the toilet and turned around, almost bumping into Hades who was nonchalantly leaning against a golden basin, forcing Poseidon to manoeuvre past him to wash his hands.

'Two family visits in one day; I do feel popular,' Poseidon remarked dryly.

Hades handed his brother a linen hand towel.

'Indeed. I just saw our dear sister departing. What did she want?'

'Same thing you want, I suspect,' Poseidon answered. 'Medusa's whereabouts.'

'And do you know them?'

Poseidon gave Hades a thoughtful look, then shook his head. 'No, I don't. This whole thing is very unfortunate. Upset some major plans.'

'Your abduction of Medusa?'

Poseidon looked up sharply, the look of surprise clear on his features.

Hades had been half guessing, but Poseidon's expression confirmed his suspicions.

Hades shook his head, tutting in soft disapproval.

Poseidon stiffened. 'You're one to talk. You stole that wife of yours.'

Hades' stomach clenched. He hated anyone suggesting that Persephone was not with him by choice, but in this case, the general belief that Persephone stayed with him against her will may actually work in his favour. Who better to confide in than someone you believed had the same positive attitude towards female abduction and enforced marriage as you did?

'Taking her against her will is not so easy with a gorgon, though,' Hades remarked. 'Is that why you disposed of the head first? Medusa without a head still offers... possibilities; without the danger.'

Poseidon shrugged. 'I'd thought about that. And maybe a few months ago that would have been a pretty good compromise, but now I have other plans that require her to be intact.'

Hades knew his best bet was to play it cool. Poseidon was as unpredictable as the sea. If he waited for the tide to be right, there was no telling what Poseidon might reveal.

Sure enough, Poseidon beckoned Hades closer.

'Medusa wasn't always a gorgon, as you know,' he said, his eyes gleaming with nostalgia. 'She was once a beautiful, beautiful woman. And like any human woman, she has human feelings.'

'Feelings like hatred. Towards you. And she's not human now. That stare of hers will be hard to avoid in close quarters, so to speak.'

Hades noticed the sly look on Poseidon's face. He knew his brother well enough to know the old sea dog had something up his sleeve. But what?

'C'mon, Poseidon, what are you planning?'

Poseidon tapped the side of his nose knowingly and then grinned. 'Perhaps I should tell you, dear brother. It would be so good to share it with someone.'

Hades grinned back. Yes, he thought, the old seaweed-smelling bastard was going to give it up. He could almost hear those existence points dropping into his bank account.

II

A Trip to the Opera

CHIRON CAREFULLY STRAIGHTENED HIS TIE AND COMBED HIS TAIL. It wasn't often that he got to welcome a true goddess of the Old World, let alone two. Yet there they were, waiting for him in his office.

Hera, he knew, must have a serious purpose to come to the Trove twice in one day, but it was Athena he couldn't stop thinking about. The minute he had glimpsed her through the teller's glass a sizzle of attraction had run through him, stronger than he had felt for any female since he could remember. Seeing her made his brain feel foggy and his heart close to bursting. She was so beautiful, so strong. A much underrated beauty, if you asked him.

Funny how he'd never thought of it before, but he really should ask her on a date. Sure, she didn't have a reputation as someone who enjoyed male attention, but maybe she just hadn't found the right half-man half-horse yet.

He opened the cupboard and selected a can from his stash of perfumed body sprays. He liberally doused himself, hopefully covering his somewhat horsey aroma. He checked his reflection one more time before leaving the managerial restroom and heading to his office.

He composed himself at the door. He couldn't look like a love-struck colt, could he? Not someone of his position.

'My dear ladies.' He shut the door behind him and headed for his desk.

'We need some information,' Hera replied, barely flicking a glance in his direction. 'Access to the credit records. Chop, chop.'

Chiron was taken aback. The credit information of his clients was of the utmost personal nature. He did not just share it about willy-nilly.

'I'm sorry. You know I respect you, Queen Hera, but if I allowed anyone to look at the records–'

'We are hardly anyone,' Hera countered. 'Athena could get a lore court order, but that would waste time and energy. Save us the bother and just do what you are inevitably going to do anyway.'

Chiron stiffened. A creature of utmost politeness himself, he was somewhat unsure how to respond to so brusque a demand.

Athena smiled apologetically. 'It would be a personal favour.'

Chiron melted into the goddess' gaze and a shiver ran from his head right down to his hooves. He trotted to the window, checked that none of his staff was hanging around outside, and drew the blinds.

'Which files? Specifically?'

'Poseidon's,' Athena cooed sweetly.

Chiron stamped his foot, an unconscious response to stress. If the women had asked to see the files of a minor deity, a faery or an elemental creature maybe, he could have acquiesced, but the God of the Sea! The last time someone had displeased that grumpy old sea-goat they had found themselves in concrete shoes at the bottom of the Atlantic Ocean. With his four legs, he would sink all the faster.

But that damn beautiful goddess was still smiling at him; there was something so irresistible about her. He wanted to say no, but...

He struggled with his conscience for another few moments.

'You'll have to keep it between us.'

'Of course.' Athena smiled and Chiron felt all of his trepidation melting away in the blue oceans of her dazzling eyes.

Five minutes later the goddesses left the centaur's office clutching a manila envelope full of spreadsheets. Hera now knew exactly where to take this investigation.

They stepped onto the street and Athena gave an audible gasp as she undid the tight-fitting corset under her dress. It had made it almost impossible to breathe, but the Girdle of Irresistibility had achieved the desired effect.

'Maybe you should keep it on,' Hera remarked. 'It has certainly come in very handy.'

'I prefer to be able to breathe, thank you,' Athena replied. 'Anyway, I promised I would get it back to Aphrodite before six. She has a big date tonight and you know how she is.'

Hera nodded and waited while Athena called Hermes' messenger service. The wing-footed god appeared in his yellow van and took the corset, carefully noting down the delivery address before disappearing into the ether.

'You ready?' Hera asked.

'Are you sure this is the best idea?' Athena said. 'They aren't the easiest creatures to deal with.'

'No choice. You said follow the credits and this is where they go.'

Athena took a deep breath. 'Okay.'

The Sydney Opera House sat as a magnificent pearl on the edge of Sydney Harbour. Said by many to be based on the sails of the first fleet of Europeans to set up a colony in Australia, the style of the building was actually a tribute to the nine creatures who made its existence possible.

The house was a strange and extraordinary piece of art. Completely impractical, of course, with its endless flights of shallow stairs and cavernous chambers that were impossible to clean. But practicality was the enemy of creativity. Art could exist only in places where logic and realism give way to wondrous flights of fancy. Which was why Hera was fairly sure that if the elusive deities they sought were to be found anywhere, at least one of them would probably be here.

Hera and Athena walked amongst the thousands of tourists, all of whom seemed to be carrying selfie sticks, snapping away at the harbour views. The guard on the stage door didn't even see them as they slipped in and climbed the rickety metal staircases to the backstage of the opera theatre. As they drew closer, Hera heard the strings of the orchestra and the sound of a diva rehearsing. Hera hurried her step, avoiding the ropes, sandbags, props and wires that created the intricate web of staging in the shadows.

The human opera singer sang the first aria and Hera had to stop and listen. Even the usually unsentimental Goddess Queen couldn't help tearing up a little at the heartbreaking notes that held like fireflies in the air, creating an invisible light that wrapped the souls of all who listened.

The song ended and the director called a five-minute break. Hera and Athena stepped out onto the empty stage and saw the object of their search floating, illuminated, above the dress circle.

Realising that she had been seen, the naturally cautious spirit darted down into the balcony and disappeared.

'Polyhymnia, is that you?' Hera called. 'It's just us. Hera and Athena.'

The luminous light emerged cautiously from the seating and hovered reluctantly in the air.

'Please, Polyhymnia, we really need to speak to you.'

Spotlights flooded the stage, causing Hera and Athena to squint in the overwhelming glare. Then the luminous entity above exploded in a burst of stars. When Hera's eyes adjusted to the brightness, she saw Polyhymnia, manifested as a small, sharp-eyed girl, sitting in the dress circle, looking down at them.

'What can I do for the Queen of the Gods?'

Hera raised her hands above her eyes 'You could kill the lights for a start.'

Polyhymnia smiled and the lights flicked off. The theatre was plunged into darkness for a moment before a soft, dim light came up, giving the whole space an ethereal feel.

'Thanks. That aria was beautiful, by the way.'

Polyhymnia, the muse of sacred music, nodded. 'I don't often get to do many of the classics anymore. Most of the time it's pop tunes and hip hop music. Still, art must progress – it's not for me to judge.'

Polyhymnia waved her tiny, child-like hands in a gesture of good-natured resignation.

'But the Queen of the Gods has not come to chat about my artistic choices. What do you need inspiration for? And what are you willing to pay?'

'We're not here for inspiration; we need information.'

Polyhymnia shrugged. 'Not my department, Athena. As well you know. You could try Clio, if it's historical in nature. She's quite busy, though, with the current fad for historical and true crime media.'

'We need to know what Poseidon paid you for,' Hera said impatiently.

Polyhymnia frowned. 'Poseidon? I haven't seen that smelly old bastard for years. What makes you think he paid us for anything?'

'It's in his financial records. A massive transfer of existence credits into the Muses' corporate account.'

'We don't talk about our clients' dealings,' Polyhymnia said. 'The creative mind is a very, very vulnerable space and confidentiality is key.'

'We understand that,' Athena replied, 'and we wouldn't ask if it wasn't really important. And it's really, really important.'

The muse stared at them, her soft gaze impenetrable.

Hera shook her head, irritated. 'Look, we need to know what Poseidon bought. We think he's connected to the abduction of Medusa.'

Polyhymnia started. 'Medusa? She's been taken?'

'Her head has. We are trying to help find it before all Hades breaks loose.'

Polyhymnia was silent for a moment.

'I know it's not your usual business practice, but we would really appreciate your help,' Athena said softly.

Polyhymnia disappeared and Athena gave Hera a look. 'I knew they wouldn't help us. No one is harder to pin down than a bloody muse!'

But before Hera could reply, Polyhymnia was standing beside them holding a large paper scroll. She threw it down and it unrolled across the stage, revealing thousands of names and requests.

'Thalia and Melpomene dealt with him. He wanted a burst of inspiration across all forms of arts, but particularly film and television. It looks like Clio and Erato did the literature and film inspirations for him.' She sighed heavily. 'Everyone wants the visual arts these days; even musicians are abandoning me in favour of one of my sisters. Did you know Erato has just opened a big talent agency in Hollywood?'

But Hera wasn't listening to Polyhymnia and her accounts of sibling rivalry. Her head was spinning from the implications of what the muse had revealed. If Poseidon was featured in a number of films, then his existence credits would get a massive boost. What was he charging up power for?

'It's odd,' Athena remarked, studying the scroll. 'That is a huge amount of exposure credits and yet I haven't seen anything featuring Poseidon come out lately. There was that Greek epic, but we were all in that one.'

'Oh no, it wasn't for him,' Polyhymnia responded. 'Says here it was for a half-mortal called Perseus. A series of children's books, a movie franchise with him as hero and a perfume named after him. All up: seven million existence points paid for the inspiration. Would have yielded maybe 100 times that. Children's fantasy fiction is the hot investment right now.'

Perseus? Hera thought. This was the second time his name had popped up in the past three hours. And Poseidon helping him was, at the very least, out of character. So, what was Poseidon paying for?

Polyhymnia began rolling up the scroll and Athena thanked her.

'I really didn't think you would help us,' she said.

Polyhymnia smiled. 'I didn't do it for you. I did it for Medusa. We owe her. More than you can imagine.'

'You do?' Hera replied surprised.

Polyhymnia nodded. 'Oh yes. She's one of our greatest patrons. Her story has inspired countless books, artworks, movies, fashion houses, and she has given us free rein to tell and retell it. Without her the Greek pantheon would have become as unfashionable as the Sumerian, or–' she lowered her voice in disgust '–the *Phoenician*.'

Polyhymnia looked around. 'I must go. The performers should be back soon and I need to work out a way to get her to drop down an octave in the final chorus. It will make the whole song *luminate*!'

The muse transformed back into a burst of light and flew into the rafters as the opera company returned.

'Hey,' the director called to the goddesses, 'what are you two doing on the stage? We've got this theatre booked for another two days.'

'Sorry, we're just leaving,' Athena replied. 'The aria is beautiful, by the way, although the last chorus may work better in a lower octave.'

The director frowned, but Polyhymnia's light flashed brilliantly a couple of times and the director clapped his hands together. 'Claudia, try the final chorus in an E.'

Athena gave Polyhymnia a thumbs-up and the muse flickered in approval before blinking out.

12

We Certainly Don't Need Another Hero!

HERA HAD NEVER CARED MUCH FOR THE SO-CALLED GREEK HEROES. Forgetting for a moment most of them were a product of her husband's numerous affairs, they were, almost without exception, a group of immature, testosterone-fuelled imbeciles with more muscles than sense. Barely a brain cell to rub between them; they always seemed to be off on pointless quests and created all sorts of havoc at the slightest provocation.

The only useful thing about their complete lack of common sense was how easy it made them to find, particularly in the age of YouTube and TikTok, where stupidity was not only tolerated but openly celebrated.

She and Athena watched Athena's laptop screen on which a young, curly headed youth rode a fire-extinguisher-propelled shopping trolley down a five-lane highway. The consequences were fairly predictable and Hera watched as the trolley spun out of control and was slammed into by a semi-trailer.

The rider disappeared under the six sets of wheels before appearing, almost completely unscathed, on the side of the road. Brushing himself off dizzily, he gave a victory salute and was greeted with whoops and cheers from the teenage idiots filming the whole thing.

Athena sighed. 'Perseus hasn't changed at all, has he?'

'Nope. Are you sure we can get a location from this? It's just a nondescript highway somewhere.'

Athena tapped and clicked through a number of screens filled with code. It all looked like gibberish to Hera, but Athena navigated easily.

'This tells us the upload address. Knowing Percy, he's uploaded from wherever he's living. It wouldn't occur to him that it could be hacked. Here it is. He's on a property on the state border.'

'Anywhere near where those farmers were petrified?' Hera asked.

Athena looked at her phone for a moment and then nodded. 'A few miles away.'

Athena copied the address into her email and sent it to her phone's GPS.

'I don't know how you keep up with all this stuff, Athena,' Hera remarked. 'I can't even get my phone to go on the internet.'

Perseus' house was a non-descript brick farmhouse hunched into a scrappy piece of land on the border of Queensland and New South Wales. Far more remote than Hera would have imagined a young man like Perseus would want to live, and a good two-hour walk from the nearest portal. If Percy had suddenly come into a lot of existence credit, he certainly wasn't spending it on this dump.

'Maybe he's having a party?' Athena said, gesturing to several vehicles parked in the driveway.

The tired goddesses picked their way across the lawn, scattered with empty beer cans, rusting car carcasses and assorted rubbish, to the front door, which was wide open behind a wooden-framed screen.

'Anyone home?' Athena called, her voice echoing through the dim and seemingly empty house.

Hera rapped on the door frame but that was also greeted with silence. 'He's not here.'

'Probably off doing another stupid stunt.'

Just as the words left Athena's lips, the goddesses were startled by an explosion from the far side of the property. Hera and Athena ran around to the back of the house, where they saw a gang of five or six young men madly scrabbling through the debris of what looked like a demolished outbuilding.

A guy of about 25, sporting a well-manicured beard and wearing a checked collared shirt and skinny jeans, was filming the operation with obvious glee.

'Here he is,' one of the boys cried as Hera saw a hand, and then an arm, claw its way out of the rubble. The other boys rushed over, obscuring Hera's view.

'I'm cool! I'm cool,' a voice shouted.

The knot of men cleared to reveal Perseus, covered in stone dust, emerging from the remains of what once may have been a brick apple store. He looked as Hera remembered him: tall and lanky with a shock of curly brown hair, which was now matted with dirt and debris. He stood up, brushed himself off like nothing had happened and made a beeline to the hipster holding the camera.

'Did you get it, Toby?'

The grinning cameraman gave a big thumbs up. 'That was *epic*, Percy!'

Perseus grinned back, then crumpled, his legs collapsing under him. The boys crowded around and heaved him up onto their shoulders, carrying him like a hero from the battlefield.

They placed him gently down on an old lawn chair where he stretched out and inspected himself for injuries. His arms were scratched and he kept shaking his head, probably to try to stop the ringing in his ears. Still, not too bad, considering he had just blown up himself and a shed with what smelled like homemade dynamite.

'What the hell is he playing at?' Athena asked Hera.

The cameraman, Toby, whipped around and caught her in his frame.

'Whoa. What do we have here? Some nice little pussycats come to help us celebrate our tenth YouTube anniversary?'

Athena stared into the camera and Toby dropped it as though it was on fire. The flip-out screen smashed when it hit the ground.

'Shit!' He picked it up and checked to see if it was okay. It wasn't. 'Goddamn it! The camera's stuffed!'

The boys turned around. 'We've got the explosion, don't we, Toby?' One of them called.

Toby shook his head. 'I dunno. I'll have to see.'

'You're a goddamn boofhead,' another of the others yelled, striding towards Toby in a menacing manner. 'Percy risked his goddamn life for that clip. You better not have stuffed it.'

Perseus wasn't paying attention to the boys, though; he was staring at Hera and Athena. Hera saw the fear on his face and she couldn't help but smile. He *should* be afraid of her.

'It wasn't my fault, it was *them*,' Toby replied, pointing at Hera and Athena.

The other boys finally noticed the two women standing in the shrubby yard near the back door. The guy who had just menaced Toby licked his lips at the sight.

'Hello, ladies,' he said. 'Not often we get such pretty visitors!'

The other boys wolf whistled and started to move towards the goddesses, encircling them with leering faces. Hera and Athena didn't even glance at them, both intent on the object of their search: the Greek *hero*, Perseus.

One of the boys, not content with just leering, made the mistake of reaching out to touch Athena's shoulder.

'Hey, ladies, you wanna come have a drink?'.'

'I wouldn't do that, Gary,' Perseus called, getting shakily to his feet. But it was too late. The boy was tossed into the side of the house, falling into a crumpled and barely conscious heap. Before any of the other men could react, Athena flicked her hand towards them. They too flew backwards, landing awkwardly across the yard.

The dazed boys stood up groggily then, regaining their senses, began backing away or helping the more injured ones to their feet.

'Bloody lesbians,' one of them called out in false bravado before Athena glared at him.

'I'd be going now if I were you,' she said menacingly.

He quickly limped away, unwilling to take her on again. The other boys quickly followed, forgetting any concern for their injured mate, Perseus, who now stood alone amid the scattered lawn chairs.

Hera pulled a couple of chairs together, indicating that Perseus should retake his seat. Perseus looked at his retreating mates, then sat quietly in the plastic lawn chair. Hera dropped down onto the one next to him, took a beer from a nearby Esky and popped it open. Athena glancing at the rings of oil covering the other seats, quite sensibly remained standing.

'So, to what do I owe the pleasure?' Perseus said with false bravado. 'Not often we get goddesses around these parts.'

'Obviously,' Athena replied, casting her eyes around the filthy yard.

From the front lawn they could hear the sound of several utes roaring out of the property as the other boys took off, leaving Perseus alone with the goddesses.

Hera sipped the beer, which was warm and flat. 'What did you do for the credits?'

'What credits?' Perseus said, refusing to look Hera in the eyes.

'C'mon, Percy. Five films and a best-selling book series? We know what that's worth.'

Perseus shrugged. 'I'm a popular guy.'

'No, you're not. You're a cretin,' Hera replied.

Perseus looked up, a hurt expression on his face.

'What are you spending them on?' Athena looked around. 'It clearly isn't home renovation.'

'You know I'm not just some loser. I'm going to be a movie star; and not just YouTube videos. You've seen them, right? Last one got 80,000 views.' He grinned at the goddesses but they continued to look unimpressed.

'Yeah, I know – they're just kids' stuff. But I'm gonna make some real films. Features. Be a big-name action star like Vin Diesel. I'm gonna direct as well, coz that really is where the power is. Maybe do a few worthy films to get the Oscar nod.' He got himself a beer from the Esky and popped it open. 'Setting up a production company is damn expensive, but.' He thoughtfully took a swig.

'And for that you stole a woman's head?' Athena asked.

'What? Nah! What are you talking about?'

'Stop with the stupid act,' Hera said, knocking the beer from Perseus' hand.

'It's not an act!'

Hera and Athena glanced at each other and smirked, causing Perseus to redden.

'Honestly I don't know what you're talking about,' he continued weakly.

'Didn't you think that stealing Medusa's head again might be a bit obvious? Clearly you were going to be one of the first people suspected.'

'I– What? No, I didn't. I– Oh fuck. Her head is missing?'

Hera slapped Perseus across the back of the head. 'Don't you swear in front of a goddess, you little bastard.'

Perseus shook his head. 'No, I promise. It's part of my Lore Court parole not to go near Medusa again. Why would I take a risk like that?'

'You mean aside from the fact that you're a goddamn adrenaline junkie?' Hera said.

'Percy, come on, you can be honest. We know Poseidon paid off the Muses for you.' Athena leaned down to pat his shoulder in a reassuring way. 'We're not here to get you in trouble. We're here to find out what Poseidon is up to and get him to give Medusa her head back.'

'Look, I haven't done anything to Medusa. Poseidon bought me a few favours with the Muses, sure. I couldn't afford it and those gals don't play around. Serious mullah, you know. Not like the old days when you just had to have talent to get a shot. So he bought me a few moments of inspiration from some Hollywood studio head and a book writer.'

'And what did you do for him in return?'

'He just wanted to help me get a break–'

Hera slapped the back of Perseus' head again. 'Stop lying! Everyone knows Poseidon is not the charitable type. So why is he now suddenly shelling out cash for you?'

'I can't tell you anything.'

Hera was suddenly up and leaning over Perseus in an incredibly threatening manner. She was tired, it had been a long day, she was damp and her legs ached, and the premiere episode of *Married at First Smite* was airing in less than four hours and she hated having to watch it on catch-up. She had no interest in wasting any more time.

'Listen, you little waste of oxygen. You know what I am capable of. I have had boys much stronger and cleverer than you turned into gnats, like they were nothing more than flies on horseshit. If you keep messing me around, I promise that whatever Poseidon threatened you or promised you will be nothing to what I will do to you.'

Perseus recoiled. He looked at Hera's stony, terrifying face and then at Athena, who cocked her eyebrow at him.

'She can't just do that now, though, can she? I mean, there are lores!'

'I'd tell her what she wants to know, Perseus. I really would,' Athena replied. 'There's no lore against smiting a Greek hero. In fact, it's kind of the basis of most of the myths for us to be allowed to do just that.'

Perseus swallowed hard and then shook his head. 'It's not what you think. I swear I didn't have anything to do with Medusa's head. But he did want something and I helped him out.'

'What did he want?'

Perseus looked into Hera's eyes and sighed.

She could see him calculating his odds of survival if he continued to mess her around.

'Look, I have to show you, okay?' he said. 'So you understand. You have to follow me.'

Hera stepped back, allowing Perseus to stand up and, as soon as he regained his feet, she grabbed his wrist in a vice-like grip. 'Don't try to be clever, Perseus; it isn't in you. If you try anything like running away or evading us, I will smite you down – demigod or not. Clear?'

Perseus nodded solemnly and Hera released him. The two goddesses followed as Perseus walked towards a small garage, his legs still a little wobbly from the dynamite impact he had recently sustained. He opened the garage and straddled one of two quad bikes parked there.

'Come on.'

'I'm not getting on that thing,' Athena replied.

'Well, if you don't, you'll have to walk.'

'Fine, we'll walk.'

Hera looked at the bike and then at her stepdaughter's determined face.

'My knees are acting up a bit, Athena,' she said as she hoisted herself on behind Perseus. 'I don't think I'm up to any more walking.'

Athena scowled. 'I'll follow you.'

'Suit yourself,' Perseus called out over the roar of the revving engine. Then he hit the accelerator and spun the wheels, spraying dry dirt and dust across Athena before taking off at full throttle, with Hera holding on for dear life behind him.

13

The Secret in the Barn

Hera dismounted the bike, spitting bugs from her mouth as she wiped the grime and dust from her face.

'You could have offered me a helmet.'

'Only mortals need helmets,' Perseus replied as he scanned the fields. There were a few melancholy cows grazing half-heartedly in the far paddock. Some grey kangaroos, who had watched alertly as the quad bike approached, hopped away into the further reaches of the cleared land as Perseus turned the vehicle off, dismounted and walked towards a dilapidated barn standing a few feet away.

Hera followed, noting that the land was poorly cleared, scrubby and probably quite unsuitable for any real farm work.

'Why do you live out here?' Hera asked. 'I've seen your existence point balance, you certainly have more than enough for a decent place to live. Maybe not a house in a major city, because I know no one can afford that now, but surely you could do better than this.'

Perseus shrugged. 'I needed somewhere isolated. Away from any natural water.'

'To evade Poseidon,' Hera said. 'Why do you want to avoid your generous benefactor?'

'You'll see.'

Before Hera could question him further, she heard steady footfalls approaching, the sound of Athena's heel-to-toe stride unmistakable even from a distance. Hera glanced over and saw Athena hurrying in their direction, a trail of fine dust behind her. As she neared, Hera couldn't help but notice that her stepdaughter still looked immaculate. They had scaled a mountain, been drenched in the Atlantic Ocean and now traversed a filthy dustbowl and still, somehow, Athena managed to look like she had just stepped out of the pages of a Women's Health magazine. Hera self-consciously patted down her own wild hair, tangled and matted. She tried fixing it up with one of her hair combs but noticed it still straggled down her back in an ungoddessly mess. She gave up.

'That was fast!' she said as Athena arrived.

Athena looked down at her Fitbit with satisfaction. 'Excllent. Twenty thousand, four hundred and fifty,' she announced. 'I'm well over my step requirement for the day. I'm training for the Valhallha half marathon, you know.'

Hera felt her smile fix in place.

Athena was always training for something or other, and she supposed it made the goddess happy, but Hera really couldn't see the point of it. Hera felt that exercise, like most human activities was a boring waste of time and resources. Deities didn't need it, they were how humans fashioned them, more or less, and considering all their supernatural powers, competitions between gods often ended badly. Even Ragnarok had begun as a 'friendly' game of cricket until the Giants had caught Odin sandpapering the balls, and they all knew how that had turned out.

'Hera, you're pretty torn up,' Athena said, glancing at Hera's skirt, which now had a rip up the right side the length of her calf. It must have caught on something during their wild ride up to the paddock, Hera thought, annoyed. Still she wasn't going to waste existence points on mending it now. She'd change it when she got home, until then she would simply knot the material together at her knee and carry on.

Perseus was opening the barn now so Hera hurried over to make sure she was with him when he entered, in case he tried any funny business. He unlatched the last lock and stepped inside, with the goddesses close behind.

It took Hera a few moments to adjust to the gloom after the harsh sunlight of the Australian bushland, and another few seconds to realise that inside the barn was another, smaller enclosure, a large, metal room, totally closed off and locked with yet more padlocks and latches. The interior building looked like it had been hastily put together, built around what may have been a horse stable and then reinforced with new corrugated iron strips and sturdy planks of wood. The door was bolted with several large padlocks.

'Why all the security?' she asked. The place was in the middle of nowhere; what could possibly be so valuable as to require this amount of hardware to keep people out?

'You'll see,' Perseus said, unlocking the last padlock and wrenching the door open on its unoiled hinges.

It was even darker inside this room than the barn and Hera couldn't see anything at all. But she could hear soft animal noises, a kind of swishing and nickering. She elbowed Athena, giving her a warning look. Any kind of monster could be locked up in here, so they best be on their guard. Athena nodded and they followed Perseus inside.

As they stepped forward a white light flickered dimly within the stall. The goddesses shielded their eyes, taking in the weakly glowing creature that stood before them.

'I thought she was a myth,' Hera breathed.

'Aren't we all?' Perseus replied dryly.

The drip-drip-drip of the water was enough to drive Hades mad. He had been sitting in this damp, dank throne room on this horribly uncomfortable coral chair for hours, waiting for Poseidon to return. He knew it was a power play; the old sea dog was testing his resolve. He himself had inflicted similar annoying delays on one or other of his useless brothers over the years. It did delight him to leave them in the stinking sulphur rooms of the Underworld while he popped out, knowing that they would have to endure the wretched stench of death, which he ducted in whenever unwanted guests arrived, until he chose to have an audience with them. But to do such a similar thing to him was simply unacceptable.

Normally he would not put up with this nonsense, but Poseidon had dropped a lot of hints about Medusa, and Hades needed to know more. Five hundred million existence credits was a strong motivation.

If Poseidon did have the gorgon's head, it wouldn't be hard to get the information from him. Poseidon had never been as charming or beloved as Zeus, but he was just as prideful and arrogant. A bit of ego stroking, the right noises about how hard done by the old sea god had been, and

Hades was sure Medusa's head would soon be his – if not actually in his possession then certainly close enough to make no difference to him claiming the reward.

So, for the sake of solving all his financial woes he could put up with a bit of rudeness from his older brother.

A young mermaid popped up in one of the several large pools of water that dotted the room and placed a tray of seafood on the rocky ledge before disappearing back into the murky water.

Hades scowled. He not only abhorred the smell and texture of raw fish, he was also horribly allergic to anything from the sea. But he was hungry – ravenous, if the truth be told – so maybe he could pick around the fishy bits?

He picked up the plate of small beautifully prepared sashimi and sifted through it, but there wasn't even a bit of parsley garnish he could munch. The fish left a sticky, oily smell on his fingers regardless of how careful he was to try to avoid touching it. His stomach rumbled and he wondered if maybe he should leave now and come back after he had eaten something more attractive to him, a steak or a lasagne perhaps. Poseidon's secrets could wait until after luncheon, surely?

Just as he had made up his mind to cut his losses and leave, a flurry of tritons entered the room, blowing on large conch shells to signal the entrance of the King of the Sea.

Poseidon had changed into a robe of luminous fish scales and a crown of delicate anemone. His beard had been washed and curled, all presumably while Hades' Armani suit had further crinkled in the damp and *his* beard frizzed up into a scraggly tangle.

Hades smiled regardless, his wolf-like canines prominent in the gloom. 'You do look marvellous,' he said cheerfully. 'All your important business taken care of now, dear brother?'

Poseidon smiled back, a picture of charm and feigned apology. 'Oh yes, I am so sorry for the delay. But there is so much to do down here, you know. I may not officially have dominion over the oceans any longer, but the tides and currents still need a lot of looking after.'

'Of course, of course. Don't you worry, I was very happy here. Gave me a chance to really have a look around your place. Remind me to recommend a marvellous mould remover before I leave. It will do wonders.'

Poseidon's smile was fixed in place. 'Yes, thank you. I forgot you were such an expert on domestic duties. But, of course, you must do all your own cleaning, I imagine, seeing as Persephone is so well known for being unable to pick up a duster or prepare a meal.'

Hades' smile faltered for just a moment. References to his wife were one of his few weaknesses. But he was not going to let Poseidon know that the needling was effective.

Poseidon waved away the tritons, who disappeared into the ponds, and the two brothers sat on coral chairs, both shifting uncomfortably on the lumpy seats. Neither of them lost their smiles for a moment.

'You were telling me about Medusa,' Hades prompted.

The sea god nodded, his face blank but for the artificial smile.

'Why are you so interested all of a sudden, Hades?' Poseidon asked. 'You never asked me about her before.'

'I have always thought the way Athena interfered with you and Medusa was appalling,' Hades replied. 'One shouldn't come between a man and his sweetheart when they are courting.'

Poseidon nodded eagerly, his blank expression disappearing as soon as he heard someone taking his side. 'That's exactly right. What does a virgin know about love? Or a man's needs?' Poseidon said. 'She was beautiful, you know, Medusa. Exceptional. And she was going to throw herself away, tending to that virgin bitch. It wasn't right. She should have been worshipping me.'

'Yes, well, the goddesses always were the most popular with the people,' Hades remarked, 'particularly the women.'

'Female gods just create problems. If we had been an all-male pantheon the world would have been a much better place if you ask me. This new one has the right idea: keep the women right out of it.'

Poseidon tossed his trident aside angrily. 'But this missing head business – if Perseus had done what he was supposed to, none of this would have happened.'

'Perseus?'

'He was supposed to bring me something on Valentine's Day and he didn't show up. And now it's all gone wrong. If he had just done what I told him; but he's double crossed me! And now he's disappeared. Impossible to find. Still, the minute he comes anywhere near water, I'll have him! I have spies in every river, stream, lake, creek, lagoon and septic tank in the world. If he so much as flushes a toilet I'll be on him! The little bastard won't evade me for long.'

Poseidon, agitated now, grabbed the plate of seafood Hades had abandoned and popped the small pieces into his mouth one after the other. He was about to swallow the very last morsel, but stopped, gave Hades a sideways look, and offered him the final piece.

'You must be famished, brother. Please have a tempura prawn. I kidnapped a Michelin five-star chef from a cruise liner last month just so I could have him prepare them for me.'

Hades shook his head politely and Poseidon's smile disappeared.

'Are you too good to share a meal with your brother?' Poseidon asked. 'This isn't the Underworld, you know. Eating something here doesn't condemn you to stay forever.' Poseidon laughed suddenly, although Hades was unsure what the joke was.

'Thank you, but I'm not hungry,' Hades replied, just as his stomach released a growl that echoed across the cavern.

'Hard to trust a god who won't eat with you,' Poseidon remarked, looking at Hades with cold, dead-fish eyes. 'I was going to open up to you – after all, we are brothers – but perhaps it's best I don't.'

Hades smiled tightly and reached for the piece of prawn left on the plate. He eyed it before looking up and seeing Poseidon's gleaming, anticipatory face grinning at him. Hades' mouth had gone dry and he swallowed a couple of times, trying to moisten his tongue and palate. He swallowed hard, then popped the shellfish into his mouth, sucking it down so fast it got stuck in his throat, causing him to cough violently and his eyes to water. He beat his chest a few times and the shellfish dislodged and fell down into his awaiting stomach.

He wiped his eyes and composed himself, ignoring the burning sensation in his throat and the fact that he could already feel his face starting to swell. Poseidon grinned, satisfied, and settled back in his coral throne.

'Good to see you are keen to be on my side. Now that Hera and Athena are meddling it could all get quite messy. We need to get ahead of them. I won't have those two messing up my plans again.'

'Is this about revenge? Do you still want to punish Medusa for leaving you?' Hades asked, still not quite understanding what Poseidon's plans actually were.

Poseidon frowned. 'I don't want to punish Medusa. I want to help her.'

'You've never helped anyone in your whole sorry life,' Hades responded, squinting through his now puffy eyes. 'Especially not a woman.' He felt in his pockets for an antihistamine. He didn't find one.

Poseidon dropped his empty plate into a nearby pool where it was whisked away by a waiting dolphin.

'I need you to follow Hera, get involved in her investigation. I know she'll find Perseus faster than I can; she's not restrained by water. Plus she's always been one hell of a detective. When she does, you tell me where he is.'

'And why is Perseus involved in all this?' Hades asked, his nose now running profusely. 'You and he aren't exactly old pals now, are you?'

'You don't need to worry about any of that. Just do as I ask. I'll make it worth your while. More than that 500 million that Shiva is offering.'

Hades coughed through his swollen throat. 'Is Shiva offering 500 million?'

'You know he is. They all want Medusa dead. But I am not going to let that happen.'

Hades thought for a moment. 'Well, I've already approached Zeus to share information.'

Poseidon stood up anxiously. 'Does he know what Hera knows? Is he in it with her?'

Hades shook his head dismissively. 'Have you ever known Hera to share anything with him? No, he doesn't know anything; as usual.'

'So why work with him,' Poseidon replied, 'when I can be a much better ally.'

'You want me to help you get Medusa so you can use her glare to finally kill Zeus, or me, maybe; that's what I think,' Hades replied.

'Why would you think such a thing?' Poseidon exclaimed. 'My plans have nothing to do with either of you.'

'We may be brothers, Poseidon, but we all know not one of us would think twice about murdering the others if we thought we could get away with it without breaking the Great Lores. No, I think we all know that a dead Medusa is in everyone's best interest.'

'No, she mustn't be killed!' Poseidon cried.

For the first time, Hades saw real fear in Poseidon's eyes. He really did want Medusa alive, but why?

'It's true; the fact is I can't stand you or Zeus. And I know the feeling is mutual,' Poseidon said. 'But this isn't about our sibling rivalry. In fact, if you help me find Perseus, I can guarantee you that Medusa's glare will never be a threat against anyone ever again. Guarantee it!'

'You have no control over Medusa!' Hades replied, annoyed at his brother's inability to accept reality.

Poseidon shook his head. 'She'll do what I say.'

It was Hades' turn to laugh. He knew his brother was demented, but this was just plain lunacy. 'You think a woman you raped and humiliated and who was then turned into a horrifying monster simply to escape you, who now has the ultimate power to destroy any god or mortal – you think *she* will just kneel down and do what you tell her? I know you suffer from male entitlement, but seriously? She hates your stinking fish guts.'

'Athena turned her against me. I told you, everything will be different soon; we'll be a family.'

Hades was beginning to think he was wasting his time. Could a man this disconnected to reality really know or do anything that could help him collect that reward money?

Revenge against Athena or Zeus, even a bit of a rampage through the mystical realms with Medusa's powerful head – that he could understand. But this romantic fantasy – it was absolute insanity.

Yet Poseidon seemed so sure. So completely assured that not only would Medusa come back to him, but that she would cease to be a monster at all. There had to be something that Poseidon knew that Hades didn't. But what was it?

'I'll help you on one condition,' Hades said finally. 'You tell me what your big plan is. How are you going to make this fanciful idea a reality?'

'Let's just say I have access to something extremely powerful.'

'Her head,' Hades stated, still unsure how this helped Poseidon achieve his romantic fantasy.

'I don't have her damned head,' Poseidon shouted.

Hades gave him a puzzled look. 'Then what do you have?'

'Something better,' Poseidon replied.

'Better?' Hades frowned. What was Poseidon going on about?

'I have our child,' Poseidon answered smugly.

Hera, Athena and Perseus stood in front of the miserable winged horse as the creature feebly looked up at them. Her glow was growing fainter, as if the effort of illumination which had greeted them as they entered the room had cost her dearly, and she looked weak and miserable, tied down in the stall, wrapped with heavy chains, her feathered wings firmly wrapped in even more bonds of silver and gold. The whole effect was horrifying. Like seeing a fragile baby bird being held alive within the jaws of a cat.

'Ladies, meet Pegasus, daughter of Poseidon and Medusa.'

Hera had heard of the legendary horse. Everyone had. Reportedly birthed of the sea from the blood of Medusa's severed head, there had been some stories of Pegasus from time to time. The hero Bellerophon had boasted that he had ridden the flying creature when he destroyed the chimera in Thebes. But none of these reports could be verified and Bellerophon, like most of the Greek heroes, was a renowned braggart and outright liar. No one had ever even seen him with the horse, but if he had somehow managed to capture her, he certainly hadn't kept her for long as Pegasus had soon disappeared entirely, leading many to question her very existence.

By the time Athena had originally retrieved Medusa's head from Perseus, stories of Pegasus had been little more than mere rumours, nothing more than the imaginings of boastful boys trying to impress the nymphs with their connection to such a rare creature. All seemed to agree that if Pegasus had ever existed, she was gone now, disappeared in grief and sorrow for the loss of her mother, or destroyed by obsessed deities who made sport of hunting and killing rare and beautiful creatures. After the fall of the Greek pantheon, even though Pegasus continued to be whispered about, most of the Greek gods and goddesses came to believe that she had never existed at all, merely a myth within a world of myths.

Yet here she was: the magnificent winged horse, said to be the embodiment of love and peace.

Athena immediately rushed to the horse and stroked her soothingly while Hera inspected the chains which held the creature down. They were unbelievably heavy, forged no doubt in Hephaestus's workshop. Divine chains to hold a divine entity, they would not be easy to remove.

'Where did you find her?' Athena asked.

'The faeries have been hiding her in their realm. They kept it a good secret, but a drunken elf let something slip during a poker game and I have been tracking her down ever since.'

Hera stepped around to the front of Pegasus and the horse raised her face. Even in this distressed and filthy condition, there was no doubt that Pegasus was an extraordinary creature. Seeing her enslaved like this made Hera's bile rise. Who could treat a beautiful being so terribly?

She turned on Perseus. 'Unchain her. Now!'

Perseus stepped back in alarm. 'No. She'll escape. You have no idea how hard she was to catch. I can't risk her getting out.'

Athena stood by the horse, bending slightly to stroke her matted mane. Pegasus snickered quietly but didn't seem to have the strength to do much else.

'You can't keep her like this.'

'I can't risk her out in the open. She may be seen.'

'Why does it matter if anyone sees her?' Athena asked.

'Because she needs to be hidden, or he'll take her.'

'Who'll take her? Percy you are not making any sense. You are the one who is holding her prisoner.'

'No, I am protecting her; *from* Poseidon.'

Hera frowned, she wasn't surprised her rotten brother was mixed up in this somehow, but how?

'Why would Poseidon want to take her?'

'I don't know, exactly, but he wanted her for something. He was there, at the poker game when the drunken elf blabbed about Pegasus. He knew he would never get away with going into the Fae realm to retrieve her, so he got me to do it. I was to deliver her to him on Valentine's Day.'

'You kidnapped her, for Poseidon?' Athena could not hide her dismay.

'He promised me the favour of the Muses if I did. I couldn't tell him no, could I?'

'Actually, you could.'

'Look I didn't even think she would be there, or if she was that I would manage to capture her. I mean, it's Pegasus. But he promised me existence points even for trying. And it was such an amazing challenge.'

He saw the hard glares of the women and changed tack. 'But then, when I found her and managed to catch her, well, I couldn't give her over. Not when... well, it's hard to explain but Pegasus makes you *be* better. The minute I brought her back here, I felt like I could do anything, be anything. It's like she takes who you are and amplifies it into this incredible focused force. My YouTube videos have never been so amazing!'

He looked at the goddesses beseechingly. 'I know everyone says she's

Poseidon's daughter because his foam and Medusa's blood created her. But she isn't, not really. I mean, if it wasn't for me cutting Medusa's head off, she wouldn't have been bleeding in the first place. I'm more of Pegasus' father than he is.'

'You have got to be kidding,' Hera snapped.

'Look, I know what you think of me, Hera. Even if I wasn't Zeus' son you would still think I was a loser, and you would be right.

'Sure, the myths call me a hero, but we all know I was just a stupid arrogant kid. Still am I suppose. But I was imagined that way. I can't help it; we heroes are mostly designed to be dickheads. But when Pegasus is nearby, well I feel more heroic, braver, more unstoppable. I can't just give her up now.'

Hera shook her head in disbelief. The entitlement of this man! Imagine thinking he had the right to keep a creature like Pegasus captive just because it made him feel better about himself. Just when she thought she couldn't think any less of this dumb, infuriating young imp, Perseus opens his mouth and her respect for him plummets once more.

'She's not yours.' Hera stated firmly, turning to inspect how to unlock the cruel, heavy chains that bound the horse.

'Pegasus would never have existed without me. That's a fact. And Poseidon isn't going to treat her well. She's just a means to an end for him.'

'What end?' Hera asked, turning slightly. A thought niggled at the back of her mind, something she almost remembered, a link, a clue, something about Pegasus and what Perseus had been saying about her, but she couldn't quite connect it yet. She should have listened more carefully to what he said, but he was so annoying.

Perseus shrugged. 'He said he needed her for some big plan.'

'What?'

'I don't know! But I *do* know he doesn't care about her. He's been nothing but a deadbeat dad her whole life. I'll take care of her.'

'Like this?' Hera gestured around the dark, filthy room. 'You don't care about her any more than Poseidon does.' She locked her cool grey eyes upon Perseus. 'All you care about is yourself, and becoming famous again. And now you're trying to play us, because you've burnt your bridges with Poseidon and you need protection. Well you made a big mistake thinking we would let you keep on doing this.'

'No!' Perseus said. 'It's not like that.'

The stony expressions on the goddesses faces didn't change and Perseus sighed. 'Okay, maybe at first, it was about the existence credits. I admit it. But he's offered me another 100k to hand her over to him, and I haven't – so you're wrong about me.'

'You haven't because you think she's more valuable than the existence points,' Hera countered. 'You haven't changed, you always were a cruel, petulant, selfish child.'

'No,' Perseus replied, stamping his foot like a petulant, selfish child. 'I'm the good guy here. I'm keeping her safe. She's mine and no one else can have her, not Poseidon and not you two."

'She's not yours,' Athena snapped. 'She doesn't belong to you. She is a living mythical creature as entitled to a life as any of us. You have no claims on her, you entitled little dickwad. No one who cared about a creature would treat her as badly as this.'

Perseus looked shocked. 'I had to lock her up for her own good. I had to keep her safe from Poseidon.'

'You stupid little boy,' Hera spat. 'Do you really think if Poseidon turned up here you will be any match for him?'

'He'll never find me here,' Perseus said. 'He doesn't have any eyes where there's no water, and this land has been in drought for decades. As long as I keep away from the sea or the lakes and rivers, and don't use any running water, his minions can't locate me.'

'The only reason you still have Pegasus is because Poseidon's too stupid to team up with one of the other deities who can search beyond the seas and waterways. But, if what you said is true and Poseidon needs Pegasus for something, then that will change, and when it does, you'll not keep her hidden for long.'

'This place is in the middle of nowhere. It's impossible to find.'

'We found you,' Athena reminded him.

Her words, softly spoken as they were, had a visibly stronger impact than all of Hera's shouting. Perseus' mouth twisted in fear.

'Did you decapitate Medusa to keep her from Pegasus too?' Athena asked.

Perseus shook his head violently. 'No. No! I told you I didn't have anything to do with that. Anyway, I don't think she even knows about Pegasus. And I want to keep it that way.'

'Of course she knows about Pegasus!' Hera said. 'She's Medusa's child.'

Athena stroked the horse's neck and shook her head slowly. 'Actually, it's possible that she doesn't,' she said. She met Hera's confused look.

'Medusa was already decapitated and blindfolded before Pegasus was even born. Then she was lost for decades. By the time Medusa was recovered, most of the world thought Pegasus was little more than a story. The gorgon sisters, even if they had known about the legend of Pegasus' birth, may well never have mentioned it to Medusa. Her child was long lost; why add another misery to Medusa's already miserable life?'

Hera nodded; sad as it was, she could see the logic of it.

The horse neighed and Athena stroked her mane again, calming her. Slowly she started releasing the chains, using focused zaps of energy to break the mystical locks. Perseus stepped forward but Hera blocked him from getting any closer.

'Don't even think about it,' Hera said as she turned and helped Athena, grateful that she had withdrawn all those extra credits earlier, because this was a huge drain of her already somewhat depleted existence energy. But there was nothing for it, and her usually frugal ways would have to be cast aside this once, as it was clear Perseus would not unlock the poor creature of his own accord.

As the last heavy chain fell to the floor, the horse scrambled to her feet and stretched out her magnificent wings, the feathered tip touching the roof of the room. Her shimmering glow brightened, flooding the space and the larger barn beyond the open door with glorious silver light.

Looking at Pegasus, Hera's heart filled to bursting. She had never known such happiness, such peace. Something about this creature melted even the most righteous anger, and she found that she could not even be upset at Perseus anymore. She could hardly blame the boy for wanting to keep such a beautiful animal.

'Are you sure Poseidon doesn't know she's here?' Athena asked.

'He'd be here if he knew. That's why I have been trying to keep a low profile.'

Hera snorted. If this was Perseus' idea of a low profile, goddess knew what he did when he wanted to get attention.

'You're not going to tell him, are you?' he said.

'No, of course not,' Hera said, and Perseus visibly relaxed.

'I knew it was the right thing to tell you two,' he said. 'I knew you'd help protect us.'

Hera waved Perseus away.

'We're forgetting about those petrified farm workers,' Athena said, turning to Perseus. 'My guess is Poseidon was looking for you and stumbled upon those poor fruit pickers instead. That means he's closer than you think.'

'You think Poseidon knows where I am?' Perseus said, shaking. 'And he took Medusa's head just to petrify me?'

Athena shrugged. 'I don't know. He should be here by now if he was that close this morning. It's not quite fitting together yet. But it doesn't matter. Those workers are enough to alert anyone that Medusa has been out here somewhere and pretty soon anyone with half a brain and a urge to hunt down Medusa will be turning up here. They might not know about Pegasus, but with Medusa's head missing, you've got to be the number one suspect, we won't be the only ones to figure that out.'

'What do we do now?'

Athena ignored Perseus' question and turned to Hera.

'We owe it to the gorgons to let them know Pegasus exists.'

Hera nodded. 'But we have to be careful. We know Poseidon is looking for her, and if he has got Medusa's head then he has already shown he can evade the security of Monsters' Realm. She won't be safe if we take her there.'

'You can't take her anywhere,' Perseus cried, moving towards the horse and throwing his arms around her neck. 'She's mine!'

The goddesses stared at him and Athena said evenly, 'She is not yours. She is her own. And she will not be caged up like this by some half-baked demigod just because you think you have some claim of ownership.'

Perseus expression hardened, anger flooding through his flushed face, but the goddesses dismissed him, turning to each other to determine the best course of action.

'I still think the best bet is Monsters' Realm,' Athena argued. 'They would have doubled security now after the breach, and with all the threats against them. Once we get Pegasus to safety, we can focus on finding Medusa's head.'

Hera nodded. 'Okay. If Poseidon has Medusa, and I'm convinced now that he does, then Pegasus is also part of whatever his fiendish plan may be. We need to get her to safety.'

Hera had barely finished speaking when she saw the blood draining from Athena's face. For the second time that day Hera felt herself yanked backwards by Athena.

'He's got a bomb,' Athena cried.

The barn exploded in light and fire as the leftover dynamite Perseus had hidden in his coat was ignited and tossed towards the side of the barn.

The goddesses were thrown back, coughing and spluttering from the fumes of the explosion.

The winged horse neighed in alarm, rearing away from the chaos. Perseus grabbed her by her long white mane, ushering her towards the fiery gap the explosive had made in the wall and urging her out into the barn and through the big double doors into the daylight. As she galloped towards the opening, he clambered up on her back.

Athena, quick as lightning, vaulted onto the horse, grabbed Perseus and dragged him to the ground.

Pegasus now totally free, ran through the open barn doors and launched into the sky.

Perseus struggled against Athena, who threw him roughly back into the dirt and kicked him in the ribs.

'Stay down,' she cried, slamming his head into the ground. 'What the hell were you thinking?'

Hera, seeing that Athena had Perseus under control, started to chase after the ascending horse. There was no hope. Pegasus, finally freed after being held captive, flew fast and straight over the horizon. Hera once again cursed her own inability to take flight. Perseus sank back into the dirt as the horse disappeared into the stratosphere.

Hera returned to the barn, sweaty and dishevelled. She knew she didn't have enough existence credit left to go after Pegasus, but she had more than enough to teach this rotten little upstart a lesson or two. She pulled him up roughly. 'Where is she going?'

Perseus shook his head desperately. 'I don't know.'

A surge of anger pulsated through Hera and she unleashed it on the youth, sending him several feet up into the air before crashing him to the ground. He fell unconscious from the impact and Hera stepped forward, intending to finish the job.

Athena put her hand on Hera's arm. 'Stop. We might need him. Can you get Artemis?'

Hera turned to Athena with a look of surprise. 'You're suggesting Artemis?'

Athena shrugged. 'I know we're not exactly best friends, but she can track any living creature – mythical or otherwise. If anyone can find Pegasus, Artemis can.'

'I doubt she'll be that interested in helping us,' Hera replied. 'You know how she feels about me, remember how she accused me of being an agent of the Patriarchy at Ishtar's birthday party a few years ago?'

'But she won't be helping us,' Athena countered, 'she'll be helping Pegasus. She's hardly going to refuse, is she, considering all her claims of caring about nature and the creatures of the Earth. But you need to hurry. We need to find Pegasus before Poseidon does.'

Hera nodded. 'Okay. Stay here just in case Pegasus comes back. And you'll need to keep an eye on Percy; we can't trust him an inch.'

Hera threw a last angry look at Perseus, who was starting to come around, coughing and spluttering in the dirt, nursing his broken ribs. 'And you! Don't you try anything, or I will unleash the powers of Olympus upon you. I might not be a queen deity anymore, but I can put a worthless little halfling like you down. Is that clear?'

Perseus nodded, defeated, and Hera turned on her heel. 'It's 50km to the closest portal, but I'll be as quick as I can getting back.'

'Don't worry,' Athena replied. 'I'll keep an eye on things here.'

Hera walked over to the discarded quad bike. After a few minutes trying to work out how to get it into gear, she got the engine to rev and then hesitated, suddenly uneasy. Was this delay a bad idea? Should she really be focusing on retrieving Pegasus, who was essentially fine and free now, while Medusa's head was still out there somewhere, possibly causing no end of havoc? Then she remembered how miserable and frightened Pegasus had looked bound and chained in that barn and knew she couldn't risk Poseidon or one of his minions finding her before she did. If Poseidon got his hands on Pegasus, it would be much, much harder to get her back to Monsters' Realm and her real family.

Hera didn't know how or why, but the Fates had somehow led her here to this barn and this horse and she knew better than to question that. The fact was that those creepy old witches never did anything without a reason, and if they had led her here, then she ignored them at her peril.

Hera revved the bike and took off. On the way she would work out what she would say to her estranged stepdaughter. It would be a difficult conversation with Artemis; after all, she had tried to kill Artemis' mother. And that was the least of their issues.

14

The Huntress

THE *YOU'RE A GODDESS WOMYN'S CENTRE*, A PURPLE AND GREEN cottage in the inner-Sydney suburb of Newtown, was nestled between a trendy vegan café and a newly-erected apartment building that dwarfed the little house. The centre's noticeboard was plastered with leaflets for sacred women's yoga retreats and a divine violence helpline.

As Hera approached, she saw Artemis, Goddess of the Hunt, an intimidating muscular woman in jeans and a RADFEM singlet, watering a tall sunflower that seemed to move its head as if searching for something in the sky. A small, mousy-looking woman stood behind Artemis, staring around nervously, like she was frightened of her own shadow.

Artemis was ignoring the woman as she tenderly patted the petals on the flower. 'You know he's not even up there anymore, right?'

The sunflower head drooped slightly and Artemis lifted it and turned it towards her. 'Clytie, you can go back to your human form if you just accept the he isn't interested in you.'

Clytie, the nymph who was a sunflower, turned her head away from the goddess and resolutely looked back up at the sky, hoping to get a signal from the Sun God that her affections were returned. She didn't get one. Aside from the fact that Helios no longer pulled the sun across the sky, he had shown no interest in the nymph for the past two and a half millennia; it was unlikely that he would change his mind now. Still, Clytie refused to give up, and so a sunflower she remained.

Artemis had watched the lovesick nymph standing for days in a field, waiting patiently for Helios to return to her. Their brief, clumsy roll in the hay meant so much more to her than it did to the promiscuous god who hadn't even bothered to ask her name before seducing her and leaving her heartbroken and deserted.

No amount of persuading would convince Clytie that Helios didn't love her as much as she loved him, and finally, fearing that the nymph would die of exposure or starvation, Artemis had transformed the girl into a tall yellow flower. Even in this form Clytie had continued to search the skies for Helios.

As the years passed, the flower nymph never gave up hope and, as much as it annoyed Artemis that a woman could be so foolish, she was also a little impressed by that level of devotion; so she had transplanted Clytie into a flower pot and cared for her across the millennia, finally planting her in this garden when she bought the house and transformed it into a woman's centre in the late 1970s.

The soil wasn't perfect for a sunflower, but Artemis made sure there was good drainage and she had plenty of sunshine, and Clytie had survived well enough. Clytie had really been the first resident of the women's shelter, although unfortunately not the last.

'I just wish you could realise that you don't need a man to be happy,' Artemis said as she finished watering the plant.

'Happy,' the small woman behind Artemis repeated.

'Echo,' Artemis said, turning to her companion, 'we've talked about this. You have to make the effort. Remember, try using a synonym instead of the actual word, okay? It's the only way you'll make any real progress.'

'Progress,' Echo replied.

Artemis sighed and then smiled in the way social workers do to hide their frustration at a particularly dense client. 'That's right. But what might be another word for progress?'

'Progress?' Echo repeated.

'Yes, but try another word.'

Echo screwed up her face in concentration. 'Word.'

'Okay, let's try something different,' Artemis said. 'How about cat? What's another word for cat?'

Echo looked around hopelessly. 'Cat.'

'Another word for cat,' Artemis prompted. 'Come on, we've done this before. You were doing well last week. Cat.'

'C...Ca...Kitten!' Echo stuttered. Then her face broke out in a wide smile. 'Kitten!'

'That's right. Kitten. Good work,' Artemis said.

'Work,' Echo replied.

Artemis' smile slipped slightly but she froze it in place and squeezed Echo's hand.

'We'll get there. It may take a few more centuries, but I believe in you, Echo,' she said.

'Echo,' Echo replied, her smile replaced with a look of complete misery.

Artemis, turning towards the centre, spied Hera standing at the gate.

'What do you want?' Artemis asked.

'Want?' Echo repeated.

Hera stepped into the garden and nodded to Echo. The nymph stepped back, fearful. Hera rolled her eyes. Why did everyone have to hold a grudge? Sure, she had cursed the nymph a few thousand years ago, but at what point would these women be able to build a bridge and get over it?

'I need your help,' Hera said, ignoring Echo.

'Group therapy for goddesses and immortals who have been abused or cheated on by the gods starts at 6pm. It gets crowded though, so I advise you to come early,' Artemis replied, walking into the centre. Hera followed, grabbing the door to prevent Artemis slamming it closed.

'Not that kind of help.'

'Really?' Artemis cocked an eyebrow at her stepmother. 'Because if any goddess needed to be at that meeting, it's you. Most of the other women are there because of Zeus too, you know. Amazing how much trauma one god can create, isn't it? Europa and Leda are lifetime members.'

Hera felt her stomach tighten. Zeus had a particular fondness for transforming into animals and using that guise to catch gentle young women unaware. He had used the same trick to get her to marry him. It had been a shady thing to do, but an effective one. Only later did she learn he had used it many times on other unsuspecting women. They, however, had not been a powerful goddess he wanted to marry. At best he had seduced and abandoned them; at worst, well, they ended up in a place like this.

'I am not responsible for Zeus' actions,' Hera stated, deliberately glancing at the sunflower standing dejected in the garden. 'Any more than you are for what Helios did.'

Artemis backed away from the door and Hera entered.

'No, but you *are* responsible for turning a blind eye to them,' Artemis replied.

'To them,' Echo repeated.

'Not to mention the carnage you left, covering up for and avenging *his* infidelities.' Artemis looked pointedly at Echo, who seemed to be creeping ever closer to the Huntress, almost clutching at her legs.

Hera waved the accusation away. Echo was weak and stupid, a regular little chatterbox who had connived with Zeus to hide his indiscretions with other nymphs. Sure, she may not have personally slept with Hera's husband, but Echo had facilitated his betrayals by distracting Hera with gossip and new ambrosia recipes while Zeus was having his way with every forest nymph he could get his hands on.

So now Echo had to repeat the last thing she heard, an apt punishment, Hera believed, for a woman who had kept secrets from her. Hera had no time for those of the female sex who betrayed other women, particularly those who helped men to do so. She thought Artemis, of all people, would understand that.

'She got what she deserved,' Hera replied. 'She didn't care how her actions hurt me.'

'Hurt me,' Echo repeated.

'You can't see the irony in that, considering how you tormented and punished women for centuries because of things Zeus did?' Artemis laughed harshly. 'Honestly, Hera, you are almost as bad as the men.'

'I certainly am not!' Hera replied, indignantly, ' Most of those stories were rumours made up by that bastard, Ovid. You know I didn't do half the harm the legends say I did. He did a similar hatchet job on Athena, and you know it.'

'Be that as it may,' Artemis countered, 'you did hound my pregnant mother until she died.'

Hera did feel bad about that. In retrospect it was poor impulse control. Although she hadn't actually killed Leto when she had the chance; and ended up helping Artemis and Apollo as much as she could to make up for her treatment of their mother. She knew she had been a bit harsh, but to be fair there wasn't such a thing as couple counselling or even a therapist she could have worked through her betrayal and anger issues with back in those days. Maybe if there had been, she would've found a healthier way to work through her rage than blaming those with whom Zeus had cheated, or fathered children with.

'Honestly, Hera,' Artemis said, breaking into her thoughts, 'I think Echo has suffered enough. Goddess knows I have, having to listen to her all day.'

Hera turned to Echo and looked her up and down. The girl shrank further back behind Artemis, trying to place the massive woman between herself and Hera.

'You know as well as I do that my curse doesn't have to survive beyond our reign as divine rulers. She's stayed like this because she wants to. She's too weak or stupid to go back to normal. That or she wants to live in a pool of her own misery.'

'Misery,' Echo agreed.

'Okay, okay, point taken,' Artemis said wearily, sitting on an overstuffed couch, one of many mismatched pieces of furniture in the small recreation room. 'Echo, go and get us some tea.'

'Tea,' Echo replied, heading out of the room and away from the Queen of the Gods. Hera didn't even glance at her as she left, turning her attention to Artemis.

The young goddess looked tired. She had taken on a lot with this centre. It couldn't be easy offering services to women harmed by gods – there were so bloody many of them. And now she was going to add to Artemis' burden, but there really was no one else as uniquely suited to assist.

'I need your help.'

'Yeah, you said.' Artemis said gruffly, glanced at Hera and then softened. 'Okay. You know I never turn down a needy female and honestly, I am glad you've finally come to your senses and left him.'

'Left him?' Hera repeated, then caught herself. Damned if she was going to become like that idiot Echo. 'Left who?'

'Zeus, of course,' Artemis replied.

'I haven't left Zeus.'

Sure, she wanted to leave the horny old toad who had treated her like dirt their whole married life, but Hera was the goddess of marriage; divorce was not something she could do without losing her whole identity. Goddess knew if it were, she would have done it centuries ago and saved her, and a lot of other women, a tonne of grief.

'Why has he been ringing here then?' Artemis asked.

'He's been ringing *you*?'

'Yes, said you had disappeared. He's been ringing around the whole family apparently, trying to find you.'

'Oh for Olympus' sake! I've been gone less than six hours! What did he say, exactly?'

'He claimed some emergency. I really wasn't listening. I just figured you had finally had enough of the old goat and he was trying to get you back.'

Hera now remembered the many calls she'd been ignoring from her husband all day. They hadn't seemed important. But if he was ringing his illegitimate children to find her, there was probably some disaster he had created that he needed her to clean up. 'What kind of emergency?'

'I don't know,' Artemis replied. 'I don't listen to the creepy old bastard, do I?'

'Okay, I'll ring him later. But that is not why I'm here. I need your help with something else.'

'Hera, I'm really–'

'Pegasus,' Hera said.

Artemis sat up straight, as if an electric current had run through her.

'Okay, I'm listening.'

Athena sat in the stifling heat of the outdoor dunny, trying to take her mind off the disgusting conditions as she evacuated her bowels. This had to be the worst toilet she had ever been forced to use, and she had camped out with the armies during the Trojan War!

She unrolled some of the sandpaper that passed for toilet tissue in outback Australia and delicately cleaned herself. She stood up, adjusted her stola and spent a few extra seconds removing some stubborn paper stuck to the bottom of her sandal. She tossed it into the filthy toilet bowl and pulled the flush. Nothing happened. She tried again and realised there was no water in the cistern and no way to connect any. Of course, Perseus had shut off all the water systems – no wonder everything was so filthy in here. With a scowl she stepped out and closed the door.

Relieved to be breathing fresh air again, she couldn't help feeling she was carrying the smell of fetid waste out into the field with her. The fact that a number of particularly attentive blowflies seemed intent on buzzing around her added to this concern. She swatted them away expertly, killing three with one well aimed slap, although she was sure more were already targeting her.

How she wished, yet again, humans hadn't been quite so detailed when imagining their divinities in their own image. Athena was somewhat fussy about her appearance and spent a great deal of her personal power making sure she always looked and smelt immaculate. Being lumbered with human bodily functions did not make this easy. Having to eject waste from her body was bad enough when able to use the gold-plated facilities of Mount Olympus. There, at least, winged cherubs kept everything spotless and stocked with toilet paper woven from clouds. But to have to deal with it on the Earthly plane in these conditions was unbearable. Usually if she was forced to spend any time on the Mortal Realm she managed without too much complaint, but one had to admit, even by mortal standards, these facilities were appalling.

Athena acknowledged she was perhaps more worried about her appearance than most goddesses. She didn't kid herself she was beautiful like Aphrodite, or the epitome of idealised girlhood innocence like Persephone, but she knew she could attain a regal attractiveness from natural good breeding and a rigorous health and beauty regime. Over the years this focus had become something of an obsession, perhaps verging on a nervous disorder, as she felt compelled to ensure her appearance was perfect at all times. If she had one hair out of place, or her stola wasn't flowing quite right, she would obsess about it until she was sleepless and tetchy.

As a result she used up a lot of her existence credit on her appearance, far more even than Aphrodite. She knew it wasn't healthy, this focus on her looks. She had never been this way when she was younger. In fact she'd never even worried about how she looked until she made the mistake of entering that god-awful beauty contest against Hera and Aphrodite, goaded on by Zeus and the other lustful gods.

She didn't even know why she had let herself be pulled into it because, goddess knew, looks were not important to how loved she had been back then. The whole of the Athenian state had adored her and her temples and worshippers dwarfed any dedicated to the other Gods, even Zeus himself.

But, somehow, she and Hera had been convinced that competing against Aphrodite in a swim suit was 'empowering' in some unexplainable way and so she'd given in. Artemis, of course, always one to recognise a bad idea, had tried to talk her out of it, warning her about the lecherous and insidious power of the male gaze to diminish even the most confident of young goddesses. But, if truth be known, Artemis' warnings had only further strengthened Athena's determination to be part of the contest, to be judged and gawked at and measured against some kind of arbitrary standards of female beauty. Why? Because Athena liked to win.

She had been pretty confident back in those days, and had naively believed that beauty was as much about quickness of mind and strength of character as aesthetic attractiveness, and this competition would prove it.

Of course, she was completely mistaken and Aphrodite had won. Hera was convinced the love goddess had used her enchanted girdle of irresistibility on the naïve young Trojan boy, Paris, who was inexplicably given the job of judging the pageant, so she had easily dismissed the whole thing as a joke and shrugged it off.

But Athena took it more to heart. After the contest she had stared at herself in the mirror for a particularly long time, noting all her imperfections: her eyes not the sparkling shade of blue they could have been, her nose slightly crooked, her skin not without a few freckles. She tried to tell herself that the determinations of some random young male didn't matter, and she was still an amazing and adored goddess, but slowly, over time, that voice started to grow fainter and fainter, replaced with one which whispered that she was not pretty enough, that she was not good enough, that despite all her accomplishments, despite her amazing mind and her incredible supernatural abilities, she was lesser than the other beautiful goddesses and nymphs and maidens around her.

That same voice whispered in the night as she lay in her bed that she was alone not because she was perfectly fine with her own company, but because there was something wrong with her, something missing. She simply wasn't pretty enough.

These feelings gnawed at her while they sat at the feasts of Olympus, they followed her as she descended into the Mortal Realm, and kept her up at night as she tried to sleep in her temple.

She told herself she was being silly – she was a goddess, for goddess sake, the envy of every woman on the mortal plane – yet the feeling of being unworthy remained.

So to quieten that voice she started buying the latest fashionable stolas and studied the other goddess' makeup techniques until she learned to powder and contour to perfection. She starved herself down several sizes and started exercising for five hours each day.

She became hysterical over any small fluctuation in her weight. Overhearing any judgemental comment about her, even from the most worthless of Earthlings, could set her on an emotional eating and purging binge lasting days. It was a vicious cycle from which she still had not managed to escape.

She spent almost half of her existence credit budget each week maintaining a perfect visage: spotless, wrinkle free and immaculate; anything less could not be tolerated. It was a hard thing to achieve, especially when she was down here on the mortal plane, but the cost was worth it. At least now she didn't hate herself *all* the time.

Now, in the sun and heat and flies and stink of this outback outhouse, she felt her sweat sticking to her back, her makeup running ever so slightly down her face. She cursed being stuck here waiting for hours with no sign of Pegasus or Hera. Time was wasting and Athena was feeling the pressure. Aside from anything else, they really needed to be getting on to Atlantis to confront that horrid old uncle of hers.

She checked herself in the fly-spotted mirror hanging on the dunny door and gave herself a quick zap of energy to fix her makeup and get her hair to flow effortlessly down her shoulders. She knew she'd already severely depleted her existence energy today, and until she could get a top up she shouldn't be wasting any more than was necessary, but when she looked at herself again she decided *this would not do.*

'Bugger it,' she said, and felt her existence points rising up from her core to give her back the rosy, dewy glow that was absolutely essential to *feel* like herself. She replaced her dirty stola for the fourth time that day, after all she couldn't walk around with a smudged hem, now could she? It made her feel a bit weak, and she realised she'd perhaps used a bit more credit than she had budgeted for, but a least she felt like a goddess again. And she could always withdraw more existence points once they all got out of this dustbowl.

She headed back across the yard to the farmhouse where she'd left Perseus nursing his wounds, hoping perhaps Hera had returned while she was relieving herself. The so-called Hero was really none the worse for the lesson Queen of the Gods had given him, but even Athena had been shocked by the severity of Hera's anger, despite her stepmother's reputation. Hera's wrath was legendary, even by goddess standards. She and Kali, the Hindu goddess of death and destruction, were known to share tips on the most effective vengeance techniques.

To be fair, Perseus deserved it. His mistreatment of Pegasus was simply inexcusable, no matter how the boy tried to justify it. To keep a mythical creature chained up in a filthy stall with no light and no opportunity to spread her beautiful magical wings... No, no one could blame Hera for her outburst, or Pegasus if she chose to fly away to the sun and never come back.

But they couldn't let that happen. Athena agreed that Pegasus needed to be back with her family, and even though she and Artemis had their differences, Athena was pretty sure Artemis would be the only one capable of finding her. The Goddess of the Hunt may be a right royal pain in the arse sometimes, but she could track anything; even if Pegasus managed to enter the almost invisible Fae Realm, Artemis would find her.

In the meantime Athena had no choice but to sit and wait for Hera and Artemis to turn up, and keep her eye on the horrid little half mortal who'd caused all this trouble.

But the house seemed strangely quiet. When Athena had gone in search of the facilties Perseus had been swaggering around, cursing Hera and acting like he was the victim in the whole sorry mess. But now the house was quiet, no sign of the petulaent little hero in the kitchen or living room. Had Perseus run off to find the flying horse after all, taking advantage of Athena's momentary absence to make a run for it?

Athena frowned. She had thought him well and truly cowed, but Greek heroes did like to throw themselves into unnecessary danger – that was the point of them – so why hadn't she realised he'd go running off the first chance he got? Athena cursed herself for lingering at the mirror and fretting about her appearance when she should have been watching the rotten little demigod.

'Percy?' She called through the house, but the place was empty. Was the little shit really going to make them chase him down? He knew Artemis was coming, did he really think she wouldn't track him and make him pay for wasting her time. Had he never heard of the last man who had annoyed Artemis? Acheron had not only been hunted by the angered goddess, he had been turned into a deer for the purpose of that hunt and then ripped apart by his own dogs. Perseus really should've stayed here with her, but there was no rationalising with heroes once they got a stupid idea into their heads.

The living room smelt of testosterone and hangovers. There were dirty clothes and pizza boxes all over the place and cockroaches scuttled across the floorboards.

Athena picked up another scent in the air. A dog? Did Perseus have a dog? She couldn't remember seeing one before. Maybe that was just what young boys ended up smelling like in the outback of Australia.

She checked the few other rooms, calling for Perseus as she opened each door, but there was no answer. Finding no sign of him inside, she headed into the front yard, searching amongst the truck carcasses and clumps of weeds.

'Perseus! You better not have run off. I am warning you!'

No response.

She walked around the wreck of a Holden panel van and there, on the other side, was an alabaster statue, so white the sun seemed to reflect off it like lasers.

'Oh no,' she said. The statue was Perseus, his terrified face a mask of granite. He, like the pig farmers, had been turned to stone.

'Percy, can you hear me?' As she said the words, she knew it was pointless. Even if he could hear, he would be unable to respond and tell her so. His body was crouched in a defensive position, his arms thrown up as if about to cover his face in an effort to shield his eyes from the gorgon's glare. He had clearly been too slow, and his horrified expression was now set in time, to forever reflect his fear as he gazed into those deadly gorgon eyes.

Perseus had been looking up at the time his gaze had been caught. The unkind may have said his posture was more cowering in terror than fighting for his life, but whichever had been the case, the assailant had been large enough to overpower and frighten him before showing him the gorgon's head.

If the head had been held aloft, that would make the attacker about Poseidon's height.

Athena shook her head, annoyed. Confirmation bias. That's what she was doing, trying to make the circumstances fit her already determined belief that Poseidon was behind this.

Still, Perseus had kept Pegasus from Poseidon even after he had paid that exorbitant amount of existence credit. Athena knew that her uncle was not one to put up with that kind of disrespect. Finding Perseus like this just confirmed Athena's suspicions that her uncle had been lying all along, and no doubt she and the other Olympians would be on his list of petrification if he wasn't stopped.

She knew she should let Hera know what had happened. Poseidon, Pegasus, Medusa and Perseus were all connected and it was no accident that the winged horse had been brought into the middle of all of this, but Athena's logical brain was still conflicted. No matter what she believed to have happened, she still had no proof of Poseidon's involvement. Nothing that would stand up in a court of lore. She had to find evidence.

Athena looked for clues, anything that could point to who could have done this horrific thing. Some of the overgrown grass had been crushed under the foot of an unknown intruder, and she bent down carefully to inspect it. A gasp escaped her lips as she recognised the print.

A rustle of movement startled her and she turned around sharply, her face forming a mask of confusion as she saw who was standing in the yard.

'What have you done with Medusa's head?' Athena demanded, but before the figure could answer, Athena was struck from behind, and the world went black.

'Sure, I'll help,' Artemis said, gathering her things. Hera was surprised. She had expected a fight, or at least the need to use emotional blackmail to get the goddess to help track down Pegasus.

Artemis smiled, sensing her stepmother's confusion. 'If what you say is true then Pegasus will be frightened, probably alone, and possibly hurt. Plus, how many opportunities will I ever have again to track a flying horse? I am hardly going to give up this chance, am I?'

'You won't hurt her?' Hera asked, worried.

Artemis threw Hera a hurt look. 'I would never hurt a creature for the sake of it! I'm a huntress, not a murderer. Pegasus has nothing to fear from me.'

Hera nodded, feeling ashamed for having doubted her stepdaughter. Artemis may be many things, but cruel was not one of them. The creatures of this world mattered as much to her as the victimised did, and in Pegasus, Artemis had an opportunity to help both.

'Where did you say you last saw her?'

Hera told Artemis about Perseus' farm and Artemis scowled; she had little time for Perseus either, agreeing with Hera's assessment that if the little bugger hadn't been a half god, he would have killed himself through simple stupidity years ago.

Before Artemis could finish her tirade against Perseus, a man in a dark blue suit entered the room. He was tall, attractive, with an effeminate style about him emphasised by the purple scarf thrown jauntily around his shoulders and neck.

'You know men aren't allowed in here,' Artemis said, blocking the man from coming further into the room.

'Do you have her?' the man replied, ignoring Artemis' protest.

Artemis shook her head. 'I don't know who you are talking about, but you have no authority here. Get out before I smack you on the arse!'

The man's face fell and he lost the expression of assured confidence. He fumbled as he dug into his pocket and pulled out a leather wallet, which he flipped open. 'It's official Entity Behavioural and Compliance Unit business, Artie,' he said shrilly.

'I don't care. You can't come barging in here. I told you before. You are not too old for me to take over my knee, Poll.'

'Yes, I am,' the man cried, but he backed away, all confidence gone. 'You can't bully me anymore, Artie. I'm an EBCU agent!'

Artemis lurched forward and the man stumbled backwards.

Hera shook her head at the display. 'Artemis,' she said, 'stop intimidating your brother.'

Artemis glanced back at Hera and then backed off slightly.

Apollo regained some of his composure and straightened his scarf.

'What exactly are you here for, Apollo?' Hera asked.

Apollo resumed his officious tone, although his voice was still edged with emotion. 'Medusa has apparently left Monsters' Realm, a clear violation of clause 1324 of the monster treaty. I have been asked to find her and...' He trailed off, looking at Artemis nervously.

'And what, Apollo?' Artemis asked, a dangerous edge to her voice.

Apollo swallowed and lowered his gaze to the floor. 'She's broken the sacred lore, Artie. You know that has a severe punishment.'

'You are *not* going to kill her.' Artemis lurched forward and shoved her brother.

'Look, if she comes quietly maybe–'

'She didn't leave Monsters' Realm under her own steam,' Hera said.

'She was stolen. Well, her head was. Her body, as far as I know, is still there. So really you have no case against her.'

Artemis looked at Hera in horror.

'Her head? Who would do such a thing?' Artemis asked as she sank back onto the couch.

'Who *could* do such a thing?' Apollo corrected.

'I have my suspicions, but I don't know for sure. Athena and I are looking into it. We are hoping to get her back before this all goes completely Vesuvius on us.'

'Too late for that,' Apollo said. 'There's a 500 million existence point reward for her. Alive or dead.'

Hera's jaw dropped. So much? Every deity and mythical creature would be hunting her now. She had to find her; they had delayed too long.

Hera's phone rang. She pulled it out from under her bra strap and saw it was Zeus. She punched the answer button angrily.

'What do you want?'

'I've burnt the house down,' Zeus replied.

15

There's No Place like Home

HERA SURVEYED WHAT HAD ONCE BEEN HER HOME WITH A MIXTURE of fury and utter desperation. The charred remains were still smouldering and what possessions had not been burnt were sitting in the debris in puddles of foam and water. She didn't have time for this. But she knew if she left Zeus to his own devices, things would only get worse. What could be worse than this, she wasn't sure, but if there was a worse, Zeus would create it. Especially with a 500 million existence point reward on offer and Zeus with no easy chair or televised Satyr football match of the day to occupy his time.

Adding to her annoyance, her husband didn't even look slightly ashamed. His expression was more perplexed and somewhat irritated, as if realising for the first time that being an ex-god of thunder didn't really help in a modern fire emergency.

The last of the fire investigators emerged from the house and looked towards Zeus. Hera wondered what the investigator saw: probably just an old man in a dirty cardigan, possibly demented, definitely a little absent-minded. She wondered if Zeus had always looked like that, his fragility simply hidden by the trappings of power.

But she didn't think so.

He had always been mature: the Olympians never had childhoods in the way mortals did; they were conceived as a certain age and that is how they stayed. But Zeus had been magnificent once, tall and dashing and full of confidence. He had not bullied her into marriage as Poseidon had tried to, nor seduced her like the mortal men who tried to gain her favour. Zeus had bided his time and watched her carefully. He figured her out and had used that knowledge against her.

After they bested the Titans, she and her brothers, as well as her sister, Demeter, were the most powerful beings in the known world. It was a heady time: lots of drunken parties, foolhardy creations and, of course, the occasional unnecessary smiting. They had it all back then, and how they had squandered it.

Zeus was already a well-known philanderer, having been twice married and divorced, and he'd copulated with most of the female Titans, every second nymph, and any other woman he could get his hands on, including Demeter; which of course meant more than several illegitimate children. But he'd barely even looked in Hera's direction until one particularly fermented nectar-fuelled evening when the two of them ended up having a deep conversation about the meaning of life while sitting on an Arctic snow cap.

She resisted his advances that night. She was not some silly little nymph whose head could be turned by a suave man. Added to that, he was her brother. That wasn't a moral issue; the Greek gods commonly intermarried between siblings, cousins, aunts and uncles, nephews and nieces. It was more the fact that she knew him well enough to know that any union with him would not be a faithful one.

She was the goddess of marriage and any partnership she entered into would be forever; there was no get-out clause for her, so she had to choose very, very carefully.

But humanity had made the gods in its image, often with the very worst as well as very best elements of themselves. So, finding a trustworthy, kind, faithful god to marry was proving a difficult task indeed.

She'd once thought Prometheus a good option; he had a kind heart and a moral core often lacking in the others. They had courted briefly but it became clear that his obsession with humankind was going to be somewhat irksome. Sure enough, a few years after she had finally accepted Zeus' proposal, Prometheus had proven her misgivings right by stealing, with Athena's help, the sacred fire to give to the huddling mortal masses on the Earthly plane.

It was inevitable – someone had to do it, despite Zeus decreeing that humankind was never to have access to fire or flame – but it had terrible repercussions for the poor guy. Zeus had, of course, reacted badly and punished Prometheus by chaining him to a rock on the very edges of the known world where a huge eagle tore out and ate his liver. For a mortal this would have been a terrible death, but for an immortal such as Prometheus, it was horrific endless torture as each night the liver grew back only to be torn out again the next day.

Hera had visited him a few times in that godforsaken place, and all things considered, he was taking it fairly well.

'It's not too bad,' he had told her. 'At least I'm out in the sunshine and fresh air, and the eagle and I have come to a good place in our relationship. Yes, he still rips out my organ, but we often have a nice chat and cup of tea beforehand, so it's not all horror and disembowelling.'

Prometheus had always been a glass half full kind of guy, which is what she had liked about him in the first place.

And it was why, over her long tiresome years of marriage to Zeus, she often wondered if marrying Prometheus may not have been the better option after all, even with his horrific situation. After all his circumstances meant that most of the time she would have been free to do what she liked, she would always know where he was at night and, as Prometheus himself enthused, the mountainside was quite picturesque, except for the all entrails and gore.

But, his kindness and good looks aside, she knew she'd never have accepted his proposal. It wasn't that he was the wrong guy, it was that really, she had not wanted to get married at all, to anyone. Men bored her at best, and at worst outright infuriated her.

Despite this, the Greek people had inexplicably decided she was to be the patron goddess of Marriage. So her father, Cronus, had set about finding her a suitable marriage partner; choosing the worst options imaginable, including another brother, Poseidon, who'd started pursuing her almost as soon as her status as a major Goddess had been confirmed. Hera had no interest at all in her fishy, sodden sibling and could not hide her contempt for him, openly ridiculing him at every opportunity, mocking his wet fish-like hands and the way he always ate with his mouth open.

'He's disgusting, rude, crude and doesn't know a woman's needs,' she told her father. 'I shall marry for love or not at all.'

She thought Cronus had finally accepted her refusal until she discovered he had secretly agreed to give her hand to Poseidon despite her wishes. That left her no choice but to join her siblings, Zeus, Hades and Demeter, who were already planning on overthrowing her parents and the other Titans, to rule over the Greek pantheon for themselves.

Such a betrayal by her father could not go unpunished, and it was the addition of Hera's substantial power, and her ability to sweet talk Poseidon into the plot, that ensured the Olympians' coup was successful.

However, even after the five had dispatched the Titans, Poseidon still felt the agreement made with Cronus was valid and insisted Hera become his bride. She refused and Poseidon, unsure how to deal with such a troublesome woman, felt the best way to win her over was to ignore her wishes completely and get his brothers, Zeus and Hades, to force her to accept their father's contract.

Hades had no interest in getting into such a fight with Hera, as he was already in trouble with Demeter over some shenanigans with Persephone, so Poseidon turned to Zeus, promising to give up all claims to the Olympian throne if Zeus forced Hera to live down in Atlantis as his new wife. Zeus had merely smiled and dismissed his brother with a wave of his hand.

'I doubt she will suit you. She is a most disagreeable woman. As for your claim to renounce the throne, by marrying Hera your claim to power becomes stronger, not weaker, so again, I am not sure I should support your request. But leave it with me and I will think on it.'

When Hera heard of this conversation, she stormed into the sky hall to confront her brother, Zeus.

'I am not a chattel to be traded!' Hera had raged. 'What right do you have to give or refuse permission for my marriage? I fought beside you against the Titans. You would not have bested them without me. If anyone is a threat to you in your sky throne, it is me.'

Zeus reddened and his eyes sparkled with fire, but his face remained fixed in a light smile. 'That is why you should marry me, Hera. Together we would create a power couple that would rival that of Rhea and Croneus themselves.'

Hera shook her head. 'I will not marry. Not you, not anyone. My heart is made of iron and shards of glass, not the soft, sticky goo of your mortal conquests.'

Zeus nodded. 'You are a hard woman, Hera, it is true. But I do not think less of you for it. One day someone will pierce that icy heart of yours and you will find love and kindness for him and he will be your true love. I intend to be there when that happens.'

Hera laughed and left the room, thinking Zeus a sentimental fool. No wonder none of his other marriages had worked out.

Yet she found herself thinking back on that night when she had almost frozen her butt off on the ice cap with Zeus until he warmed her with the heat of his lightning.

Soon she was sneaking glances at her brother when they feasted in Olympus or when they got together to play cards on a Saturday night. He was a surprisingly good bridge partner and she found herself more than once pairing up with him to beat Hermes and Hestia, who always seemed to squabble over the trumps.

Hera knew, compared to the other goddesses and nymphs Zeus constantly had on his arm, she was not his type. They were soft, well spoken, submissive and kind, whereas she was hard and brittle, sharp-tongued and uncompromising. But still, the memory of their snow-top rendezvous kept popping into her head, distracting her at the most inopportune moments.

In fact she was thinking of Zeus on a visit to her temple in Mikonos and was so distracted she almost stepped on a small, fledging bird which was lying, chirping in distress upon the path.

'You stupid bird,' she said. 'You'll be eaten lying on the ground there. Has your mother abandoned you to your fate?'

The bird, a baby dove, turned its head towards her and cried out again in a sweet, sad coo. It tried to spread its wings and move up towards her, but its left wing had been damaged. The bird cooed again, an edge of panic and pain tingeing its beautiful song.

'Don't look at me; I'm not a nature goddess,' Hera said. 'It's not my job to help you.'

The bird tried again to get to its feet and fell on its side, emitting a sound of pained surprise as it tried to flap its broken wing.

A small hawk settled in a tree a few feet away, eyeing the bird but unwilling to make a play for it while Hera stood so close. The dove, panicked, rustled its feathers, desperately trying to get to its feet.

Hera sighed and looked around, checking to see if anyone else was within sight, but the pathway was deserted.

'Oh, all right,' she said, scooping up the bird in her gold-threaded stola and cradling it in her arms. 'But only until you're better. Then it's off with you, you hear?'

The chick snuggled into the folds of the fabric and looked somewhat smugly at the hawk, who screeched with frustration before flying away in disgust and disappointment at losing its evening meal.

Once in her chambers, Hera placed the bird on her dressing table and got it some small pomegranates. She hand-fed the chick some of the sweet seeds, which it gobbled up greedily.

'Oh, you are a hungry little thing, aren't you?' She laughed as it pecked softly at her fingers. 'But you should remember not to bite the hand that feeds you.'

The bird swallowed the last of the fruit and looked up at her, cooing happily, and Hera found herself petting the animal before pulling her hand back. 'That's enough now. You're just here for a little while until you recover or die. I have too much to do to spend my time looking after a silly little bird like you.'

The chick cooed again, watching attentively as Hera disrobed and put on a silken nightgown. It continued to watch her as she climbed into her large floating cloud bed.

As she settled, the bird began cooing aggressively, louder and louder.

'Shut up, I'm trying to sleep,' she grumbled, but the bird ignored her and continued with its noisy protestations.

Hera threw her bedclothes off and stormed over to the bird. 'If you don't let me sleep, I'll roast you in a pie and eat you for dinner,' she said.

The creature looked up at her with big brown dove eyes and cocked its head to one side, increasing its cooing as it awkwardly tried to move itself towards her. She picked it up and the minute it was in her hands the bird stilled and nestled up against her, closing its eyes.

Hera rolled her eyes. 'You want to stay with me, do you?'

The baby bird nestled in deeper and looked up at her with one sharp but sweet-looking eye.

'Okay, but just one night, you hear me?'

Hera carried the bird back into her bedchamber and fell asleep with it lying on her breast.

Over the next few days, she set the chick's broken wing and ordered her servants to bring the best seeds, fruits and insects from the grounds. She did not let the servants touch the bird, preferring to hand feed it as it sat on her hand or shoulder.

Over time her nurturing ways seemed to pay off and the baby bird gained strength, flying around the chamber and confidently perching on the bed head or the vanity as Hera prepared for her busy day as a beloved goddess. On her return it cooed her a sweet song as she rested her head against the pillow, never failing to lull her into a serene slumber.

Hera knew the time had come when the bird could go back out into the meadow, but she resisted directly sending it, preferring to leave her window open to allow the bird the freedom to choose its own path. Occasionally she would come into the room and find the bird gone, and her heart would sink a little. But it always returned, often with a beautiful flower or stolen trinket that it would lay before her.

She accepted these gifts without comment, but deep down she was truly touched. No one had ever cared about her in the way that this dear little creature seemed to and she found herself taking the bird with her whenever she visited her temples or roamed the human world, often giving it treats like sesame seeds or pieces of ambrosia.

One night as she lay drifting off to sleep, the bird nestled against her, she whispered to it, 'If only I could find a man as sweet and loving as you, dear one. Then maybe I would marry after all.'

The bird's feathers ruffled and it flapped its wings mightily, shaking off the bedclothes and causing the dust to stir around the room. Hera sat up, wide eyed and frightened, as the bird seemed to melt and shake before her eyes. It transformed into a human shape and she realised her naked brother Zeus was now lying beside her in place of her beloved dove.

'You have found such a man,' he said, wrapping her in his arms.

Hera fought him off. 'It was you? All along?'

Zeus stretched out on the bed, luxuriating in his nakedness, and nodded. Hera jumped out of the bed and started throwing whatever was at hand at him: pillows, a lamp, glassware. *How dare he trick her so!*

Zeus merely laughed and easily fended off her attack. 'I did not trick you,' he said. 'You loved me by your own choice, no one forced you. '

'I didn't know it was you!' Hera replied hotly.

'But you didn't know it wasn't me,' he replied.

'That doesn't even make sense,' she said. 'Get out of my room right now!'

'Of course, if you wish it. But I love you, Hera, as you loved that little bird. Which was me. We should marry. I will be faithful to you as a god, just as the bird was faithful to you. I will be what you need and want, for all eternity.'

As Zeus said those words he got up and embraced her, his lips brushing her neck. She felt herself giving in, melting into his body.

'You promise?' she whispered.

'Cross my heart and hope to die,' he said softly as he nibbled her ear and pulled her towards the bed. As Hera sank down onto the soft mattress and felt his hard body up against her, she thought *He cannot die, he's an immortal* – then the thought was gone and she was lost in a sea of pleasure.

And he had kept his word, for a few weeks anyway, which was an eternity for Zeus. He couldn't help himself when it came to chasing women; he was, as he so often told her, literally unable to keep it in his toga.

And here he was *again*, having burnt down their house, trying to chat up a particularly pretty firefighter. But Hera, so plagued by jealousy during the early days of his philandering, couldn't even bring herself to be slightly concerned now, after all these thousands of years. She had nothing to be jealous of really. Like so many other women in recent years, this one was simply humouring Zeus, giving him the sort of look she probably reserved for her slightly creepy old uncles. Hera bustled up and inserted herself between them, noting with a dull satisfaction the look of relief on the young firewoman's face.

'So, is any of it salvageable?'

The firefighter shook her head. 'I'm sorry. Whatever did this was fast and incredibly hot. It looks as if it started as just a small oven fire but, if I didn't know better, I'd say it was like you had some kind of really localised electrical storm or lightning strike. But nothing like that has been reported in the area.' She shrugged. 'Must be some sort of electrical fault, I guess.'

Hera gave Zeus a glare, which he pretended to ignore as he pulled himself up to his 6'3 height and snorted imperiously. 'What are we supposed to do now? I haven't even had my dinner.'

'You'll need to find some emergency housing,' the firefighter said. 'Do you have relatives you can stay with?'

Hera had a momentary flash of the Olympian family, none of whom would throw their arms out in welcome to them. Worse still, one of them could be hiding Medusa's head, waiting for a chance to have Zeus or herself vulnerable and at their mercy. No, Hera realised, it wouldn't be a good idea to let the family know they were helpless and homeless. The best thing was to get him out of harm's way. A low-key motel room would do very nicely for the moment; the fewer gods and goddesses who knew where they were, the better.

'That's okay, we have somewhere to stay,' Hera assured the firefighter and then dragged her protesting husband away.

'I am not staying in some fleabag hotel,' Zeus whined, knowing instinctively what Hera had planned. 'Why can't we stay with Aphrodite; and Hephaestus?'

Hera turned around sharply, noting the hesitation between the names of her stepdaughter and husband. She knew full well why Zeus wanted to stay there. Aphrodite, the most beautiful and sexually open of Zeus' illegitimate daughters, was a favourite of the lightning god for reasons other than family loyalty.

'You'll stay in a motel and keep your head down,' Hera replied. 'There's a lot going on and I need you to stay inside and not tell anyone where you are. Especially any of your brothers.'

'Is this about that gorgon business?'

Hera started. 'How do you know about that?'

'Hades called me about it.'

'What did you tell him?'

'Nothing. I don't know anything. He said there was a bounty on the head and we should pair up to look for it. Seemed to think you knew something about it, though.' He eyed her shrewdly. 'Do you?'

Hera shook her head, but her brow was creased with worry.

'I should go out and start looking,' Zeus said. 'We could do with those points.'

'Don't be an imbecile. Why do you think someone stole her in the first place? You could be a target. You should stay right out of this, like the other gods are doing. Most of them have gone into hiding.'

'Because they're all cowards,' Zeus said. 'In times of crisis, it is true gods like me who need to take the lead.'

Hera rolled her eyes. Of course, now he would want to get involved, and become a thorn in her side. She may not have wanted to be pulled in this whole sorry cocked-up business, but now that she was, she definitely didn't need more cocks in her way.

But she knew keeping him out of it would be tricky. Zeus was a proud man, even if he didn't rule the known world anymore, and over the past few millennia his pride had taken a buffeting.

Being the major deity for several thousand years across the studious Greek civilisation into the barbaric but ambitious Roman world had made Zeus believe himself to be the first true eternal god. Zeus loved it when his adopted people conquered the lands of the Egyptian, Celtic and Germanic gods. He particularly enjoyed lording it over Osiris at the annual all-deity conferences and peace talks. To suddenly lose his status because of the beliefs of some long-haired hooligans who took their orders from a flaming bush had really knocked his confidence.

Sure, it was hard, but everyone else had managed to move on. Everyone except Zeus and his idiot brothers who were still pining away, believing they may rule the sky, land and sea again one day. They refused to accept they were now no better or worse than the Mesopotamian sun god or the Aztec goddess of maize; all of them now remembered only as stories.

Zeus needed to understand that the mortals didn't owe him anything. Goddess knew he had cared little for them when he had reigned. Truth was, Zeus had no more entitlement to divinity than any other mythical being. They were all at the mercy of human fashion and belief, and mortals were incredibly unpredictable.

It was a good thing she'd left Artemis and Apollo in the car; Artie would not put up with this Greek god entitlement nonsense, that was for sure.

'Zeus, I don't have time for this right now. Medusa's head is being investigated by the Entity Behavioural and Compliance Unit.'

Zeus looked aghast. 'Those pencil-pushing scum are dealing with this?'

'Yes,' Hera said. 'Do you really want to get involved, given you did just set fire to a suburb with your lightning rod? I am sure they'd be very interested in investigating that. You know the fines are astronomical.'

Zeus hesitated. 'But it's a 500 million point reward.'

'You know you still have outstanding fines from the time you turned that TV evangelist into a talking duck,' Hera reminded him.

Drunk and feeling a bit down on his luck at the time, Zeus had zapped the woman without even thinking. The EBCU had managed to cover it up reasonably well, sending out the story that it was a television special effect, and Hera had managed to convince Zeus to transform her back, but the whole sorry mess had been extremely costly. Zeus had his transformation powers taken off him by the Divine council and they had to pay a fine of 40,000 existence points.

'Goddamn!' he said. 'That was totally justified. She was spouting off that only one true god nonsense!'

'Apollo is sitting in my car right now.' Hera pointed to Artemis' little blue Toyota where the goddess was drumming her fingers on the steering wheel while Apollo slumped in the seat behind her. 'Do you really want him to know you are meddling in this?'

'Are you working with them? Is that what is going on? Are you with the EBCU now, Hera?'

'Um, kind of.'

'Well, make sure they give you the reward,' Zeus said, his eyes gleaming.

Hera sighed. 'Yes, yes, of course I will.' Hera steered him towards one of Hermes' cabs, and deposited him in the back seat before telling the driver to take him to a hotel in the western suburbs.

'Aren't you coming with me?' Zeus asked.

'I can't. If I'm not there when they find Medusa, I won't get the reward, will I?'

Zeus looked alarmed. 'Oh no, best stay with them then,' he said quickly. 'Oh, did you pick up any beer while you've been out? I'm dying for a cold one.'

Hera smiled tightly. 'No, I didn't. But I'm sure there will be drinks at the hotel.'

Zeus' eyes lit up with greed. 'Open mini bar?'

Hera nodded, and handed him their existence credit card, realising what a pounding this was going to cost their existence cache, but it was worth it, if it kept him out of her hair until this whole thing was over.

The cab pulled away and Hera sighed again. One problem down, several million left to solve, not the least of which was sitting in Artemis' car.

'How did the fire start?' Apollo asked from the back seat.

'Electrical fault,' Hera replied as Artemis pulled out into the queue of rubberneckers.

'He used his lightning again, didn't he? Clause 2789 of the Deity Co-habitation with Humans statute specifically states—'

'He didn't use his lightning, Apollo,' Hera snapped as Artemis honked her horn angrily at a four wheel drive that was refusing to let them pull out into the gridlocked traffic. 'Anyway, don't you have more important things to investigate?'

Artemis made a threatening face at the recalcitrant driver and the traffic cleared enough for her to pull out.

'You're right,' Apollo said. 'This Medusa business could make my career. I could be promoted to head of Monster Infractions. That's only one step down from director of Mythical Misdemeanours.'

Artemis and Hera shared a look. Hera knew she had to distract Apollo from his pursuit of Medusa. Once the EBCU got its bureaucratic mitts all over this, it would be impossible to keep Medusa safe, even if they did manage to retrieve her.

'I always thought you wanted to be in the cryptozoology department,' Artemis said.

Apollo nodded. The cryptozoology branch of the EBCU was where the best and brightest made their careers. Its role was to create new and mysterious phenomena and creatures by spreading rumours over the internet, creating found footage and writing quasi-scientific reports of sightings, using the newly-created existence credits to supplement the pensions of its agents.

'I've applied six times. You know they'll never let me in.'

'But what if,' Hera said, understanding where Artemis was going, 'you brought in proof of a previously dismissed mythical creature?'

Apollo looked up, his interest caught. 'That would be amazing. But no one has done that since Agent Macha found a real changeling in a hospital in Northern Wales 200 years ago.'

'Exactly. It would be a definite coup,' Artemis said.

'Yeah, but it's a fool's errand. There are no long-lost mythical creatures left to find, they're all extinct, or already documented,' Apollo said. 'No, my best bet is to stick with this Medusa thing.'

Hera considered her next move. She didn't want to reveal too much yet, but she needed to string him along for a little bit. All she needed was enough bait to distract Apollo from his quest to find Medusa. Maybe she wouldn't even have to mention Pegasus by name, just drop some hints.

'What if I told you that Pegasus has been sighted?' Artemis said.

Hera grimaced. Artemis never had been one for any kind of subterfuge.

Apollo's eyes nearly popped out of their sockets. 'The mythical winged horse of Greek legend? She's extinct.'

'Not extinct,' Artemis said. 'Very much alive.'

'Many at the EBCU have posited her existence, but she's been gone for thousands of years. You'll take me to her?' Apollo asked.

'Well, it's not as simple as that. But if you promise to leave Medusa to Hera, we will let you be part of bringing Pegasus back into the Greek legends.'

Apollo clapped his hands in excitement. 'You have a deal. To be completely honest, I didn't fancy going after Medusa. She turns guys to stone, you know.'

'Yeah,' Hera said as Artemis took the freeway on-ramp heading towards Perseus' farm. 'We know.'

16

The Plot Thickens

WHEN THE THREE GREEK DEITIES FINALLY ARRIVED AT PERSEUS' farmhouse, they found it deserted. The front door was locked and the windows shuttered.

'Are you sure Athena was waiting for us here?' Artemis asked.

'Yes, she was going to make sure Perseus didn't run off after Pegasus by himself.'

Apollo wandered down amongst the car wrecks and assorted debris. 'Hey, I think you should come and see this,' he shouted.

The two goddesses hurried to join him and found Apollo standing next to the squatting stone form of Perseus.

'I think we might be a bit late,' Apollo said grimly.

Hera scanned the garden. 'Can you see Athena?'

The twins looked around but there were no other statues amid the weeds and rubbish.

'Maybe she left before this happened, or went after the attacker?' Artemis suggested.

Hera wasn't convinced. Such a powerful goddess would not have let this happen if she could've stopped it, and yet it looked as though Athena had not been cast to stone.

Hera kicked through the weeds around Perseus' frozen form and spotted something shiny in the grass.

'What is it?' Apollo asked, looking over Hera's shoulder.

Hera picked up a broken neon-blue Fitbit. 'It's Athena's,' she said as she examined the tiny device carefully.

'Maybe she didn't realise she dropped it?' Apollo suggested.

'Athena wouldn't go anywhere without this ridiculous thing,' Hera said. 'She is obsessed with her step count. She'd have had to be dragged away without it.'

'Hera!' Artemis called from the other side of the yard, where she held up a few strands of seaweed while giving her stepmother a knowing look.

'You two go find Pegasus. I'm going to go and see my brother,' Hera said, her fists clenched with anger. 'He's gone too far this time.'

Hera sidestepped the whole underwater portal and boat travel to Posedions Realm and apparated directly into the throne room of the damp kingdom, expecting to find Poseidon sitting on his uncomfortable chair and eating sealion sandwiches. What she did not expect was the scene of complete chaos that awaited her.

The room was in disarray: the coral throne was smashed to pieces; platters of prawns and sushi were strewn across the floor; there was scattered whalebone furniture everywhere; and misplaced seagrass matting lying in fetid puddles of sea water. The God of the Sea was cowering in a corner, struggling to keep his eyes covered as two gorgon sisters tried to wrestle his hands away from his face.

The tritons who had bravely tried to come to their king's aid stood stony and frozen in postures of attack. Or in the odd case, retreat.

And standing in the centre of the room, a whirlpool of angry vengeance, was the cause of all this destruction, her back to Hera as the mighty serpents on her head hissed and writhed.

'Medusa!'

At the sound of her name, the most famous of the gorgons spun around. Her iron collar securely holding her head very clearly upon her shoulders.

Medusa hissed, and Hera dived behind the smashed ruins of the throne, a second before their gazes could meet. The light filtering through the crevices above illuminated the dark still rock pools in the cavern, turning them into reflective mirrors in which Hera could see the reflection of Medusa looking at her.

'Hera,' the gorgon hissed. 'You're early!'

Medusa's sisters relaxed their grip on Poseidon, who slid lower against the phosphorescent wall, his arms thrown up across his eyes. They looked at Medusa nervously as she focused her wrath on them.

'Can't you idiots do anything right?' Medusa yelled.

'You said you wanted her here,' Stheno protested.

Medusa shook her head angrily, and Hera, peering around the statue now that Medusa was turned away from her, saw the back of Medusa's head wobble a little unsteadily within the collar.

'She wasn't supposed to be here until he was turned. We had to set the scene.' Medusa turned to Stheno. 'What kind of clues did you leave?'

Stheno stared at the ground. 'Some seaweed.'

'What? Seaweed? Where?'

Stheno seemed to shrink under her sister's angry glare. 'In the yard where Perseus was stoned.'

'You imbecile. That's hardly cryptic, is it? That would take two seconds to work out.'

Euryale gave Stheno a stern look. 'For goddess' sake, Stheno, why would you do that? You know the plan needed Hera to come in a few hours.'

'She wasn't at the property when we scoped it out. How was I to know when she was coming back?' Stheno replied.

'But Athena was there,' Euryale said. 'You should've known better!'

Stheno couldn't meet her sister's eyes. 'I'm sorry. It's just, I have a date with Jacko at 7pm. I wanted to be through with this by then. It's our anniversary.'

Medusa looked as though her 'newly recovered' head was going to explode with rage.

Euryale stroked Medusa's shoulder soothingly. 'It's okay, Medusa. It's going to be okay.'

'How can it be? She's here early. She's seen everything.'

'Well *that's* an understatement,' Hera said. 'And I know exactly what is going on now. Medusa's head was never stolen, was it? You made it all up. But why?'

Medusa laughed, a horrible hissing sound, like air escaping from a punctured pool lilo. But she did not turn to Hera as she answered, keeping her deadly gaze averted from the goddess.

'Why? *Why?*' Medusa demanded. 'He was never going to leave me alone. Never. No matter what I did, what I said. I thought the threat of turning him to stone would be enough. But he turned up last week and whispered from the shadows that he had figured out how to steal my power. Turn me human again so I couldn't keep fighting him off.'

'Don't you want to be a beautiful woman again, Medusa, like you were?' Poseidon asked from his cowering position in the corner.

'When has being beautiful ever been a blessing for a woman? It just makes you men behave worse than you normally do: possessive, jealous, lustful. Why would I want that?'

'A woman's role is to be wanted by a man,' Poseidon responded.

Hera felt herself twitch with irritation. The god was an idiot. Had he never learnt to read the damn room?

Medusa strode towards him and picked him up by the scruff of his neck, holding him so close to her that Hera could see the gorgon's spittle spraying on the god's tightly closed eyelids as she spat out her next furious words.

'You mean enslaved by a man. A plaything to a god. *I am not* your plaything, Poseidon. I am not your lover or your slave, and I refuse to again be your victim. I should have turned you to stone when Athena first gave me this power. But I didn't. I listened to her, and the other goddesses, who said it was safer to go away rather than enact the vengeance you deserved, and draw the wrath of your fellow gods.'

Poseidon whimpered in her grip, turning his face away from her.

'And I could've lived with that; I could have. But you couldn't leave well enough alone, could you? You had to come back. Skulking in the shadows, whispering that it was all going to start again. I would never be free of you. If you think I am going to sit by and let you destroy my life by turning me human and enslaving me, you are very, very wrong.'

Hera stood up, positioning herself to run if she needed to, and continued to look at Medusa via the reflective pools that dotted the floor.

'Medusa, I understand your anger. But he can't turn you back into a human. The old powers are gone. Even Athena couldn't make you a human again, if you did not wish it.'

Medusa turned to Hera, uncertainty and anger moving in waves across her serpentine face.

'That's not true!'

'Yes, it is. Only you have the power to decide what you want to be. Don't let him ruin your life by doing this. No matter what he has done, if you turn him to stone, the EBCU will have no choice but to hunt you down. You know that.'

'Of course I know that,' Medusa snapped. 'Why do you think I had to go to all this damn trouble? No matter how heinous a god is, how many people he rapes, murders, enslaves, he's a god and he's immune to all justice. The EBCU was set up to protect them, not us. No one cares what happens to a woman, especially a monstrous one.'

In the reflection, Hera saw the tears of fury and frustration pool in Medusa's fluorescent-green eyes.

'But I'm not playing by those rules. Not anymore! I have a life now, I have freedom. I don't care if he is a god; he is not getting away with this again.'

'Medusa,' Hera said soothingly. 'He can't turn you back into a human. He's not that powerful.'

'Yes, I am,' Poseidon cried, still suspended in Medusa's claw-like grip, his eyes still tightly closed to protect him from her deadly glare.

'Poseidon, shut up,' Hera yelled. It occurred to her to wonder why she was bothering to try to save the idiot's life. But then she wasn't – it was Medusa's life she was trying to save. However much satisfaction killing Poseidon might allow the gorgon, it was not worth her own death sentence, which was exactly what the EBCU would ensure happened.

Medusa dropped Poseidon and slumped down in one of the few upright coral chairs.

'He's been threatening me for months,' she said. 'Coming around to Monsters' Realm, hiding in the bushes and whispering to me, stalking me, taunting me! I don't know how he can do it, but he believes he can turn me human. And so do I.'

Hera thought about the curse she had cast on Echo, which the nymph herself perpetuated long after Hera's magic had worn away. Athena's spell on Medusa was stronger, but it could also be weakened by time.

Maybe that was why Poseidon had taken such a risk in abducting Athena, hoping he could somehow use her to force Medusa to let go of her goddess gift. If that was true then Athena was most certainly still alive.

'Poseidon, you need to release Athena and leave Medusa alone. If you do that, you may have a chance to survive this.'

'Athena? Why would I want that virgin bitch?' Poseidon replied, opening his eyes in surprise and quickly closing them again before Medusa could turn her glare once more in his direction.

'To try to reverse her spell on Medusa,' Hera said, but even as she was saying it, she realised it made little sense.

'What? That sanctimonious trollop would never help me get Medusa back. You think I haven't tried that in the past? You goddesses think you are so important, going around transforming women so we can't get our hands on them, then refusing to turn them back, even when we ask nicely.'

Hera had to admit, Poseidon wasn't powerful enough to overpower Athena. So what had happened to her stepdaughter?

'I don't need Athena to get my Medusa back.'

Poseidon turned to Medusa, taking a quick glance at her direction, catching the side of her face.

'*And get you back I will!*' He got shakily to his feet, his eyes again tightly squeezed shut.

Medusa leapt from the chair and grabbed him, trying to force his eyes open so he would have to look at her.

'Medusa! Stop,' Hera cried. 'I understand what you want to do and why. He is an odious, horrible creature who does not deserve the power he has been given. But he's lying; he can't change you back. And if you harm a god, every deity in the Divine Realm will come after you. Even I can't protect you from that.'

Medusa stopped what she was doing and turned towards Hera's voice, her face writhing with anger.

Euryale put a comforting hand on her shoulder.

'You know Stheno and I will stand by you, whatever you decide. But Hera is right. If you kill him now, the other gods will never let you live, not even in Monsters' Realm.'

Suddenly all the energy left Medusa's body, her face slackened and she dropped Posedion like a sack of potatoes to cover her own face with her hands, sobbing with frustration and anger.

'I can't go back to being a human. I can't.'

The two other gorgons looked at each other uncertainly, unsure how to console their sobbing sister. Medusa met Hera's eyes in the reflection of the seawater pool.

'It was the perfect plan. I convinced my sisters that my head had been stolen and they came to you for help, which I knew you wouldn't give them.'

Hera flushed guiltily. Suddenly she understood why the gorgon had insisted Hera, and not Athena or Artemis, be the one they asked for help. Medusa just needed to set an alibi. She didn't want someone *actually* investigating, certainly not visiting her at Monsters' Realm. Medusa had banked on Hera's reputation as someone who did not put herself out for the females in her realm. How Medusa must have panicked when she and Athena had turned up at the Gorgon's cave, running an actual investigation.

'Did you two know the whole time?' Hera asked the sisters.

'Not at first. Not until you and Athena left Monsters' Realm,' Euryale admitted.

'I didn't want to get them involved at all,' Medusa said. 'But I tried to go after Perseus without them and ended up accidently petrifying those stupid humans. Luckily for me I'd just arrived home to ask them for help when you and Athena arrived at Monster's Realm. I barely had time to get back to the cave and stash my head before you were poking your noses into my bedroom.'

'We thought her body had just wandered off aimlessly,' Euryale said miserably, we had no idea she had planned any of it.

'After I knew Athena was involved, I had to come up with a new plan, and I needed to involve my sisters. I just had to hope we could get to Perseus before you to set our plan in place.'

'Why did you go after Perseus at all?' Hera asked.

Medusa spat. 'Perseus decapitated me! He flew me around as a party trick! He deserved being turned to stone, and so does this bastard.' Quick as lightning, Medusa grabbed Poseidon again. He cowered in her steel grip, his eyes so tightly closed they were almost invisible behind his clenched cheeks.

Hera had to try to keep Medusa talking, because if Poseidon was turned to stone everything would be over for all of them.

'And Athena, did she deserve your wrath?' Hera said. 'She's done nothing but help you.'

'Athena? I would never hurt Athena. I mean, I was surprised when you dragged her into it. I really didn't think you would do anything at all. But once Athena was involved, well, yeah, the plan had to change. But I figured out how to use even that to my advantage.'

'What do you mean, your advantage? She's never going to help you break the Great Lores. Even if she wanted to, she couldn't lie for you; you know that.'

'Exactly. She was the perfect witness. Well, she would've been, except you turned up too early.' Medusa looked around the cavern. 'And without her. Where is she?'

'That's *my* question.' Hera said.

'She was at the farm when we got there, Medusa,' Stheno said. 'We all saw her go into the toilet before you stoned that boy.'

Euryale looked at Hera. 'Wasn't it Athena who found the clue we left?'

Hera frowned. 'No. Athena was gone when I returned. Artemis found the seaweed. We assumed Poseidon had taken Athena.'

It wasn't like Athena to wander off, and if she *had* seen Medusa stone Perseus, she would've interceded. So what had happened? Her Fitbit indicated she had been in the proximity of the Perseus statue, but not when. Maybe she'd left before Medusa attacked. Maybe she had found Pegasus, or had gone off on some other line of inquiry. The whole situation was a mess, but another thought nagged at Hera.

'If you knew we were going to follow the clue here,' Hera said, 'how did you think you would get away with this? Especially if you knew Athena was involved.'

'Don't you see? Athena was the key to the whole new plan.' Medusa smiled, her snake hair writhing in smug satisfaction. 'You arrive here *after* I have turned old fish-breath, and find my head lying in the shadows. You would naturally assume he had petrified himself accidently, doing something perverted with my head.'

Hera realised that was exactly what she'd have thought. It would fit with everything they knew, or thought they knew, about the situation and her debauched brother.

'It would appear to you and everyone else that I was just an innocent victim, stolen and ill-used. The EBCU wouldn't be able to prosecute a case against me.'

'You're forgetting the stoned Percy,' Hera reminded her, 'and those humans.'

'I would say Poseidon used me to settle an old score and petrify the half son of Zeus. Everyone knows Poseidon is a vindictive old bastard. And incompetent enough to get a load of humans caught in the crossfire.'

'Hey,' Poseidon called out.

Medusa didn't even bother to look at him this time, just delivered a swift kick to his groin that sent him stumbling backwards.

Stheno picked him up off the floor and held him roughly against the wall.

'And I had you, and more importantly the ever truthful Athena, to testify to the fact I was an unwilling hostage in the whole thing. My head gets returned to my grateful, dismembered body and all is right with the world,' Medusa said. 'It would have been perfect, if Stheno hadn't buggered it up!'

'Well, you should have done it yourself then,' Stheno muttered.

Hera felt bad for the gorgon. It *had* been a good plan indeed. But timing, as they say, is everything.

Euryale wrapped her arms around Medusa's shoulders, their serpent hair intermingling as she tried to comfort her.

'It could still work,' Euryale said quietly, meeting Hera's watery gaze. 'We could all still make it work.'

17

The Medusa Situation

HERA LOOKED DIRECTLY INTO EURYALE'S EYES, SEEING THE HOPE there. She shook her head sadly. 'I can't.'

'Yes, you can. You are not bound to the truth the way Athena is. You need only go away, just for half an hour or so, forget what you saw here. And when you come back you can bring Athena and pretend that this is the first you knew of it.'

'I can't,' Hera repeated.

'Yes, you can,' Euryale stated more firmly. 'No one need ever know it didn't go down exactly as Medusa said. Particularly if Athena sees what we want her to see. She is the perfect witness because she doesn't know the truth; she hasn't seen this. She can testify and you can back her up. No one in the mystical realms will dare question Athena's word. We can still do this – and keep Medusa safe.'

'I don't know where Athena is,' Hera said. 'She's disappeared.'

Medusa looked genuinely worried.

'We will help you find her,' Stheno said, 'if you help Medusa and do as she has suggested.'

Hera looked at Stheno. There was no love lost between that gorgon and Athena, but Medusa was still a devout follower of the warrior goddess, despite or perhaps because of all that had befallen her. Hera knew that the gorgons would leave no stone unturned to find Athena if they were allowed to complete their own plan first.

The gorgons were silent, hopeful.

Hera looked at Medusa's slightly turned profile and saw not a monster, but a terrified, desperate woman. One who had been used and abused; attacked, mutilated, demonised. A woman almost destroyed simply on the whim of a pair of men who cared nothing about anything but themselves.

Could she blame Medusa for seeking vengeance? Had she not done worse acts herself? The difference was that, unlike Medusa and her monstrous sisters, Hera was a goddess; her privilege meant her acts of vengeance went largely unpunished.

Hera moved her gaze towards the ghastly gorgon, almost daring Medusa to turn her head, catch Hera's eyes in her deadly stare and remove the need for her to make such a hard decision. But Medusa kept her head turned, almost as if she was ashamed to look at the Queen of the Gods, afraid to hope that Hera might change her mind.

And Hera was tempted. Despite the legend, Medusa was not an evil thing. She was a young woman who had once had dreams and hopes, who had loved the goddess Athena enough to commit her life to serving her. Medusa was not the monster in this room. She never had been.

But to allow her to kill a god, even one as awful as Poseidon? It was the ultimate crime against the Great Lores. Something that could not be forgiven. Even if that god had attacked and rampaged his way through history, destroying any female he encountered, he was still a deity and the most important lore of all said they could not be harmed by a lower entity.

Hera was torn. Could she turn her back? Could she let herself abet such a gruesome and possibly world-changing act?

'Killing a god is not without consequences,' she said, almost to herself.

'You did it,' Medusa said quietly. 'You helped overthrow the Titans. Your own parents, Hera. They were gods. Does Poseidon deserve better than your own father; your mother?'

Hera drew breath sharply. 'I didn't kill them!' Yet the jab had found its mark. Medusa had targeted and hit the great sense of guilt and loss Hera had felt ever since she and her siblings had risen up against their parents and the other ruling Titans.

The image of her mother's face when she realised her own children had betrayed her, flashed into Hera's mind unleashing shame in shuddering waves.

Yes, Hera had wanted vengeance on her father for promising her to Poseidon, but the attack against her mother was never part of her plan. And so it was Hera who had insisted that Rhea and Cronus not be killed, as Zeus had demanded, but imprisoned. And she was the only one of their children who bothered to visit their parents in Tartarus, the prison realm into which they had been flung once the Olympians defeated them. She was the only one who still called them on their birthdays and festival days. No one else cared. But Hera had acted against reigning gods, and Medusa knew it.

Hera straightened her dress, her decision made. She opened her mouth to tell the sisters, but before she could form the words, the room was disrupted by a mighty howl and a gigantic black mass appeared in the middle of the room.

Before anyone could react, the monstrous creature grabbed Euryale and Stheno in two of its three gigantic mouths and threw them into the air. Both gorgons struck the stalactites on the ceiling with incredible force, and were unconscious when they hit the floor in messy heaps.

Medusa turned towards the beast, but she was too slow and its massive paw struck her down, separating her head from the collar around her neck. It sailed across the room and landed face down in a large puddle.

Poseidon, hearing the splash, opened his eyes and looked at the beast. His fear turned to a grin as he recognised the monster. 'Cerberus!'

Hera, unseen in the melee, shrank further back in the shadows behind the ruins of the coral throne. The huge dog either did not sense her or did not consider her its primary target as it turned towards Poseidon. The sea god, sure of his rescue, started to stand, holding himself up against the wall on the far side of the cave. Cerberus growled menacingly.

'Cerbie, it's me: Uncle Poe.'

At the sound of Poseidon's voice, Medusa's head spluttered and her body tried to find its way towards her head. But, blinded and separated, she was no match for Cerberus, who smacked her body down and started sniffing the back of her helpless, disembodied head. When her serpent hair hissed and bit at him, he stepped back, growling.

A moment later the room was filled with the acrid smell of sulphur and dark earth as Hades appeared. He stood beside Cerberus and looked smugly at Poseidon.

'Hades, my dear fellow. You arrived just in time.' Poseidon cried, limping towards his brother. 'These bitches were trying to kill me!'

A deep Cerberus growl stopped the Sea God in his tracks so he nonchalently brushed himself down to regain some dignity.

'You never have been particularly lucky with members of the fairer sex, have you, Po?' Hades said, observing the scene in front of him.

Poseidon smiled humourlessly. 'Yes, well, as I said: good timing. How did you know I was in trouble?'

Hades brushed the question aside. 'I must say this has worked out nicely. I had my doubts, to be honest, but I'm pleased to have been proven wrong.'

'Yes, well, I am very grateful. And now you have tamed Medusa I can set about my original plan.'

'Your plan? Hmm, I don't think I am here for *your* plan, old man. I may, in fact, have plans of my own.'

Poseidon's smug expression was replaced with one of worry. 'Well of course I will reward you, Hades. We are brothers after all.'

'Yes, brothers. I seem to recall coming to you a few thousand years ago asking you to be a brother to me,' Hades said.

The colour drained from Poseidon's face. 'I couldn't go against Zeus,' he stammered. 'You know that.'

'Yes, so you said at the time. The two of you ganged up on me quite happily though, didn't you. And of course, you got a sweet deal. God of the Sea and all that, while I was relegated to the netherworld. Never to feel the sun on my face, never to enjoy the breeze in my hair or frolic in the water with nymphettes and mermaids.'

'Come on, Hades, it's not as bad as all that. God of the Underworld is a very prestigious position.'

'Really?' Hades cocked his eyebrow and surveyed his brother. 'Is that why you specifically requested it be given to me, while you lorded over the most important resource on the planet?'

Poseidon shook his head and laughed uneasily. 'Stop being an ingrate, Hades. We are all forgotten gods anyway. And you can frolic in the sun or the sea as much as you like now.'

Hades considered this for a moment. 'True; long lost and forgotten. Who really cares for us anymore? The time of pantheons is long gone. One supreme god is what the people want now, isn't it?'

'Hades, I don't know where you are going with this.'

'That was our mistake, dear brother. Too many of us; too confusing for the simpletons. They like things streamlined, efficient. We really just needed one key narrative. That's what most of the more popular ones have now. The crowd want something simple, direct. We could've been that, but we missed our chance.'

'Hades, stop with the *woulda, coulda, shoulda*. We are better off than most. We still have power, can do whatever we like–'

'Can we? Whatever we like? Yes, I suppose you're right.'

Hades walked over to Medusa's body, which was still struggling under the weight of the hellhound's paw. Despite her strength, without her head she was no match for the giant dog so, satisfied that she was unable to attack him, and that her sisters were both unconscious, Hades began to search for the Gorgon's newly disembodied head.

He spotted it, still face down in the rockpool, Medusa's protests and rage muffled by the water. Hades pulled a glittery pink eye mask from his pocket and, with his other hand, picked up her head by her serpentine hair careful to keep her face averted from him. He slipped the mask over her eyes, enduring several snake bites as he did so.

He then drew some golden threads from his other pocket, threw them at Poseidon and told his brother to tie Medusa's hands and legs securely.

'These paltry bonds won't hold her,' Poseidon said, looking at them with dismay.

'Yes, they will. They're from the Golden Fleece. I use it to secure Cerberus to the gates of Hades, so I am sure it will keep Medusa in check. Now do hurry, brother, we have no time to waste here.'

Poseidon did as he was asked, kneeling over Medusa's prone body, his face blasted by the hot breath of Cerberus who was still holding the gorgon down.

With a few short knots the binds were tied and Poseidon stepped back, gazing at Medusa's struggling, vulnerable headless body with a proprietary expression

'Thank you for this, Hades,' Poseidon said, holding out his hand. 'I will reward you for this assistance, and for helping me reunite with my beloved.'

Cerberus growled menacingly. Poseidon stepped back from Medusa, slightly confused, but smiled hopefully at Hades.

'Now if you will just hand me her head, I can get back to my original plan.'

Hades smiled. 'Like I said, Fish Pie, I have my own plans.'

In one quick, skilful movement, the God of the Underworld directed Medusa's face towards Poseidon and flipped up the mask.

Poseidon, taken totally by surprise, had no time to close his eyes or turn his head. He was hit full force with the angry gorgon's glare. The water god was immediately turned to stone. Hades, quick as a flash, flipped the mask back down over Medusa's eyes and stepped away from her writhing body.

Hera let out a cry of surprise and Hades spun in the direction of the throne.

'Who's there?'

Hera considered staying quiet, but knew she didn't have enough power to apparate out before Hades saw her. She, like Poseidon, had no defences against Medusa's gaze should Hades force her to look into the creature's eyes, so she had to play this very carefully. Gathering her sopping, muddy skirt about her, she stepped out into the room.

'Hera. I should have known you'd be here.'

'Are you going to kill me too?' Hera asked, her voice only slightly quaking.

Hades just stood there, still holding Medusa's head by a handful of her snakes until one bit his arm so savagely he dropped it. The head bounced twice before rolling to a stop beside Cerberus' huge haunches. The dog leant down, sniffed the face, and then the giant serpent on his own tail subdued Medusa's hissing reptiles into submission.

Hades quickly scooped the head into a sack.

'I have no quarrel with you, sister; we've always been cool,' Hades said. 'It's Zeus I intend to kill. Before collecting the reward, of course.'

Before Hera could react, Cerberus leapt forward and raised his paw. Her world went black.

18

Flying Horses and
Miserable Fish Dungeons

As the world swam back into focus, Hera realised she was no longer in the throne room.

It was dark, but she could make out two other figures – or was it three – on the other side of the room. They were blurry and unclear, but she was definitely not alone.

'I think she's awake,' one of them said, but Hera passed out again.

The second time she came to, there were two figures hunched over her. The gruesome visages shocked her into consciousness faster than a bucket of cold water would've done, although she realised a few seconds too late, one of them was about to do just that.

The cold seawater hit her like a slap and she bolted upright. Euryale and Stheno crowded around her.

'Give her room, give her room,' Euryale said as she pressed her face almost into the goddess' nose.

Stheno put down the bucket and helped Hera to her feet.

'Where are we?' Hera asked.

Stheno grimaced. 'Wherever sea monsters come to die would be my guess, judging by the smell.'

Hera had to agree. Even for Atlantis, the dead fishy smell was pretty foul. The room was gloomy, lit only by the bioluminescence of the marine algae lining the damp walls. The luminous glow was just enough to reveal the shadowy piles of fish skeletons and decomposing sea creatures littering the floor and heaped against the walls.

'It's Poseidon's garbage room,' Hera said, rising from a mound of stinking fish heads. She tried to ignore the smell as she looked for a way out. She pushed against a large iron door that seemed to be the only exit.

'Oh, good idea,' Stheno said. 'Because it never occurred to us to just try to push that open.'

Hera turned away from the unmoving door and shrugged. 'Sorry for insulting you by making an effort.'

'There's no way out that we can find,' Euryale said. 'The door is barred by something even our strength can't budge. I think it's been sealed with spells as well as hard iron and lead.'

'No windows, drainage grates? Anything?' Hera asked, deciding the gorgons may not appreciate her checking for these things herself.

'Nope, nothing. Just the door. And it's impenetrable.'

Hera shook her head. Nothing was impenetrable. She was a bloody goddess!

'I have to get out of here.'

'Oh, do you? Because we're keen to stay and have a picnic on rotting fish guts and dried squid carcasses,' Stheno said.

Hera gave the snarky gorgon a dangerous look. 'Stop being a bitch and help me think of a way out. It's your fault I'm here in the first place!'

'Come on you two. We're all stressed, but let's not turn on each other,' Euryale said. 'Hades took Medusa's head. She's not doing well.'

Hera realised the other figure she'd glimpsed when she first woke was the headless Medusa, blindly walking repeatedly into the wall in the furthest corner of the room.

'I thought Poseidon bound her,' Hera said, watching the unrestrained gorgon's body feel it's way around the room.

'Hades took the fleece threads after he threw us in here. I guess he needed them for something else.'

'Well can't you get her to sit down? She's giving me the creeps wandering around like that.'

'We have tried to settle her, but she's beside herself,' Euryale said.

As if to prove this point, Medusa's headless body stumbled and fell in a heap, then scrambled to her feet and tried to feel her way towards her sisters.

'None of this would've happened if you had all just stayed in Monsters' Realm!' Hera hissed at the gorgons.

'We couldn't! Medusa needed our help. She was convinced he was going to turn her into a human again,' Euryale said

'He can't,' Hera cried, exasperated. 'He couldn't before and now he really can't. And now there's a rogue god out there with Medusa's head, and all of Medusa's plans are going to end up delivering her right to the EBCU. Probably *after* she kills my husband too.'

'I wish Poseidon could have turned us all human,' Stheno said under her breath.

Euryale turned on her, eyes blazing. 'What in Hades is your problem? You want our sister to be enslaved to that selfish bastard?'

Hera stepped between the sisters, holding her hands up. 'Come on, I don't need you two at each other's throats. There is enough mess to clean up as it is.'

Stheno slumped to the floor, her eyes filling with tears, making her seem almost human. The effect was quite frightening.

'No, no, I didn't mean it. It's just, well, look at her.'

Medusa's body was crawling around on hands and knees trying to figure out how to get around a large barrel full of discarded fish oil, that she could neither see nor, Hera thought enviously, smell.

'Over two millennia of that. And it's actually better when she doesn't have her head.'

Euryale patted her sister on the shoulder and sat down next to her. 'I know you don't mean that.'

'It's our 100th anniversary tonight,' Stheno said. 'Did you know that?'

'You and that giant fella?' Hera asked, realising what really may be behind Stheno's outburst.

'Yeah, Jacko. He was hinting he might pop the question tonight. But now I'm going to accidentally stand him up, and he'll probably think I don't love him, and he'll leave me for a Siren or an Ogress. Goddess knows it hasn't been easy for him, dating someone from a family like mine.' Stheno frowned, fighting back tears. 'Maybe if I'd still been human, it could have been different. But marriage and happily ever after isn't for monsters, is it?'

Stheno threw an angry glance at Medusa's body, which was currently feeling up and down the wall.

'*She* did this. Not me. Not you, Euryale. Her! She wanted a life without men and we had to sacrifice our lives for her!'

'Henny, come on now. It's not so bad.'

'It is! It *is* bad. You were engaged. He was a dickhead, but still you may not have been entirely miserable. But then she made us these... these things! All because *she* wanted it.'

'She was trying to protect us.'

'She wasn't. She wanted us to be like her so she wouldn't be alone. Do you really think I was ever in danger of being attacked by a lustful god? I was as plain as sand! I hadn't even had a date before she turned me into this thing. Honestly, I was in no moral danger whatsoever! And now this. I think she made up this whole thing about Poseidon just to get attention. Or maybe to break up me and Jacko.'

'No. No, Medusa wouldn't do that. She likes Jacko.'

'Does she? She won't even let me invite him to dinner. And she refers to him as Ole One Eye, no matter how many times I tell her that's rude! Because of her we have to sneak around Monsters' Realm like a pair of teenagers. Sure, it was fun at first; but one hundred bloody years of it! If it wasn't for the fact that I'm stuck in this rotting hellhole with you two, I'd be glad that Hades took her away. Let her bully him for a while.'

Euryale said nothing, just rubbed her sister on the back as Medusa fell over once again behind them.

The sun was high in the sky by the time Artemis and Apollo navigated through the dense shrubby bushland of Northern NSW and across the border into Queensland.

'She's come through here,' Artemis called to Apollo, who was limping along behind her, desperately trying to keep up.

'How do you know?' He called back.

'Shift in atmospheric pressure. There has definitely been a disruption of the air flow currents through this area. Too low to be aircraft. Too big to be a bird.'

Apollo grunted, then collapsed into the shade of a nearby wattle tree.

'Can we rest for a minute?'

The pair had been tracking the flying horse for hours, all the way from Perseus' farm, over 85km of rough terrain and steep hills. On foot. Even for a deity, that was hard work, although Artemis seemed totally unconcerned by the relentless sun or the scrubby, thorny bushland. She kept the same, steady pace, while Apollo huffed and sweated and sat down behind her. She shook her head and ploughed ahead, ignoring his obvious exhaustion.

'You've been sitting behind a desk too long, Polly,' she chided. 'Get a move on or we'll lose the trail!'

Apollo, breathing heavily, with a huge effort, pulled himself up and lumbered beside his sister, putting a sweaty hand on her arm. He didn't know if deities could have heart attacks, but if they could, he figured he must be on the brink of one as he struggled to force air into his lungs.

Artemis turned and frowned at him, but even she couldn't ignore his obvious pulmonary distress. 'Okay, a few minutes,' she conceded. 'Honestly, Polly, I thought you were in better shape than this.'

'No one is in this kind of shape!' He slumped against another tree, while Artemis did some stretches. 'This is stupid. We're never going to find her this way. And even if we do, she can just fly away. Even *you* can't give chase in the sky, Artie.'

Artemis turned to her twin and nodded. 'Yeah, I've been thinking the same thing,' she said. 'The carrots and sugar may tempt her over.'

Apollo shook his head. 'Not if Pegasus has been as ill-used as Hera said she had been. After how Perseus treated her, I'd be surprised if she ever trusted anyone ever again. I think we are on a fool's errand, Artie, I really do.'

Artemis looked into the sky, squinting at the afternoon sun.

'Apollo...' Artemis began.

Apollo looked up sharply. Artemis only used his full name when she wanted him to do something he didn't want to do.

'No,' he said pre-emptively.

'You don't even know what I was going to ask,' Artemis replied.

'Whatever it is, no.'

'Don't be such a pain, Polly.'

Apollo shook his head. 'Okay, ask.'

'The chariot–'

'No!'

'Come on, Polly. It's the only way we're going to be able to do this.'

'No!' Apollo's face hardened.

Artemis sat down and put her arm around his shoulders. 'We only need it for a few hours, then you can put it back wherever you hid it. No one need ever even know we used it.'

Apollo shook his head. He was never ever going to let that dreadful thing see the light of day again. Artie knew how he felt about it!

Artemis squeezed his shoulders. 'Apollo, those days are gone now. You'll never have to go back to that. But the sky chariot is the only way we are going to be able to properly chase down Pegasus, and you know it.'

Apollo's face crumpled.

Artemis squeezed him again sympathetically. 'I know how much you hate it, but it really is our only option.'

'Do you know how long it took for my skin to recover from all that sunburn?' he asked, but there was a pleading in his voice now, not the absolute conviction of someone who would not be swayed.

'Only you and I will know we got it out. And no human seriously believes the sun is pulled across the sky by some fella in a toga anymore. You won't be trapped doing that again. I promise.'

Apollo shuddered as he remembered how his promotion to a sun god under the Roman mythologies had, at first, delighted him.

For Apollo had not always been a sun god, in the early days of the Greek world he was appointed God of Arts and Music. A nice enough gig at first, as it entailed mostly lazing about in fields reciting poetry to pretty young nymphs, until he discovered he was also required to deal with actual writers and poets. That wasn't quite so much fun. Poets were, everyone agreed, extremely loathsome creatures, with their flowery phrases, teary earnestness and propensity to start fist fights with their editors over a replaced comma.

That damned awful Homer was probably the worst of them. Apollo remembered all the hours spent struggling to read through that epic snorefest, *The Iliad*. Such a complicated, overwritten plot with absolutely no historical accuracy. Why people liked it so much was beyond him. He much preferred the erotic lines crafted by the lovely Sappho, written in late night, drunken bouts of self-reflection.

But, while it was fun cavorting with nymphs and a talented poetess, he was often derided by the other gods as lacking in any real masculine energy, so when the Romans wanted him as their solar deity, he jumped at the chance. The sun, after all, was an important celestial body. Sun gods in other religions were often the most beloved and powerful, so it seemed like a huge step forward, or up, for a god of the Greek pantheon, who was often sniggered at and treated as too soft and silly for any real divine work.

So, Apollo handed his artistic duties over to his daughters, the Muses, and marched into the sun chariot stables. He quite rudely pushed the Greek sun god, Helios, aside, telling him he'd no longer be manning the wondrous sky chariot, because from then on he, wondrous Apollo, would drive the bright sun-horses across the heavens to give the people of Earth their light and heat.

In his haste and arrogance, Apollo failed to notice the expression of pure relief that flashed across Helios' face.

'Of course, Apollo, of course,' the newly-retired sun god had said quickly, gathering up his things and scampering out of the stables at a pace Apollo had wrongly assumed was motivated by fear, or reverence for Apollo's new stature.

Apollo climbed into the magnificent gold chariot, hitched to two dazzling orange horses with manes of pure flame.

'Yeee-haah!' he yelled, urging them upwards. The horses flew into the sky, bursting into a scorching red-hot mini sun that seared Apollo's face and hands.

Apollo threw up his hands to protect his face, his eyebrows singeing from the heat, his beautiful alabaster skin turning pink then ruddy red as the sun-horses' heat burnt through his outer dermis.

Twelve hours later; hot, sweaty, exhausted and looking several years older than his previous youthful appearance, Apollo and the chariot came to rest on the other side of the world.

As he made his way in the dark of night back to Mount Olympus, Apollo realised he would no longer be frolicking in the fields of Elysium playing his lyre, chasing pretty young nymphs, or writing dense symbolic poetry. Instead, he'd be trapped in a fiery, flying heat lamp for eternity. What had seemed like a promotion was a life sentence of burning torture.

And so, over the centuries, Apollo pulled the staggeringly hot sun from horizon to horizon until his skin was as tough as old leather. He kept a semblance of his boyish good looks through several trips a week to the goddess of youth, but even Hebe found it hard to battle against the constant and unrelenting sun damage the new sun god's skin had to endure. By the end of the Roman Empire, she was really just removing the skin cancers and trying to keep him at least slightly moisturised.

When the Romans finally converted to Christianity, dumping their polytheist gods and goddesses into the world of myth and fable, Apollo had openly celebrated. Finally, he was able to relinquish that bloody chariot and those searing horses. But, to ensure neither he nor anyone else would ever have to urge those stinking, skin-destroying sun-horses through the sky again, he unhitched the steeds and hid them and the chariot in a secret place he would never divulge.

This was the chariot Artemis wanted him to resurrect. It was simply not on.

'Come on Polly,' Artemis tried again, 'It's *one* trip. And we need not go anywhere near the sun–'

'No, Artemis. If you are such a great huntress and tracker you shouldn't need those demonic nags.'

Artemis gave him *that* look. The look she had used on him ever since they were very young. The look that said Apollo was being a child.

The fact that Artemis and Apollo were twins, and therefore exactly the same age, never stopped Artemis from treating him like her little brother. Her sense of superiority was, to be fair, reasonable when he had been a directionless youth wandering around Olympus, spending his days drinking nectar and seducing maidens, while she was off avenging violated women and protecting the natural world. But he had grown up a lot since then. He was now a senior operative for the EBCU, for gods' sake! When would she stop treating him like a child?

Artemis' face darkened. Apollo felt the air around him crackle as she held in her annoyance.

'You owe me!' Artemis said, her tone stern and authoritative.

Apollo grimaced. He hated how Artemis kept bringing up this so-called debt. So what if, as a newborn baby herself, she had helped bring him into the world as their mother, hounded by Hera and abandoned by Zeus, lay comatose and dying on a deserted island. He had never asked to be born, never mind be delivered by an overly precocious twin sister who, even at the age of a few hours, had displayed a resilience and strength no other god or goddess had come close to equalling.

'That was a long time ago, Artie,' Apollo said weakly, but he was already defeated. He knew he was unlikely to be strong enough to resist Artemis if she really had set her mind on something. What's more, he knew she knew it too.

Apollo sighed and stood up. 'We'll need to find a portal.'

Artemis smiled. The tension in the air eased. 'Good boy.'

19

Into the Sky

ARTEMIS FELT THE HEAT LONG BEFORE THEY WALKED OVER THE lip of the volcano's crater. The monstrous Australian summer they had left behind seemed virtually Arctic when standing at the edge of this blast furnace.

Apollo's face was a mask of dismay as two flaming balls of lava jumped out of the open mouth of the volcano and flung themselves towards them. Artemis instinctively braced, holding up her arms in a defensive gesture, though exactly how she intended to defend herself from two sentient balls of flaming molten earth was unclear, even to her.

Thankfully she never had to consider that question in any real depth, as the fiery projectiles transformed into two majestic orange-hued steeds with eyes black as the abyss of Tartarus, and long flowing manes of fire.

Artemis felt her skin prickle with the heat, then start to sear, as the horses cantered up to Apollo with what could only be called joyful enthusiasm. Her brother held out his hand to halt them and the two fire-steeds stopped obediently in front of him.

'Clearly their recollections of you are not as negative as yours are of them,' Artemis said as the fearsome creatures snickered and scratched at the ground, gazing at Apollo adoringly.

'Yeah, they aren't too bad when they turn the lights down a bit,' Apollo agreed. The two horses instantly dimmed their dazzling orange hue and their manes settled into a cosy flicker.

Apollo patted them, then moved past and jumped down over the rim of the volcano. Artemis, amazed, just watched, unable to get anywhere near as close to the volcanic heat as Apollo could. He reappeared a few moments later tugging an elaborate two-wheeled chariot.

'A little help would be nice,' he called.

Artemis hesitated, then moved forward. Her skin was turning a dark shade of pink and the beads of sweat on her face turned into rivers.

'How do you handle this heat?' she cried, grabbing quickly at the closest handle on the chariot. She instinctively cried out, realising she was holding metal that had just been salvaged from an active volcanic mountain. Just touching such a thing should burn through all the layers of her skin – but it didn't. The chariot was eerily cool to the touch.

Feeling foolish as Apollo gave her a puzzled look, Artemis grabbed the rim of the seat with her other hand and the twins quickly lugged the chariot up and over the lip of the volcano and onto the ground, where it rolled easily on its beautifully crafted silver wheels.

Without direction, the two horses walked calmly over to the chariot and waited patiently while Apollo fastened them, using the flame-proof bridles and harness attached to the device.

Artemis looked at the golden chariot and the impressive but fairly regularly sized horses and shook her head. 'People actually believed this was the sun?'

Apollo shook his head. 'No, we never were the sun. We just had to look like we were pulling the sun. So we rode along right in front of it. To the people below it looked like we were part of it, lugging the main bit behind us.'

'And no one ever caught on?' Artemis replied, hoisting herself up into the chariot next to her brother, who was already taking the reins.

'Humans aren't that bright. When a couple of the ancient scholars suggested the sun was a star and not a god, I thought that might free me, but it didn't convince anyone. A few others had a go at explaining it was a celestial body with no connection to chariots or horses, or whatever other god they were worshipping by that time, but most of them were crucified for heresy. People don't like their beliefs questioned, no matter how stupid they might be.'

'Hey,' Artemis said, 'you shouldn't complain. Where would we be if humans didn't feel the need to explain perfectly natural phenomena with incredible and outlandish stories?'

Apollo urged the horses up into the sky. 'True that,' he cried over the roar of the wind as they ascended with alarming speed.

Once up in the air, Apollo eyed his sister as they flew across the sky, following the trail of the other mythical flying horse. He knew he needed her help or he'd never find Pegasus, but this presented a problem. Once the creature was found, Artemis would never let him take Pegasus to the EBCU, no matter what she had promised to convince him to help her.

He badly needed something to impress his fellow EBCU operatives. Artemis didn't understand how important it was to be impressive. She, along with most of the other deities, detested the EBCU, thinking it more of a bureaucratic nuisance than an important policing unit.

They may be right; these days, at least. It was true most of Apollo's day-to-day activity was spent logging sightings of bunyips and preparing fire-safety presentations for dragons. Occasionally he did get out from behind the desk – intervening in bar fights between Asgardian deities who'd drunk too much mulled wine, or issuing notices and fines to gods who used their precognition to foresee lotto numbers. Mostly, though, his main focus as an operative was ensuring all interactions between the Divine Realm and the human world remained, by and large, non-lethal.

It hadn't always been like that. He remembered the heady days when the Entity Behavioural and Compliance Unit had been established. Was it so long ago? Only the middle of the 16th century, if he remembered rightly. It was just after a particularly bloodthirsty series of witch trials and religious crusades had seen believers of many of the old gods burnt, drowned, staked and tortured.

The goddesses in particular were incensed and demanded something be done. If this continued, they argued, there would be no humans left to believe in anyone. So, after much debate, the Great Lores were passed: no deity could do anything to encourage or abet any human in any act of violence or encourage it to be done in their name.

Of course, many, including the war gods like Ares and Thor, as well as demons and dark creatures, appealed against the lore, arguing their very existence relied on the violent desires of mankind. They were overruled and spent the first hundred years trying to thwart and undermine the lore at every turn. So the EBCU was established to police the gods, goddesses and creatures to ensure they did not use their power and influence to destroy the followers of other religions or believers in other entities.

The violence and insanity down on Earth settled down somewhat, though never completely disappeared, as the enlightened Age of Reason began, during which several smaller terms and treaties, agreements and lores were written and passed. Even the Divine Realm, once the most warlike of all the realms, managed to find a balance between the enormous egos of its residents and the importance of keeping humankind in existence.

Apollo firmly believed that was due, in great part, to existence of the Entity Behavioural and Compliance Unit, because it – with the exception of the Great Courts of Lore – was the only authority that all the realms feared and obeyed.

But human beings soon began using other excuses besides religion for their dastardly behaviour. Things like nationalism, racism, sexism, general arrogance and, of course, basic greed all became openly celebrated ideals on the mortal realm. Apollo often thought the religious ardour that too many humans loved to embrace was only ever a pretext for exerting those other prejudices in the first place.

The big problem, as the EBCU became more successful at keeping the mythical and the mortal removed from each other, was the unit itself became less necessary and opportunities for glory and advancement within it became scarcer.

Apollo had been on only two truly interesting cases in the past hundred years, both of which he'd failed to close before his arch rival, the goddess Nemesis, swooped in at the last minute and claimed all the credit.

As the goddess of vengeance, she had a lot of really useful contacts and the ability to sniff out wrongdoers long before most of the other EBCU operatives had finished their breakfasts.

And so, despite his painstaking investigations into the great gnome disappearance of the 1950s, it had been Nemesis who'd discovered the gnomes had been kidnapped by enterprising ogres, who dipped them in cement to be sold as surprisingly popular garden ornaments. Humiliating though this had been, it paled in comparison to the awards she had taken from him when she broke the Loch Ness Monster case.

That was especially galling as he'd been the one to bring the case to the EBCU when human scientists decided to ultrasound the famous loch and prove once and for all that no giant creature lived within.

Nessie had been ropable, determined to not only be present when such a test was undertaken, but use the opportunity to eat as many of these interfering scientists as she could.

It was a potential PR disaster either way. The Loch Ness Monster was one of the most famous and beloved creatures of Monsters' Realm, personally accounting for at least a tenth of all the realm's existence credit. Proving her to be *non*-existent could not just ruin the Monsters' economy but throw all of the mystical realms into complete chaos.

But the lore expressly forbade any monster to prove their existence beyond any doubt. The dilemma had stumped the EBCU cryptozoology team; and Apollo, desperate to be part of the most important branch of the EBCU, was determined to crack it.

But it was Nemesis *again* who beat him to it and came up with the perfect solution. Using her network of gossips and envious rumour mongers, she spread the information that Nessie was not, as had previously been the agreed upon cover story, an ancient dragon, but was in fact a shape-shifting creature similar to a Celtic water horse.

It was a stroke of brilliance. If Nessie could indeed shape shift, then any evidence supporting why she was not presently or always in the loch could be easily dismissed by monster and conspiracy enthusiasts as inconsequential. She could literally be anything – a rock, a mountain, a shark, or a school of fish if she wished. Thanks to Nemesis, Nessie's mythology remained and it was the goddess, and not Apollo, who was offered the coveted open spot on the cryptozoology team.

But now, today, he had a chance to really prove he was more than a glorified pencil pusher. Pegasus was *the* most legendary of legendary creatures. Finding her would get him a spot on the team for sure – may even give him a shot at running the whole department. Trouble was, he needed to bring Pegasus in to the unit to prove his claim, and he knew Artemis was never going to let him do that. She and Hera had not shared their full plan with him, but he understood enough to know they had reasons of their own to capture Pegasus. He knew it had something to do with Medusa – just what, he was unsure.

'There she is,' Artemis cried, breaking Apollo's train of thought.

Apollo reined in the sun-horses and turned them slightly to the west, where he could just see the outline of the dazzling white horse between the clouds.

If he hadn't known what he was looking for he may missed her completely, she was so white and flawless.

'Ah, well,' he thought to himself as the chariot made a beeline towards Pegasus, 'I shall just have to make sure I take possession of her, and not let Artemis bully me again.'

20

The Kraken Awakes

THE SLOW DRIPPING OF SEAWATER WAS GETTING TO HER. HER HAIR had never been so frizzed. Even Aphrodite's beautician skills would be unable to do much with it now, Hera thought as she tried to drag her fingers through the unruly mess.

The gorgon sisters had all but given up trying to find a way out of the fish dungeon and instead busied themselves with trying to calm Medusa, eventually lulling her into what looked like a state of fitful rest, although without a head it was hard to tell if she was asleep, awake, or even dead for that matter. It was all rather creepy, this headless creature falling about or lying on the floor like a decapitated corpse, so Hera avoided looking at her. Ironic really, now that looking at the gorgon was no real threat at all.

A noise outside roused Hera from her reverie and she hurried over to the door. The sound was heading away and no one responded to her calls, but whomever had been walking past had been carrying a lantern or torch, as a crack of reddish light shone momentarily through the tiny, almost invisible gap underneath the heavy door.

Not much of a gap, it was true: a mere sliver. But a sliver was all Hera needed.

She wondered if she had enough power left. She cursed handing their only existence credit card over to Zeus and wished she'd mastered the remote banking Gondaline had tried to sign her up for. But it had all seemed so complicated. So much easier just to go into the Trove and make a withdrawal to top up her power. But now Hera regretted her resistance to the new technology. When she got out of here – if she got out – she was going to sign up for that service as soon as she could.

She tried to calculate how much power she had in her tank. Throwing Perseus across the farm and apparating into Poseidon's throne room rather than using the portal had been a little wasteful perhaps, but both had seemed necessary at the time. She scanned her mystic centre and, as she feared, her mystical power core was almost empty. If she did what she was planning, she may go into core existence debit and that would mean disappearing into the ether forever, little more than a memory – not really the escape plan she had in mind.

'Stheno, Euryale,' Hera called across the chamber. 'I need to borrow some of your existence points.'

'What do you need them for?' Stheno asked.

'I can shapeshift, but it takes a lot of power. There's a crack under the door. If I had enough points, I could turn myself into an ant and crawl through, then unbar it from the other side.'

'Don't you have enough points of your own?' Stheno sat up straight, the possibility of escape motivating her to lose some of her lethargy.

'I've run out of what I withdrew yesterday,' Hera said, and even in the bioluminescent gloom she could see Stheno roll her eyes.

'Can't you just withdraw some more?'

Hera shrugged. 'I never signed up for remote withdrawal.'

'What?' Stheno asked.

'I never signed up. I didn't think it was necessary and there's a real threat it might be hacked.'

'Oh, for goddess' sake,' sighed Stheno, 'you older generations are such a bunch of technophobes.'

'Who are you calling old? You must be 6000 if you're a day!' Hera replied.

'I'm 5330, if you must know,' Stheno replied. 'And I have been told I don't look a day over 3200!'

'Can we not fight over every little thing,' Euryale cried.

'Okay, so just spot me some of your existence points and we'll be out of here in a jiffy,' Hera said, turning her back on Stheno.

Euryale looked up with regret. 'I'm sorry. We can't.'

'I'll pay you back,' Hera snapped. 'You know I'm good for it.'

'It's not that,' Stheno growled. 'We don't have any.'

'What? No existence points?'

'Only enough to stay breathing. Who do you think even remembers Medusa's sisters, let alone our names or stories?' Euryale replied. 'We have no real way of generating any income.'

'But then, how do you survive?'

'Medusa gives us an allowance every month,' Euryale said. 'It's more than enough to keep us going,'

'So lend me some of that,' Hera said.

'With all the excitement, and the fight in Poseidon's cabin, we are both extremely low. We don't have enough to spare.'

'Well can't *you* get a top up?'

'We have to ask.' Stheno said grumpily from the corner. 'Medusa doesn't just let us have unfettered use of her account. Even though she has more existence points than she could ever spend.'

'Okay, so ask.'

'And how exactly do you intend us to ask her?' Stheno replied. 'She'll have a slight problem hearing our request, won't she? Having no head tends to make communication just a tiny bit difficult.'

Hera slumped back against the door, defeated. Stheno was right. She was about to give up and try to come up with another plan when she noticed Euryale was looking decidedly uncomfortable and giving her the side eye.

'What is it? Euryale?'

'Well, I'm not supposed to mention it.'

'Mention what?'

'If I mentioned what, I would be mentioning it,' Euryale replied.

'Oh, for monster's sake, Euri, what are you talking about?' Stheno said. 'Do you know something that could help us get out of here?'

Euryale's face was a mixture of emotions, but finally she nodded. 'I can ask Medusa. We have a system, she set it up, in case her head ever got lost again and we needed something.'

'Almost like she knew her head was going to go mysteriously missing,' Hera said dryly. Euryale nodded.

'And she never thought to tell me about this system?' Stheno said, getting up and striding towards her older sister.

'It wasn't necessary for both of us to know—'

'Bullshit! She didn't want me to know because she doesn't trust me, right? Well, what is it? What's this system?'

Euryale bit her lip, clearly torn between betraying her sister's confidence and possibly getting them out of here.

Hera sat beside Euryale, taking the gorgon's clawed reptilian hand in hers. 'This isn't just about you and your sisters and some stupid made-up abduction anymore,' Hera said. 'A god has already been petrified and Hades is going after Zeus now. You *may* possibly have gotten away with petrifying Poseidon – goddess knows he was never the most popular god in the Divine Realm – but Zeus is well loved across all of the heavens. Though for the life of me, I can't understand why.

'Anyway, the other gods won't let you or Medusa survive if Zeus is harmed, and who knows if Hades will hand her head in after that. If he's figured out he could become the one surviving deity by unleashing Medusa across the whole of the Divine Realm, we could have a full-scale war of the gods on our hands. I don't think Medusa was hoping for that, do you?'

Euryale's face slowly paled as she considered Hera's words. Then she nodded curtly and approached Medusa's prone body.

Taking one of Medusa's hands, Euryale gently unfurled her sister's fingers. At first the touch clearly frightened Medusa, but Euryale soothed her with a few strokes on the arm and the body relaxed. Euryale slowly and deliberately started drawing a complex series of symbols on the outstretched palm.

After a moment, Medusa's other hand came up and felt towards her sister, who guided the hand to her own upraised palm. Medusa wrote a responding series of symbols.

Euryale responded with another short burst of strokes and then placed her hand down carefully beside her sister's body. 'She has agreed,' Euryale said holding out Medusa's outstretched arms to Hera.

Hera took Medusa's hands and felt the energy transfer. A deep warmth flowed from her toes, up her legs into her stomach, chest, arms and finally into her cranium, where it settled like champagne fizzing around her mind. She had never felt such strong power before. Her own seemed like flat lemonade compared to the fizzing joy of Medusa's energy.

But there was no time to ponder or revel in this now. Feeling a little drunk on the influx of points, Hera focused her mind, shrank herself into a black fire ant and scuttled under the door. Once in the corridor she pulled herself together, resumed her human form and surveyed the door. It was barred with a great iron rod, which she could easily dislodge. Not so easy to navigate was the row of ornate locks which had been used to further secure the door from the outside. Hera glanced around the murky hallway, hoping to see something that might help her open the locks, but there was nothing. If there were keys, they were not kept anywhere near the basement.

She suspected Medusa's borrowed existence points would be more than enough to blow the door off its hinges, if she had to, but doing so would no doubt alert any guards and make it much harder for them to get away without being noticed. And they needed to get away clear. Her best chance was to try and manifest a divine Skelton key. She needed something to transfigure, and luckily found a few dropped fish bones further along the hallway which would serve her purpose. She knew the magic, and it would take a huge amount of energy to create, but she had to try.

She concentrated on the bone in her hand and pushed the gorgon's borrowed power into its sharp jagged form. To her surprise the bone manifested itself into a skeleton key immediately. Feeling energised, rather than drained, Hera slid the key into the locks one by one, each turning without resistance, and within moments the door swung open.

The quality of Medusa's points was extraordinary. But as much as she enjoyed the feeling they gave her, an uneasy thought occurred to her. With this kind of power to give away, how much did Medusa really have access too? What real damage could she do – not just her glare, but as an entity in her own right?

Thankfully each deity or creature's existence points couldn't be used to generate any ability that the creature was not originally assigned, just as Hera couldn't use her points to fly or indeed break through another deity's curse. But with this much power, Medusa could surely transmit her glare across miles, fathoms, maybe into space?

Hera realised no divine personage, either old or new, could stop Medusa if she really unleashed her rage. Yet despite her justified anger, the gorgon had not used her power to destroy all of the divine and human realms. She had not even turned it against Hades or Cerberus as they held her down on the floor of Poseidon's throne room.

She hadn't remotely blown up Poseidon's kingdom, even though she probably could've from the comfort of her own bedroom. Instead she chose to come and confront Poseidon directly in his own lair. She hadn't even blown his eyelids off and forced him to look at her, allowing him, time after time, to avoid her gaze. Why?

Was it because Medusa was simply not aware of her own abilities? Or because she knew exactly how powerful she was, and was reluctant to unleash it. Did Medusa, perhaps because of the injustices and violence wreaked upon her, find it difficult to justify the use of her own terrible destructive force?

If that was true, Medusa had more humanity and compassion than most gods or goddesses combined.

Euryale and Stheno moved towards the open doorway, guiding Medusa, as Hera regained her focus, alert for any guards. The corridors were empty; it seemed the place was all but deserted. Maybe the petrification of their king had given the sea creatures other things to worry about besides guarding a bunch of women down in the dank depths of the city. Then she remembered it was Hades who'd imprisoned them, and Poseidon's minions had no quarrel with them.

'Come on. We need to get to the portal,' Hera said.

'Hera? Is that you?'

Hera stopped dead in her tracks. 'Athena?'

The door to her left was locked and bolted in the same way as the one she'd just opened. 'Are you in there?'

'Yes.'

The gorgon sisters helped Hera remove the heavy bar, then she used the skeleton key again to unlock the door, releasing the Goddess of Wisdom who, irritatingly, still looked immaculate and professionally coiffed.

'What happened to you?' Hera asked.

'Cerberus knocked me out. Hades had him at Perseus' farm. I think he had Medusa's head, because Perseus was petrified when I found him!'

Stheno and Euryale glanced nervously at Hera who smiled tightly and then changed the subject.

'How long have you been locked in?' Hera paused. 'Why didn't you shapeshift your way out?'

'I'm low on existence points,' Athena admitted. 'I didn't realise how much we'd be using in this damn fool adventure, and my hair was quite frizzy this morning.'

'You don't do remote banking either?' Euryale asked.

'I've been too busy to set it up,' Athena muttered.

Euryale rolled her eyes, but the sound of something falling distracted her from commenting on such foolishness from a goddess of wisdom. She realised Medusa had wandered off.

'Where's Medusa?' Euryale cried, looking down the long, dark, empty hallway.

'Medusa is with you?' Athena asked, surprised. 'You found her? Oh, thank heavens. I thought Hades had her.'

'He does, just not *all* of her,' Hera said, thankful that it was not an actual lie. She hadn't decided how much to tell Athena yet, so it was best to keep all information as simple and undetailed as possible. It was not that she was going to necessarily lie for Medusa, but she hadn't decided what to do about that. And for now, at least, she didn't have to.

After a short search the women found Medusa's body in a crumpled heap at the bottom of a small flight of stairs.

'Honestly, Stheno! You need to keep an eye on her,' Euryale said.

'Why is that my job?'

'Because I can't do everything–'

'Ladies, please. I think you should be helping your sister rather than squabbling,' Athena scolded, and the two sisters glared at each other before guiding Medusa back on her feet.

Athena pulled Hera aside. 'Why is Medusa's body here? Last time we saw the sisters they were all in Monsters' Realm?'

'Listen, Athena, I'll fill you in later, okay,' Hera said. 'Right now we have to find Hades. He's already petrified Poseidon; and he's going after Zeus.'

Again, not a lie. After all it *was* Hades who'd actually petrified Poseidon, even if it hadn't been his original plan. Athena didn't need to know more than that, because she may refuse to help, and Hera knew they wouldn't get far without Athena's clever thinking.

'What?' Athena demanded. 'Poseidon? What the–'

'As I said I'll explain later.' Hera turned to the three gorgons. 'Come, we need to get to the portal. Hades has a massive head start on us.'

Once the women emerged from the dungeons, they found Atlantis in complete chaos. Tritons, nymphs, and even a few humans in diving gear were running around the island in complete panic.

'Queen Hera,' a young mermaid called out. 'Is it true? Has Poseidon been petrified?'

Hera stopped by the young blonde creature and nodded solemnly. 'Yes. I am afraid so.'

The mermaid considered this for a moment, her face blank. Then she turned around and yelled to the other mer-people basking on the nearby rocks, 'The old bastard's gone! Queen Hera just confirmed it.'

Whereon *all* the mer-people turned their happy faces towards the goddesses.

'About time!' an old triton responded from behind them, before blowing his horn to bring the rest of the island's inhabitants running or swmming towards the shoreline.

'He's been pertified!' the triton yelled to the awaiting masses. 'Poseidon, king of the sea is no more.'

For a moment there was a shocked silence, during which Hera nervously expected a sudden attack by Poseidon's loyal minions. Instead, the crowds of sea folk erupted in a chorus of cheers and hurrahs, and the mer-people dived and frolicked in the ocean, all seemingly delighted by the demise of their dictator.

'Shouldn't you be worried?' Euryale asked one of the mermaids. 'There's no one to watch out for you all now.'

'Oh, we'll be fine,' she said, with a grin. 'The lecherous old bugger never did any of the actual work. Just creeped around groping us and setting off the occasional tidal wave. Much better without him, honestly.'

'Come on, Euryale; we don't have much time,' Hera said, pulling the gorgon away from the celebrating mer-people, and towards the undersea portal.

With a gasp, Hera raised her head above the churning waves. A moment late Athena and Euryale popped up beside her.

'Didn't you bring the boat?' Athena asked.

'No. I apparated from the mainland,' Hera replied. 'I thought it would save time.'

Athena pursed her lips at such a flagrant waste of existence points. 'No wonder Hades was able to overpower you.'

'He overpowered you too,' Hera replied crossly, spitting up the seawater she just swallowed.

'We have a boat,' Euryale said.

'Excellent.'

'Only it's gone.' Euryale added looking across the empty sea.

Hera shook her head. 'Hades probably took it, or sank it.'

Euryale and Athena looked around fruitlessly as Stheno, dragging a flailing Medusa, joined them.

'There's no boat,' Euryale told her.

'Oh, for goddess' sake!' Stheno frowned at Hera and Athena, dogpaddling beside her. 'How did you lot manage to rule over all of humankind for so long? Here, sis, hold Medusa for a minute.'

Euryale hooked her arms under Medusa's armpits, as Stheno raised herself and looked around. She plunged her hand back down into the water, grabbed a large fish and slapped it against the surface three times. The goddesses clung to each other to avoid being thrown around in the froth and foam of the massive wave that rippled across the ocean.

'What in Hades are you doing?' Athena cried, spluttering as she tried to keep herself above the chaotic sea.

Before Stheno could answer, the water turned a dark black as if a great shadow was passing beneath, then suddenly a mass of grotesque tentacles breeched the waves – followed by a huge pink head, the size of an aircraft carrier. The great creature rose up, towering over the women and staring down at them with its one great monstrous eye.

The goddesses frantically splashed away. They both knew exactly who this was: the deadly Kraken, monster of the deep.

'Stheno? What are you doing here?' the Kraken asked the gorgon, who showed no terror or even surprise at its arrival.

'I need some help, Kracky. If you will give us a ride, I'll forgive all those existence credits you owe me from the last poker night.'

The Kraken turned its one-eyed gaze to the other women, resting on the headless woman held aloft by Euryale's strong arms. 'Is that Medusa?'

'Will you help us or not?' Stheno snapped.

'Sure, don't get your knickers in a twist. Where do you need to go?'

Stheno swam up to the Kraken and patted its spongey, slimy head. 'Mortal Realm, fast as you can.'

'Ooh, Mortal Realm. I haven't done that for a while! I reckon it's time I scared the skin off a few sunbathers huh?'

The monster grinned, revealing a gleaming row of razor-sharp teeth in its soft, squishy mouth. The effect was chilling.

'Try not to eat too many of them,' Stheno advised. 'You know how humans get.'

'Sure, sure, just a few surfers and a couple of English backpackers, I reckon. No one ever misses them,' the Kraken replied.

The creature wrapped a tentacle around Euryale and Medusa, raising them onto its neck, then offered another for Hera and Athena to clamber onto. As soon as Stheno climbed up beside her sisters the Kraken took off at a terrifying speed towards the horizon.

As they plunged under and over and under the waves, Hera realised she'd need a serious conditioning treatment for her hair when this was all over. All this sea water was not doing her split ends any favours.

22

Sibling Rivalry

HADES WALKED UP AND DOWN THE STREET FOR THE THIRD TIME, checking the house numbers against the address in his black leather book. The sack containing Medusa's head was getting heavy so he dumped it on the footpath, while he stared at the house in front of him in dismay.

Yes, this smoking pile of charred timber was definitely once 351 O'Hara Street. It didn't matter how many times he checked, the reality of the situation was not going to change. Zeus was not here, and neither was his house.

An elderly Greek woman, dressed head to toe in black mourning clothes, walked up the street pulling a decidedly uncooperative shopping trolley. She hesitated in front of the house opposite the burnt remains of Zeus and Hera's home, whereon Hades tied his precious sack to his brother's singed front fence and hurried to open her front gate.

'Here, let me help,' he said, reaching out to take control of her trolley, which was trying to roll away down the street.

The woman looked up at him and smiled. 'Thank you. This arthritis really got its claws in today.'

'You are most welcome, madam,' Hades replied in the old language and the woman looked at him, surprised.

'You're Greek?' she asked.

'Indeed I am.'

The woman's smile became tinged with suspicion as she eyed him up and down. 'Do I know you?' she asked in their old language.

'No, but I believe I may have met your husband.'

'My husband has been dead for almost 10 years,' the woman said sadly.

'My condolences,' Hades said smoothly, moving aside to let her walk past him.

'May I ask, do you know what happened to 351?' He nodded towards the ruins of Zeus and Hera's house.

'Oh, burnt down this afternoon. An electrical thing, I heard. Went up fast as lightning.'

'Did you know the occupants?'

The woman considered, then leaned forward and whispered, 'I don't like to gossip. They kept to themselves mostly, but there were lots of strange goings on over there.'

'Yes, I can imagine,' Hades said.

The woman glanced up. 'Do *you* know them?' she asked.

'Oh yes, I'm family. I'm trying to track them down. We haven't spoken for some time.'

She nodded and her smile faded completely as she pulled away.

'Do you know where they went?'

The woman shook her head. 'No, I don't. The lady was pretty upset with her husband when she seen what happened. Such cursing! I never heard the like of it.'

The woman made the ancient sign of the evil eye as a mark of protection. 'I certainly wouldn't want to be on the wrong side of that woman, I can tell you. She was fearsome, the way she carried on, as though it was all his fault. I thought she might have beaten him right out here on the street. Course, couldn't blame her. Lost everything, they did.'

Hades smiled and closed the gate. 'Thank you for your help, madam.'

'My Dmitri left the oven on once, but I was home and caught it in time. All we ended up losing was the dinner.' The woman's eyes misted over. 'That's Dmitri Costopoulos,' she said, looking steadily at Hades. 'You'll make sure he's okay, won't you?'

Hades started.

'I know who you are. I know who *they* are too. I'm from the old country. I remember the old gods.'

Hades nodded. 'I'll check in on him, make sure he's okay.'

The woman nodded, satisfied, and lumbered to her front door on painful legs. Before she entered, she turned back to Hades. 'Don't suppose I have long for this world, do I?'

Hades pursed his lips, considering what to say. 'It's not really up to me.'

The woman nodded. 'Well, I'm not afraid of death. Don't think I would care to live forever. I suspect life could become quite tiresome.'

'Yes, forever isn't what it's cracked up to be,' Hades acknowledged. 'Not what it's cracked up to be at all.'

The immortal King of the Underworld returned to the now writhing sack, tapped it lightly to settle Medusa's serpents, and slung it over his shoulder. He headed for Marrickville train station, wondering how he was going to find his brother now.

Pegasus flew in great looping swoops through the air, revelling in her freedom. If she was suffering any ill effects from her time chained up in Perseus' barn, Artemis couldn't detect them. The flying horse seemed, to all intents and purposes, as happy as any creature the goddess had ever encountered.

Apollo pulled the fiery horses to a halt, causing the chariot to hover in place a few feet away from Pegasus.

The winged horse spotted them, turned and glided closer, neighing gleefully.

Artemis held out some fresh carrots and Pegasus stopped a few centimetres away, flapping her magnificent wings and eyeing the treat cautiously.

'It's okay, Pegasus,' Artemis cooed, 'no one here is going to hurt you. We want to help you.'

The horse snickered softly, grasped the carrot quickly and then took off, circling high above the fire chariot.

'Pegasus,' Artemis called. 'We're here to help you. We want to reunite you with your mother.'

The horse stopped, seemingly suspended in mid-air, then fell gently towards them, pulling up next to Artemis' upraised hand.

Artemis stroked the horse's beautiful mane as Pegasus snickered questioningly.

'I promise, we only want to help. You know who I am, don't you?'

The horse nuzzled against her hand and Artemis smiled widely.

'That's a good girl. Follow us, Pegasus. I promise no one will ever chain you up again.'

The horse neighed in agreement and Apollo flicked the reins to get the sun-horses to resume their suspended flight.

'Polly, take us to Pan's refuge. It's the safest place for her until we hear from Hera.' Artemis said, retrieving more carrots from the foot of the chariot to give to Pegasus during the journey

Apollo gritted his teeth and urged the horses on, checking that Pegasus was following.

Artemis frowned. 'Pan's refuge is east.'

Apollo pushed the horses faster, steering them due west. Artemis tried to grab the reins and he pushed her off.

'Polly, what are you playing at?'

'I am taking Pegasus to the EBCU.'

Artemis turned on him sharply. 'No! You know they'll just lock her up. Or worse.'

'But it's Pegasus. She's been on the EBCU most wanted list for eons.'

'We promised to reunite her with her mother!'

Apollo scowled. 'You promised you would help me get into the cryptozoology branch!' He had suspected Artemis would not keep to her word, but was still disappointed to have his suspicions confirmed.

Artemis frowned, but before she could respond Apollo slapped the reins heavily against the sun-horses' flanks. 'I am officially commandeering this mission. Now stop arguing with me. Once I log Pegasus in with EBCU and fill out the necessary paperwork, we can look at whether Medusa has any claim to the animal and–'

Apollo's next words were cut off as Artemis slapped him brutally across the face and wrestled the reins from him. She urged the horses to turn back towards the eastern mountains.

Apollo, stunned, stood still for a moment, then grabbed the reins and tried to pull them out of Artemis' vice-like grip.

'Artie, you have to respect my authority,' he cried in a whiny tone, tears springing to his eyes. 'I'm a senior EBCU operative!' He wiped the tears away quickly, hoping Artemis would think they were caused from the slap and not from his anger and frustration at once again being ignored by his twin sister.

'Back off, Polly. Pegasus is going to Medusa and that is that.'

'But the EBCU!'

'I don't give a flying centaur about the EBCU!' Artemis spat. 'They're a bunch of officious, useless pencil pushers. No one takes them seriously, and I am certainly not going to give that bunch of mean-minded little has-beens a creature as glorious and rare as Pegasus.'

Apollo's face contorted in dismay. 'I'm one of those mean-minded has-beens.'

Artemis gave him a side eye and slapped the reins harder on the sun-horses' flanks.

Fury overcame Apollo and, without thinking, he pushed Artemis aside and grabbed the reins again.

Artemis reacted by pushing him back so hard he almost went over the side of the chariot. He steadied himself and then shoved back, twice as hard. He wasn't going to give into her again. Not this time!

Suddenly it was on. The twins began hitting each other, their hands nothing but blurred movement as they fell into a slap fight that rocked and creaked the metal chariot.

The reins were dropped and the sun-horses, unsure what was happening, flew up towards the troposphere, then the chariot hovered and swayed as each horse chose a different cardinal direction to try to pull away from the fighting siblings.

Apollo, overcome by years of frustration and resentment at his sister's imperious attitude, and Artemis, equally enraged by Apollo's lack of gratitude at how much effort she had put in to looking after him for millennia, ignored the horses' actions.

Slap. Slap–slap. Apollo took a belter across the back of the head. *Slap, slap, slap.* He broke through Artemis' defence to land a loud painful crack across her right shoulder.

'Ow!' She countered quickly, grabbing his upper forearm and administering an eye-watering Chinese burn. Apollo screamed and poked her in the eye.

Artemis let go and Apollo tackled her onto the floor of the chariot, pinning her down for a few moments before she used her mighty thighs to flick him over and pin him beneath her muscular bulk. She started hawking up her spit.

'No!' Apollo protested, as Artemis rolled her saliva up into her lips and let a long string to fall from her mouth towards Apollo's shaking face.

'Arggghhh,' he cried, unable to avoid the spittle as it landed on his reddened cheek.

'Say you give up!' Artemis said through gritted teeth, then prepared her next spit bomb in the back of her throat.

'Never,' Apollo yelled, eyes scrunched closed, as he tried to push his much bigger and stronger sister from him. Both of them knew he was going to lose this fight, but for the first time in a long time Apollo wasn't going to just give in to her. He was sick of being bullied. In a final act of resistance, he drew all his strength and gave a mighty shove.

It probably wouldn't have been too successful except that, at that very moment, the two sun-horses tore away from each other, ripping the chariot's harness apart as each was freed to fly off in their own separate direction. The chariot, separated from the steeds' power, started plunging to the Earth, taking the fighting twin deities with it.

The chariot toppled and overturned, flinging Apollo and Artemis clear before disappearing somewhere in the soft desert sands below.

Artemis recovered first. Bruised and aching, she found her brother's sandaled feet sticking up out of a nearby dune, kicking about as he tried to free himself. She trudged over and yanked him out of the sand. He lay next to her, breathing heavily, his mouth bleeding, and made a half-hearted attempt to slap at her. She batted him away wearily and the two collapsed, exhausted, next to each other, looking up at the empty sky. No sign of the sun-horses or, more worryingly, Pegasus.

'Look what you've done now,' Artemis said.

'Me!' Apollo rasped. 'You're the one who tried to commandeer the chariot. If it wasn't for you, we'd be almost at headquarters by now.'

'You are *not* taking Pegasus to them. I told you.'

'And who died and made you the boss?' Apollo replied.

'Mum!'

Apollo was stunned into silence. The memory of the death of their mother was still powerful enough to bring up fresh, overwhelming grief.

'She wouldn't have bullied me like you do,' Apollo finally said.

Artemis looked over at her brother, his face obscured by the sand that had stuck to her spit.

'I don't bully you. '

'Yes. You. Do!'

'No, I don't. I look after you, Apollo, because you refuse to grow up! Did you ever think of that? I had to give up my whole life to make sure you were okay. I didn't get the life of lazing about reciting poetry in the fields of Elysium. I had to go out there and work, bring home the bacon.'

'You're the Goddess of the Hunt – that's what you are meant to do!'

'Yeah, but that doesn't mean it wouldn't have been nice to have a break occasionally, or come home to some gratitude when I not only caught the dinner but cooked and served it as well.'

Apollo shook his head. 'That's not fair. You never let me do anything. You were always refusing to let me come hunting.'

'Because you were terrible at it. I didn't want to end up with an arrow in my back because you got startled by a wood pigeon.'

Apollo pulled himself up. 'I'm not useless, Artie. I can look after myself. I got into the EBCU despite your efforts to talk me out of it. I'm someone now in the new administration and you hate it.'

Artemis also got to her feet and scraped sand from her chest and legs. 'And you're proud of being part of that disgusting police state?'

'Yes, I am,' Apollo said. He knew many in the Divine Realm saw the Entity Behavioural and Compliance Unit as a negative thing, but he truly believed it did good work. Without it they would be in chaos.

'And I suppose you support their complete denial when Gaia shows them proof of climate change? And what about their inability to stand up to the actions of people like Midas who continue to amass more than 80 per cent of the world's existence points while not supplying a single ounce of divine guidance?'

Apollo shook his head. 'Every system has problems.'

Artemis shoved Apollo into the sand. 'And their continual support of the one male god and erasure of female divinity? I suppose that's just a system glitch, is it?'

Apollo looked up at Artemis' enraged face.

'You can't blame me for that. I don't agree with that policy and you know it.'

Artemis turned away, disgusted. 'You've never done anything about it though, have you? You've always been too emotional and easily led, Apollo. It's your greatest weakness.'

'It is not!'

'You wander through life never taking any responsibility for anything while you benefit from all the injustice and cruelty around you. There is no way I'm letting you give them Pegasus just so you can get a promotion. They will destroy that poor precious creature like they do every other thing in the mystical realms.'

Apollo cowered before Artemis' anger, expecting a blow, but saw the intense sadness that fueled the rage. Artemis was not just angry; she was heartbroken. He had never seen that before.

'Pegasus is Medusa's child,' Artemis said. 'You know better than anyone how hard it is to be without a mother. We both do.'

Apollo shook his head, 'You never even grieved our mother.'

Artemis looked at him with obvious shock. 'How could you say such a thing?'

'Because it's true. You just got on with it, like it was perfectly normal. You brought me into the world and then moved on, like Mum's death meant nothing. You never cried. You only ever mention her to remind me how much I owe you because you looked after me when she was gone. You don't care at all about her, or me.'

'I didn't have the luxury of crying,' Artemis shouted. 'You got to cry and get sympathy and attention from everyone while I had to make sure we survived. Don't you think I wanted to break down and mourn my mother? Don't you think I felt lost and devastated just like you?'

'Then how could you be friends with Hera now? You know it's her fault our mother died.'

'No, it isn't,' Artemis replied. 'Not entirely. I know I blamed her too, but over time, you start to see things differently. Hera didn't like our mother, and maybe she could have helped more, done more for her, but it was Zeus who abandoned our pregnant mother and didn't lift a finger to stop Hera from trying to find her. He even egged her on, loving the fact women were fighting over him. It was Zeus who left mum to die in childbirth on that rocky island and it was he who claimed we weren't his kids and had no right to any divine membership. Hera at least showed some remorse over what had happened and insisted we become Olympian gods. Maybe it was guilt over what happened to our mum, or maybe it was just the right thing to do, but Hera looked out for us. Without her protection, we never would have survived.'

Apollo shook his head as if to clear it. He'd never heard his sister defend Hera before; had always assumed she blamed the Olympian queen, as much as he did. But it was true, Zeus never stood up for any of them, not even their mother who he claimed to have loved. Thinking about it now, he wondered if any of the story of Hera hounding Leto was even true, they only had Zeus' word for it. Either way, he had to admit, Hera had shown him and Artemis, indeed all of Zeus' illegitimate children, far more affection and care than he ever had.

'Okay, maybe I am wrong about Hera, and about you,' Apollo said. 'But I have to take Pegasus in. Someone is bound to do it eventually, and it's my only chance at the cryptozoology department. You and Hera said so yourselves!'

'Why do you even want to be part of that stupid department? They never do anything useful.'

'If I get on the cryptozoology team, I would finally get the respect I deserve. They all think I'm a loser, just like they did back on Olympus.' He looked down, unwilling to meet Artemis' eye. 'Just like you do.'

'I never said you were a loser.'

'You don't have to say it,' Apollo replied. 'You think I'm weak and useless. You make no bones about your hatred for all men and I'm a man, Artie.'

He looked at Artemis' shocked face and sighed. 'I know, you have your reasons to hate men, and I don't even blame you. Most men, particularly gods, are bloody awful to women. Even I haven't been the most thoughtful. But I'm your brother, your twin, and you have always thought of me as nothing but a burden.' He slumped down on the sand and looked up into the sky, tears glistening in his eyes.

'That's not fair,' Artemis said, sitting beside him. 'I had to step up because you didn't. And I don't hate you. I was protecting you. Like I protect the women and creatures in my care. That doesn't mean I hate anyone.' She stopped for a moment. 'But, yeah, I suppose I have always resented you. I worked hard while you composed poetry and frolicked in the fields. You could've stepped up any time and taken over the load of looking after us. But you never did.'

'You never let me!' Apollo cried.

'I shouldn't have to *let* you, Polly!' Artemis retorted. 'Just once you could've stopped fooling about and helped me with something. Or done *anything* without being asked a hundred times.'

Apollo sat sullen and frowning, realising what Artemis said wasn't untrue. Maybe he had, *did* take advantage of the fact his sister could be relied on to do all the hard stuff. Maybe he liked that he got to be the fun, sensitive god while she built a reputation of being hard and unemotional.

'Yeah, well, I always did appreciate everything you did for me, Artie,' he said sulkily. 'I just never really had a chance to tell you before.'

Artemis gave Apollo a sideways glance, her expression softening slightly.

'Yeah, well, I never really minded looking out for you,' Artemis said. 'I like how you write poetry and stuff. Some of it isn't even half bad.'

The siblings looked at each other, not yet quite sure if they could drop their defences, but both badly wanting to.

'You know, I wrote a poem about you once,' Apollo said. 'But I was always a bit frightened of showing it to you, in case you laughed at it.'

'Do you remember any of it?'

Apollo nodded.

> *'Sister mine, fearsome and strong*
> *You protect the weak and right the wrongs*
> *Done to those lost and feckless*
> *Forever determined, never reckless*
> *Like your spirit, your aim is true*
> *I wish that I was more like you.'*

Artemis couldn't help but smile. 'That's pretty awful, but I kind of like it.'

Apollo laughed. 'Yeah, not one of my best ones. But a poem can only be as poetic as its subject.'

The two smirked at each other and then Artemis got to her feet, dusted the sand off her jeans and emptied it from her sandshoes.

'I'm sorry if I gave you a hard time growing up, Pol,' she said without looking at him.

'Well, I probably wasn't the easiest brother in the world,' he said, holding his arm out for her to help him up. 'But I do think you are kind of awesome.'

She sighed and heaved him upwards. 'Yeah, I got that from the poem.'

The siblings hugged each other, long and deep for the first time since they were children, and it felt good.

'Why have we never spoken like this before?' Apollo asked as they finally broke their embrace. 'If we had, maybe we wouldn't have spent the last few centuries fighting so much.'

Artemis shook her head. 'I don't know, but maybe we should do it every century or so. You know, clear the air and have a quick hug, just to keep us on track.'

Apollo laughed and nodded. 'Sure thing, sis.'

'Well, as great as this mending of sibling relationships is, we still have the problem of finding Pegasus, and when we do, what we do about her,' Artemis said.

'The sun-horses will probably come if I call them, but I've no idea where the chariot landed. Believe me, you do not want to be riding one of those fire horses bareback!'

Artemis blanched at the thought. 'We'll have to think of something. Maybe we can convince a griffin to fly us around?'

'Those foul creatures are just as likely to take us right into the sun!' Apollo said, recalling a particularly unfortunate incident with a griffin in the 18th century when he'd tried to ride one for a dare.

Artemis shrugged. 'We may have to risk–'

A soft nicker prompted the siblings turn in the sand. Pegasus, wings spread, stood on the dune only a few feet away.

'Pegasus,' Artemis cried in surprise. 'How long have you been there?'

The horse gazed at her with kind, beautiful eyes.

'I have a feeling she was watching us this whole time,' Apollo said.

'You think so?'

'Yeah, I think that might have been why we were able to talk to each other like we did. You got to admit, that is not the way we usually communicate.'

Artemis approached the horse cautiously. 'Did you do that, girl? Did you help Apollo and me sort ourselves out?'

Pegasus just looked at them both, her peaceful expression filling the twins with a sense of calm and happiness they rarely experienced.

Artemis stroked the horse's mane and Pegasus rubbed her head affectionately against Artemis' shoulder.

'This is what she does, I think,' Apollo said, joining his sister. 'She helps people be better. Isn't that right, girl?' Apollo stroked the horse's neck and she nuzzled him.

Artemis' gaze shifted between her brother and the horse. 'I don't think she makes us nicer exactly, because otherwise Perseus never would have kept her locked up like he did. I think she amplifies who were *really* are. I mean we do love each other, Polly, even if we sometimes forget to show it.'

'Yeah, I suppose we do.' Apollo handed Pegasus a piece of carrot from the pocket of his suit. 'I guess her power might be to blow away the pretence, you know all the bullshit we build up.'

Artemis frowned. 'If that's true, I get why she wanted to avoid being anywhere near humanity for the last few centuries.'

'What do you mean?'

'Think about it. If she makes it impossible for you to hide who you are, that's not a good thing when she's faced with the selfish, greedy psychopaths that make up the human race.'

Apollo raised an eyebrow. 'Or the gods they created. Do you *really* think she left the world because of how horrible it was?'

Artemis nodded. 'Think about it: the first person Pegasus ever knew, was a total sociopath. As soon as she was born, she was captured by Perseus, who'd just decapitated her mother. Then the obnoxious little snot used her to fly about the known world destroying gods and humans. He then abducted the princess Andromeda only to abandon her, pregnant and terrified, on a deserted island. Wouldn't you want to escape a world like that too?'

Apollo nodded.

'And then she was taken by Bellerephon,' Artemis continued. 'He was a piece of work. Do you remember he was the first of the so-called heroes brought to judgement during the Monster Reconciliation Truth and Justice Tribunal.'

Apollo knew the case well. He had been part of the EBCU committee that heard the testimony of over two hundred monsters and creatures, and their families, who had been attacked, killed, captured or otherwise mistreated by Greek heroes. It had been a controversial initiative, and even now many in the divine realms felt the Heroes were well within their rights to kill, capture or harass any monster they liked. But when the Preservation of Monsters Act was passed, the EBCU committed itself to helping Athena run a mediation session, or a truth and restorative justice tribunal, where the Heroes were held to account for all the carnage they had created.

One of the first of Athena's targets had been Bellerephon, whose murder of the Chimera – an animal with the body of a lion, a goat and a snake tangled together – had been widely celebrated in myths and legends. But the 'legendary act' had been nothing more than the horrific and senseless extermination of a unique creature – for a trophy.

Pegasus was long lost by the time Bellephron's testimony was given before the committee, and many did not believe he'd ever been in possession of the famed winged horse during his exploits.

Something Bellerephon said in the proceedings haunted Apollo now.

'While I was on Pegasus, controlling her with my steel bridle and golden spurs, I felt like I could do anything,' he had testified. 'Killing the Chimera was just a part of it. I also laid waste to villages, destroyed farmlands, beat and whipped that damned winged horse in my pursuit of the Chimera. I was invincible. Yet once Pegasus was gone – she ran away as soon as I jumped off her back, you know – well once she was no longer below me, I lost that feeling; I never felt quite so indestructible again. In fact, I have never managed to defeat another monster.'

After Bellerephon's slaughter of the Chimera, many heroes searched for Pegasus, hoping to harness her power for their own ambitious and bloodthirsty quests. Yet she was never again found. Until now.

Hmm, Apollo though. If she *had* amplified Apollo and Artemis' love for each other, perhaps Pegasus had also amplified Bellerephon's blood lust, or Perseus' need for attention? If so, Pegasus could be one of the most dangerous or liberating creatures ever created, depending on who was around her.

Pegasus nodded her magnificent head as if affirming Apollo's unspoken thoughts.

Artemis urgently gripped her brother's shoulder, almost as if she'd had the same revelation. 'We have to make sure Pegasus doesn't fall into the wrong hands, Polly. You understand that, don't you?'

Apollo bit his lip and stroked Pegasus' snowy mane. 'Like those of pencil-pushing officious little EBCU agents?' he asked.

Artemis said nothing. She didn't need to. Apollo might want to be part of the EBCU, but he wasn't like them, not really. Despite his many faults, Apollo knew in his heart he was a poet, not a bureaucrat.

'We should take her to Medusa,' he said.

Artemis grinned and slapped Apollo on the back, then sobered suddenly.

'It would mean you never get a promotion at EBCU,' she said, 'It's one thing to not have Pegasus, but if the EBCU find out you had her and let her go, they'll never let you in the cryptozoology department no matter how hard you try. You might even lose your job entirely.'

Apollo shrugged. 'Yeah, I know. But it's only a job. This is bigger than that, isn't it?' He stroked Pegasus' flank. 'If the EBCU don't get that, well they can shove their cryptozoology job.'

Artemis grinned broadly and hugged her brother, then pushed him aside roughly, slightly embarrassed by her continuing emotion. Apollo laughed and pulled her back into an embrace.

'No way, sis, you and me are huggers now!' He held her fiercely for a good 30 seconds before releasing her. And damn if she didn't hold on for a second or two longer than that!

'Pegasus, are you happy to come with us now?' Artemis asked as she turned away from her beaming brother.

Pegasus nodded, and nuzzled Apollo again.

'I would say that was a definite yes,' Artemis said, patting the horse's back. 'Trouble is, we have no idea how to get out of this place.'

Pegasus looked at Artemis with what seemed like reproach and then folded her massive wings together and knelt next to the goddess.

Artemis looked at Apollo in amazement.

'I think she's offering us a lift, Artie,' Apollo said.

Artemis clambered onto Pegasus' wide back and Apollo followed suit. As soon as they were comfortably seated, the horse stood, flapped her massive wings, and took off.

Apollo clutched his sister's waist as they ascended into the clouds.

'What an amazing feeling,' she remarked and Apollo had to nod; his heart was bursting with love for his sister, hope for the future and love for all the vulnerable and frightened creatures below. It was an intoxicating feeling, and he suddenly understood why so many tried to possess this beautiful horse, and why none of them ever could.

22

Persephone's Domain

DRIPPING AND EXHAUSTED, HERA STUMBLED UP THE BEACH AT Bondi. Several impossibly tanned sunbathers and surfers watched her with ill-concealed amusement. *What a sight she must look.*

She fished a small sea perch out of the front of her blouse and tossed it into the ocean. She saw her stepdaughter emerging from the water and was surprised to see Athena looked as bedraggled and miserable as she felt. The wise goddess' hair, usually pinned up in a complicated, flattering bun, was hanging in scraggy ringlets across her shoulders. Her face looked tired and harassed, and Hera could almost feel the burning itch of the sunburn developing on her stepdaughter's nose and shoulders.

Athena noticed Hera's startled expression and tried to pat her hair and fix her appearance, her embarrassment obvious.

Hera smiled at her kindly and held out a hand to help Athena stumble up the sand. Hera had always envied Athena's effortless elegance and impeccable grooming. But now, seeing her daughter less than perfect, she remembered the young woman Athena had been, fighting toe to toe with the other gods, protecting her beloved humans while covered in the sweat of battle and the mud of the earth. Where had that Athena gone? Lost behind perfect makeup and low self-esteem.

'I don't have enough accessible points to tidy up,' Athena whispered, her eyes downcast.

'You look great,' Hera said. 'Stop worrying about it.'

Athena flushed but managed a quick smile.

Hera smiled back and then, feeling the champagne fizzle of Medusa's power still strong within her, said, 'I can give you a quick makeover, if you like?'

'I thought you had no existence points left,' Athena said, patting her sodden hair and wringing out her filthy clothes.

'I borrowed a few. I think I can spare some to tidy you up.'

Hera unwrapped a ribbon of seaweed that had curled around her legs, using it to expertly bind her own wild hair back off her face. She noticed Athena looking at her in a weird way.

'So do you want the zap or not?' Hera said.

'Nope.' Athena picked up a stray piece of seaweed and tied back her hair in an imitation of Hera. 'I think there are going to be more important things to use those points for.'

Hera yanked another fish from her bra, throwing it towards the ocean, where it was snapped up mid-flight by the Kraken, who was emerging onto the shore.

Pandemonium broke out on the sand as humans scrambled towards the road where drivers, who had seen the monster's arrival, were slamming on brakes and crashing into each other in a chain of insurance claims that would make the local smash repairers a small fortune.

'Don't kill any of them,' Athena warned as Kraken and Stheno pranced up and down the beach, threatening anyone not fast enough to get out of their way. 'You know the terms of the treaty.'

'You never were any fun, Athena,' Stheno called as she broke into an abandoned picnic basket and gobbled down the goat's cheese and beetroot salad that the fleeing hipster couple had abandoned under their appropriately vintage-looking beach umbrella.

Athena pulled Hera aside. 'Do you have your phone? We are never going to beat Hades to your house, but we could warn Zeus now that we are back in range.'

Hera shook her head. Hades had taken her phone when she was unconscious, just as he had taken Athena's.

'We could use a payphone?' Athena said.

Hera doubted it. They were as likely to find a payphone in a public street as they were to meet a velociraptor. It didn't matter anyway; Hera had never bothered to learn Zeus' mobile number; it just came up in her contacts. It was amazing how reliant even a goddess was on technology nowadays.

'What's the plan then?'

Hera thought for a moment. The simple truth was she didn't have a plan. As a goddess she always believed that it was the Fates who decided the outcomes, not her. She'd always found it best to take some kind of action and see how things played out. Things generally worked out because, well, she was a goddess and the world was essentially ordered that way. Something would turn up, or it wouldn't.

'We need to stop Hades,' Athena said. 'Regardless of how you feel about Zeus, we can't let him be petrified.'

Hera scowled. Was it so obvious she wasn't really bothered if her husband ended up a marble statue? It wasn't as if she was actively trying to harm him, but if he wasn't saved – was that the worst outcome in the world?

'It's not just about Zeus,' Athena said, reading Hera's mind in the uncanny way she had. 'You know if Zeus is attacked there will be no saving Medusa or any of the other monsters. This will see the end of the Preservation of Monsters Act, and it will be all-out war on Monsters' Realm. We can't let that happen.'

Hera tuned into the fizz of Medusa's power surging through her and wondered if maybe the monsters could defend themselves better than Athena thought. But it wasn't worth taking the risk. Medusa may be uncommonly powerful, but most of the creatures on Monsters' Realm existed on superficial fable or legend points, not the potent power that Medusa seemed to command. The gods had tolerated them, mostly because the monsters presented a united front through the formation of the realm and had a few staunch divine supporters like Athena and Artemis. But if push came to shove the wrath of the gods could probably destroy many of them, or at least weaken them enough to take Monsters' Realm away.

Hera nodded. 'Don't worry, Athena. Hades has no idea where Zeus is.'

'Yes, he does. We all went to your housewarming. Everyone knows exactly where you live. That was a great night, by the way. Did you get the card I sent as a thank you after it?'

Hera rolled her eyes. Only Athena would bother to follow up on a thank you card from 60 years ago. 'He's not there. He burnt the house down.'

'He what?'

'It doesn't matter.' Hera said, walking up the beach towards the street, 'The point is he isn't there, and he's nowhere that Hades would think of looking for him.'

Athena pulled Hera's arm, slightly. 'What about Pegasus – did you find her?'

'No, but Artemis and Apollo are still out there looking, maybe they have by now.'

Euryale was suddenly at Hera's side, wide eyed and grabbing at her shoulder.

'Did you just say Pegasus?'

Hera started. She'd forgotten the gorgons were with them. She flicked Euryale's hand away. 'Yes. Pegasus. Perseus had her.'

Euryale looked perturbed and glanced at Medusa, who was sitting, headless but seemingly happy, making what she thought was a sandcastle but was actually an uneven pile of sand. Horrified but curious bystanders recorded her on their phones before being scattered by Stheno roaring up to them.

'Pegasus is real?' Euryale asked quietly, almost to herself.

'Yes, she's real,' Hera replied irritably, ignoring the fact that she had asked almost exactly the same question when Perseus had first shown her the mythical horse.

'That must have been what Poseidon was planning,' Euryale muttered, looking again at her pathetic, headless little sister. 'He must have known Pegasus was back.'

'Yes, he did. He was the one who sent Percy off looking for her,' Hera said, looking at Euryale suspiciously. 'Do you know why he did that?'

Euryale bared her teeth in sudden anger. 'I didn't believe Medusa when she told us Poseidon was coming after her. I thought he was just taunting her, or she was reading too much into it. But if Pegasus is real, then Medusa was right to be worried. That bastard *was* coming for her. He was going to make her human.'

Athena and Hera looked bewildered. 'What are you talking about?'

'There's something I have to tell you, but you can't breathe a word of it to anyone else. Especially Medusa.'

Hera and Athena listened carefully as Euryale explained the situation, the goddesses interrupted a few times to gain clarity, but mostly just listened, silent and amazed. The gravity of what they were hearing slowly dawned on both of them.

'We need to contact Artemis. Right now,' Athena said.

Euryale called to Stheno across the now deserted beach. 'Come on, we have to go.'

Stheno paused mid throw. The multicoloured beach ball dropped far clear of the Kraken's spiky tentacles, where several previously thrown balls were spiked, punctured and deflated, like some weird plastic jewellery.

'No,' Hera said. 'Athena and you can help me with Medusa.' She turned to Stheno. 'You go to your dinner with Jacko. We can't have you missing that proposal.'

A look of pure delight filled Stheno's face, making her, not pretty exactly, but certainly less hideous than she normally looked. 'Really?'

'Yeah. As the goddess of marriage, I can't stand by and let you remain a spinster for the rest of your life, now can I?'

Stheno ran up and pulled Hera into a crushing hug before pushing her away with such force that the goddess fell to the sand.

'Are you sure? Medusa is still a prisoner and your husband is still in danger.'

Hera nodded. 'We have a plan now, and if you would prefer to see your fella then we can spare you.'

'Kracky, stop messing around. We need to get back to Monsters' Realm. Like yesterday,' Stheno yelled, almost before Hera had finished her sentence.

The Kraken grinned and allowed Stheno to clamber again on its back before plunging into the water.

'Are you sure it was wise to let her go like that?' Euryale asked, helping Medusa to her feet. 'We could've used her help.'

Hera waved the idea away. 'The last thing we need is her lumbering around harassing everyone. It's better she's out of it. And if I'm right, we have a bit of finessing that needs to be done, and Stheno has the finesse of the proverbial bull in a china shop.'

'Shouldn't we have asked her to take Medusa then?' Euryale asked.

'No,' Hera said. 'If this plan has any hope of working, we need Medusa with us.'

'Yee-hah!' Stheno's voice carried back all the way to the beach as the two monsters broke the surface and crashed into the incoming waves. Stheno was sitting topless astride the Kraken, waving her shirt above her head in triumph.

'Mama's getting some lovin' TONIGHT,' she screamed, seconds before the beast dived again and disappeared into the Pacific Ocean.

Euryale rolled her eyes, but she was smiling. Hera and Athena were too.

'So, what *is* the plan?' Athena asked.

Hera fished out a sopping business card from where she'd tucked it into her bra strap earlier that day. On it was the number for the Goddess Womyn's Shelter and in one corner a private mobile number for Artemis.

'We get Artemis and Pegasus here as soon as possible.'

'I thought you said it'd be impossible to find a public phone,' Athena reminded her.

Hera searched the seafront, her eyes lighting up as she saw what she was looking for.

'The Fates decide what is possible or not,' Hera said, marching towards a lone, forgotten payphone on the promenade, 'not me.'

Artemis and Apollo, dusty and exhausted but invigorated, slapped the dirt from their clothes and shut the paddock gate. Just as it clicked into place, Artemis' mobile rang.

'Yes, Artie here,' she answered, not recognising the number that flashed up on her phone. 'Oh Hera, great! I've been trying to call you but your phone was off.'

Artemis scrunched up her face at the response 'Okay, okay, sure. Yes, we found Pegasus. We've got her at Pan's mythical beast sanctuary. She's an absolute sweetie. Once she knew we were there to help she's been no trouble at all.'

As if to prove the point the winged horse reached over the fence and neighed gently into the phone.

'Yeah, I can do that. Probably a few hours from here. But why–' Artemis pulled away from the corral in order to hear the static-tinged voice on the other end of the call.

'Okay, I think I know where that is. But I can barely hear you,' Artemis yelled. 'It sounds like you are talking on an old-fashioned public phone.'

Hera hung up in her ear and Artemis thought she should be annoyed, but in Pegasus' company it was so darn hard to hold any kind of negative emotion; even against Hera. In fact, she found herself feeling only empathy for the goddess. It sounded as if she had been through an ordeal, and Hera wasn't as young as she used to be.

She really should treat Hera to a trip to Hebe's Spa and Health Retreat when this was all over. Spend a bit of quality time with her stepmother. Do a bit of family healing. She might even treat herself with a cheeky little mani-pedi.

Apollo, walking up with hay and a large bucket of water, interrupted her thoughts. 'Was that Hera?'

'Yeah, she wants us to head out with Pegasus right away.'

'I thought we were keeping her here where she's safe.'

'Apparently not. It's really important that we take Pegasus to her. She wouldn't say why, just hung up on me.'

Apollo smiled. He too found it impossible to be annoyed with his stepmother, who in ordinary circumstances he rather disliked.

'So where does she want us to take Pegasus?'

'You're not going to believe this...' Artemis began as they fed and watered the lovely creature before preparing her for the next part of their adventure.

As Artemis and Apollo headed towards their destination, Hera, Euryale and Athena were undertaking a more perilous journey.

'Are you sure about this?' Euryale asked anxiously, as the river Styx appeared before them, flowing with black, inky water and stretching endlessly into the even darker blackness beyond.

'We need Persephone on board or the whole plan fails,' Hera replied. Not really the convincing response she'd intended, but it seemed to do the trick, as Euryale didn't question the idea again.

'You and Medusa should wait here,' Hera advised the gorgon. 'As divine beings, Athena and I can come and go, as long as we don't eat anything. But I'm not sure the same is true for monsters. You may be stuck down here if you aren't careful. The last thing we need is to add a rescue from the underworld onto our to-do list.'

Euryale nodded, clearly relieved. Even a fearsome gorgon got nervous when contemplating the land of the dead.

Athena tapped a withered, crumbling tree three times and a dark, shadowy boat appeared almost instantaneously in the river, heading towards them with silent but impressive speed.

Euryale stepped back and hid herself and her headless sister amongst a cluster of rocks as Charon docked the boat and tied it to the shoreline.

'Charon,' Hera said, trying to supress the feeling of creepiness this old man, with his greenish, hollowed-out face shadowed by his rough, black cape, always elicited within her.

Charon didn't respond straight away, just looked the two goddesses up and down, then held out his hand, palm up, and waited patiently.

'Do you take points?' Hera asked.

'Cash only.'

Athena dug into the folds of her stola for spare change but came up empty. No one carried actual money anymore.

Hera considered for a moment then, realising she still had Medusa's points flowing through her, conjured two small gold coins and dropped them into Charon's palm. His thin, bony fingers wrapped around the money and he held one of the coins to his mouth, testing its authenticity by biting down on it with one of his three remaining teeth.

Satisfied, he pocketed the coins and stepped onto his boat. 'One way,' he stated.

'Return,' Hera corrected him.

The old man looked up with watery, phlegmy eyes that crinkled with a thousand creases as he smiled humourlessly.

'Don't guarantee return,' Charon replied, standing on the bow of the boat and taking up his long iron pole. 'It's not a journey many make back again.'

Hera and Athena jumped on board, the boat barely rocking on the glass-like river.

'We will be the exception. We are visiting Queen Persephone. You will wait for us and you will bring us back or you will find yourself at the bottom of this river,' Hera said evenly.

Charon looked at the goddess then nodded curtly, a mirthless smile frozen on his face. 'Of course, Queen Hera.' Then, almost inaudibly under his breath, he added, 'If Queen Persephone wishes it.'

The kingdom of Hades was beautiful in a dark, terrifying kind of way. The river flowed long and deep, enclosed on both sides by sheer, jagged cliffs on which steely eyed vultures watched the progress of the small raft with obvious interest.

A few moments into the journey and the island of the magnificent Cosmic Tree came into view, the mighty tree of knowledge on which the ambrosia of the Greeks, the Norse Apples of immortality, and the soma of the Persians grew. Hera and Athena bowed low to the tree as they drifted past, and even Charon slowed his rowing and nodded his head in reverence. As the gods were the divine beings for humankind, so it was this tree the gods worshipped. It was the Cosmic Tree, the Tree of Knowledge, the Tree of Eden, which bore the fruits of knowledge, immortality and wisdom.

The giant tree stretched up to the heavens, connecting the Underworld with the Upworld and the infinite space beyond. The tree held all the great mysteries of life and death within its branches, kept safe and hidden even from the gods. Hera could see the life force of the world pulsing through the gnarled trunk, through the intertwined branches and beyond, where even her divine eyesight couldn't see.

The land around the tree brimmed with life, contrasting sharply with the black emptiness of the Styx that sustained it. The huge branches bent from the weight of the endless fruits and blossoms, spices and riches. Every food ever known, imagined or yet to be discovered sprang from the tree, providing not just sustenance for the world but also the fruits and foods of immortality that gave the gods their power and eternal life.

The Charosh, fierce dogs with the wings and claws of owls, stood guard at the base of the tree, snarling as the three Greek deities drifted past.

Yet Hera knew that other, even more horrifying creatures made their homes in the branches. The Keres, vicious sisters of the Greek god of death, Thanatos, perched high in the foliage awaiting their call to collect the bodies of murder victims and others who had died by violence. Their reward for this service was the flesh from the bodies of these tortured souls, which they hung in long bloody strips in the uppermost branches of the Cosmic Tree to dry out before being greedily devoured by the three women.

Higher again the Golden Fleece, once retrieved by the human hero Jason, glistened amongst the branches, and higher still, sitting like a statue, almost too bright to look at in the murkiness of the Underworld, was the legendary Phoenix, its flaming plumage lighting up the air around it.

Athena tapped Charon on the shoulder and the rower obediently stopped and gently nudged the boat onto the small piece of land that surrounded the tree.

Athena, her eyes glistening with tears, her face a rapture of emotion, stepped off the boat and onto the land. The Charosh growled as she passed them, but the dog-creatures made no move to stop the goddess from touching the sacred tree. As the goddess of wisdom, this ancient tree of knowledge was more than just a provider of life and sustenance, but the source of her own divine understanding. The opportunity to see it, never mind touch it, was as rare for her as seeing a god was for a mortal, and Hera understood why Athena needed a few moments of contemplative silence to reflect on the great forces within it, which even immortals would never truly understand.

After a moment Hera called to her stepdaughter. 'Athena, we have to go.'

Athena nodded but still she stood there, unable to remove her hand from the bark, feeling the life of the universe flowing within it and also within her. It was intoxicating, extraordinary.

'Athena, I'm sorry, but we have to go,' Hera repeated, and her stepdaughter finally lifted her hand from the tree, the feeling of loss immediately apparent on her face. Whereas a few moments ago she had been connected to life and the infinity of the universe, now the world was small and dark. The sense of grief was palpable.

Hera helped the goddess back onto the raft and Charon pushed off again, heading towards the caverns that opened up just beyond the tree's island.

They sailed along at a sedate, reflective pace, both goddesses lost in their own thoughts as the river carried them towards the Underworld.

Suddenly the river disappeared from beneath them and they found themselves falling, falling down deep into the very bowels of the Earth.

Charon seemed completely unperturbed as the raft plunged into the darkness. Hera held on for dear life, an inhuman cry of terror escaping her lips. Yes, she was immortal, but that didn't mean that falling into a seemingly endless abyss was not going to scare the crap out of her. She was thankful she'd not had lunch. Athena also looked more than a little green around the gills.

The dimness in front of them lightened and Hera could vaguely make out the glassy surface of the lower part of the Styx. It was coming up fast. Too fast for her liking.

'Charon!' she cried, but the ferryman didn't hear as her voice was snatched away by the mighty updraught. She closed her eyes, steeling herself for the inevitable crash. Could immortal's bones break? She expected so, for gods could feel pain. Prometheus certainly did. One thing the *Clash of the Titans* had taught her was, immortal did not mean unbreakable or invulnerable.

'Hera?'

The goddess, eyes still tightly closed, heard her stepdaughter as though through a megaphone. Then she realised all other sound was completely absent. It wasn't just that it was quiet or even silent. It was as though they were in a vacuum where sound itself did not – could not – exist.

She opened her eyes to find herself sitting on the raft, white-knuckled and terrified, while the boat sat still and serene on perfectly smooth water.

Charon was looking at her with his deep, black wells of eyes, waiting for her to disembark onto the small dock at which they were moored.

Athena was already waiting on the wharf, her face a mixture of worry and anticipation.

'Last stop,' Charon said matter-of-factly, his voice rumbling through the hollow air like a loudspeaker.

Hera held her arm out for assistance. Charon, whether deliberately or unknowingly, ignored the goddess' outstretched arm and Hera clambered out of the boat unaided.

Charon started to row the boat back out onto the river.

'Wait,' Hera said, her voice high and angry. '*You will wait!*'

Charon, his back to the goddesses, slumped his shoulders and placed the oar down on the boat without an argument. Satisfied, Hera and Athena walked up the wooden platform towards the next and possibly most intimidating hurdle they would encounter on this trip.

The gates of Hades rose 1500 storeys high and were embedded into dense stone that wound around the Underworld from every possible angle. This entrance was the only way in or out and one of the few mystical destinations that was not accessible by a travel portal. Hades was not a place known for hosting or indeed tolerating visitors. If you were coming here, chances where you were never going to leave.

Slobbering and growling behind those gates would be the hound, Cerberus, tasked with making sure that no one got in and no one got out without a good reason.

Knowing they did not have an invitation, Hera and Athena's only hope was to lull the dog with the music on the Nano shuffle they'd picked up on the beach at Bondi, no doubt dropped by a terrified bikini clad backpacker. To Hera's horror, the playlist seemed to consist almost exclusively of amateur Australian rap bands mixed inexplicably with Justin Bieber songs. She was more than a little worried that this kind of music had more chance of enraging the hellhound than soothing it into sleep, but it was all they had so they were going with it.

Justin Bieber's weirdly feminine voice echoed thinly across the eerie silence. Both goddesses expected the three-headed dog to descend on them without mercy and rip them both to pieces. But the gates were deserted. The monstrous hound was nowhere to be seen.

Hera looked around nervously, but even the dog's great chains were not visible. She turned off the music and breathed a sigh of relief.

'Charon, where's Cerberus?' Hera called to the ferryman, who just shrugged, back still towards the goddesses.

'Is he anywhere around? Has he got off the chain?' Athena added.

The ferryman turned around slowly and gave Hera one of his dead-eyed stares. 'The Master has taken Cerberus on an outing,' he said.

So, Cerberus was still with Hades. Hera was surprised.

'But Persephone is here?' she asked.

'Oh yes, she's in all right. She always seems to be in when visitors arrive unexpectedly. Has a bit of a knack for it, she does.'

Hera was relieved. Without Persephone their whole plan fell down. But Charon was right, Persephone was always present when visitors came to Hades. Always.

'You know it's an infringement of the Underworld code for the gates to remain unguarded,' Athena said. 'Even though Hades is no longer the main Afterworld, there are still residents floating around inside, so the rules apply here.'

Charon laughed. 'These gates don't need no guarding. Those that are in there prefer to stay in there and those out here prefer not to enter, unless they don't know no better.'

Hera ignored this last comment, reaching forward for the large, ornate door knocker, which she rapped imperiously. The reverberations in the empty realm were almost deafening, but within a few moments the gates swung open and two wraiths appeared to lead Hera and Athena to Persephone's throne room.

Charon watched the two goddesses walk through the iron gates and shook his head. He would wait a couple of hours; after that, if they did manage to get out, they would be on their own – goddesses or no goddesses, he had work to do.

'Aunty Hera!' Persephone said, clapping her hands with delight as Hera and Athena entered the throne room. 'It's so good to see you.'

As ever, Hera was struck by the contrast between her niece and the foul, dingy world she'd been forced to inhabit. Persephone literally radiated health and wellbeing in her Diane von Fürstenberg original wraparound dress and Christian Louboutin high heels. Her naturally yellow tresses were frosted with lighter silver tips that seemed to circle her face like a golden corona in the darkness of the room.

'Persephone, we need your help,' Hera said. 'Hades has done something very stupid.'

Persephone's brightness dimmed for a moment, until she forced a smile back on her face. 'Whatever is the matter, Aunty?'

'Hades has turned Poseidon into stone and we believe he is intending to do the same with Zeus. Is he here? Have you seen him?'

Persephone, wide eyed and bewildered, clapped her hands over her mouth and shook her head. 'Poseidon is petrified?'

'Yes. Do you know where Hades is?'

Persephone shook her head again, a small flush rising prettily from her neck.

'No, no, I haven't seen him all afternoon,' Persephone replied. 'You really think he'd be so foolish as to go after Zeus?'

'I wouldn't have thought so before today,' Hera answered, 'but that's what he told us he was doing.'

'He told you?' Persephone replied, a shadow passing over her face, gone so fast Hera would have missed it if she hadn't been studying the Queen of the Underworld so intently. Persephone flushed again and smiled. 'That doesn't sound like my Hades.'

'Well, it's what he said, only a few hours ago.'

'Hours ago? Oh my, maybe it is too late. Maybe he has already found my dear uncle and slaughtered him. Maybe it's all too late.'

Persephone jumped out of her chair and flung her arms in the air in a gesture of horror. 'If he has, then what shall become of Olympus? Who shall rule the ancient pantheon?'

'He won't find Zeus. Don't worry about that. But we need your help to find Hades.'

'Why won't he find Zeus?' Persephone asked, dropping her arms and looking at Hera with a surprised air. 'My Hades is a very clever fellow.'

'Because he's not where Hades expects him to be. The only person who knows where Zeus is, is me. And I don't intend to let Hades know.'

'Oh, that is a relief,' Persephone said, dropping her dramatics and sitting down on her black pearl-encrusted throne. 'I can't imagine what the other immortals would do if Hades attacked Zeus. I would hate for my little love muffin to go to jail.'

'He may go to jail anyway,' Athena said. 'Like Hera said, he's already attacked Poseidon.'

'Yes, yes, you're right,' Persephone replied, 'but I'm sure the courts would give him probation for that. I mean, it was only Poseidon, after all.' Persephone's mouth twisted in dismay. 'But everyone would be most upset if Zeus was harmed,' she added quickly.

Hera wasn't sure everyone would be that upset, she herself had been secretly imagining a life where Zeus was just a frozen figure in the corner of her living room. He would probably be a more agreeable husband that way and certainly a more useful one, but Hera thought better of voicing that out loud.

'Still,' Persephone said, 'no one did anything when Hades kidnapped me from the above world and brought me down here all those years ago. So maybe no one really cares what happens to us deities.'

'That's not true,' Athena said. 'Your mother caused a right old stink. And you were always up in the above world as I recall. Hardly spent any time down here at all.'

'A flower needs some light in order to bloom, Athena,' Persephone said, her eyes sharp in her otherwise smiling face. 'Anyway, you said you needed my help. I am happy to, of course, but I'm not sure what I can do.'

'Tell us where Hades might be.'

'I don't know.' She shook her head innocently. 'Honestly, he never tells me anything. He does as he pleases.'

Persephone looked at Hera. 'Are you sure it's Hades who is after Zeus? I mean, he loves his brother. Maybe someone is framing him?'

'We saw him attack Poseidon with our own eyes, Persephone,' Athena said. 'There is no doubt it's him.'

Persephone sat back, disappointed, and her face fell into a pout that did nothing to detract from her general prettiness.

'Oh dear, he has been very stupid then, hasn't he?' Persephone said in a childlike voice. 'I really don't know what I should do with such a stupid man. It's a good thing Zeus is safely hidden away. He is safely hidden, isn't he, Aunty?'

'Oh yes, don't you worry about that,' Hera assured her niece. 'Zeus is safely stashed in an old motel on the highway near Sydney airport. It's even named after him, which I thought was a nice touch. But Hades will never even think of looking for him there.'

'How very clever you are, Aunty.' Persephone beamed. 'I've always thought very highly of you, you know. As my mother does also.'

Hera smiled at the compliment before they were interrupted by a small group of zombies carrying silver platters piled with fruits and sweets, including several ripe pomegranates.

Persephone waved them over and selected one of the fruits.

'Would you like some?' Persephone asked. 'I don't know about you, but I'm starving. I haven't eaten since breakfast.'

'No, I don't think so. We all know what happens to goddesses who eat anything from the land of the dead,' Athena replied. 'In fact, you should know better than most, shouldn't you, Persephone?'

Persephone blushed and dropped the pomegranate back onto the platter. For a moment she looked like the 3000-year-old goddess she was, but then the moment passed and the young, beautiful girl was back, smiling at them serenely.

'Oh yes, well, you know, I never could resist a good pomegranate,' she said, delicately waving the zombies to leave the trays on the wooden side tables before they lumbered away.

'Can you get in contact with Hades? Get him to call it off?' Hera asked. 'If anyone can convince him to do anything, it's you.'

Persephone giggled and twirled her hair in a coquettish manner.

'I would try, but I have no way of contacting him. Unless he comes home. He doesn't like me to call him while he's working – you know how men are.' Her eyes widened in an attempt to convey her own naughtiness at saying anything bad about her husband.

'If you do see Hades, try to keep him here, and call us as soon as you hear from him, okay? I have a new phone, so I'll write down the number. Neither of us want him in any more trouble, do we?' Hera scribbled her number onto a cloth napkin. 'We have to work together if we are going to save these stupid men from themselves.'

The smell of the roasted pheasant on the table beside her was causing Hera to salivate. She realised she hadn't had a thing to eat since this whole sorry business began.

'Of course, Aunty, of course. I'll do what I can. But I'm sure that if Hades is determined to do something, there is nothing I can say to stop him. I'm only a woman after all.'

Hera supressed her irritation at Persephone's fatuousness. She tried to get up but felt Athena's hand on her arm, pulling it down.

'Hera!' Athena cried out sharply and Hera realised that she had almost placed a steaming, delicious leg of roasted bird in her mouth. She threw the piece of meat away from her face, forcefully braining a small zombie who had been sitting, quietly knitting a beanie, in the far corner. The creature fell over unconscious.

'By the goddess, Persephone! Why must you offer food here? You know how dangerous it is!'

Persephone blushed a lovely pink peach colour and looked bereft. 'I'm so sorry, Aunty, it's so silly of me. But my mother would be very cross if I didn't show the proper hospitality to my guests.'

Hera rolled her eyes and gestured Athena back out towards the river, leaving Persephone fussily picking through a particularly delicious-looking tray of fine and tasty morsels, but dismissing each piece of food in turn. Hera's stomach growled; she really should think about getting something to eat – this running around on an empty stomach could prove dangerous.

24

Persephone and Hades

THE GIANT DOG WAS ALMOST PULLING HADES' ARM FROM ITS SOCKET as they rushed about, zig-zagging across the Divine Realm. Hades had already searched Asgard, Olympus and was now combing the Eighth Heaven, and still no sign of his brother.

'Cerberus, heel. *Heel!*' Hades cried at the hound for the hundredth time. Unexpectedly the monstrous dog stopped and looked at Hades, tongue lolling out of its gaping mouth, causing Hades to fall forward from his own momentum. The strong golden threads that held Cerberus securely in Hades' grip slackened for the first time since they had begun the search in the divine realms. Hades took the opportunity to loosen his fist and dust himself off. Then he held out a bit of old toga for the dog to smell once again.

'This smell: Zeus. You understand? I need you to find the man who smells like this. Do you understand?'

The hellhound sniffed the material indifferently then looked around the heaven, holding its nose up high in the air as if trying to get a scent.

'Good boy!' Hades said encouragingly. 'You find that scent, Cerbie, and you'll get a whole roasted pig for a treat.' The dog sniffed the air a few more times then got up and started to growl, pulling on the fleece lead.

'Okay, good,' Hades said, strengthening his grip on the threads. 'You show me where he is, okay. You show me.'

The monster dog took off, dragging Hades behind him at breakneck speed towards a huge bodhi tree, whose branches reached over the cloud-like mountains of the ancient heaven state. Hades pitched forward, holding tight to the lead with his left hand and grasping his toga and the hessian sack with Medusa's head in his right.

As they ascended the cloud mountain, Hades felt his feet leave the ground and realised Cerberus was running at such speed, Hades was now airborne. Startled, Hades loosened his grip, and the thread slipped from his hand. With nothing pulling him along, gravity did its job and Hades crashed face first into the cloud at his feet. Heavenly clouds, as every deity knows, are far harder and more uncomfortable than they look to humans and Hades' face scraped along a particularly rough piece of stratus before he rolled on his back and regained his breath.

Cerberus raced off, jowls covered with frothy slobber, as he headed towards a group of five unsuspecting minor Asian goddesses picnicking near their sacred fig tree.

Hades thought about calling the dog back, but knew it was useless. As he watched the goddesses scramble up into the branches, he decided it was better if they thought he'd deliberately unleashed the monster dog than suspect he did not have the power to control it.

Hades considered where his brother could be. Despite his struggles with Cerberus, he had managed to hold onto the gorgon's head throughout his fruitless search for Zeus. But the task had taken a toll and he was dirty and sweaty, and the silver chains that attached the sack holding Medusa's noggin to his belt had been broken somewhere between Asgard and the Happy Hunting Grounds and he didn't want to use the few strands of fleece he had to hold onto Cerberus. But he'd have to do something about securing it because he couldn't risk accidently leaving the gorgon behind somewhere.

He dropped the sack, which moved in a rather unpleasant way as Medusa's serpent hair hissed and snapped inside. He sat next to it on the slightly damp cloud floor and pulled it towards him.

'You'll never get away with this,' a raspy but surprisingly calm voice said from the bag.

Hades started. He had assumed Medusa would be unable to speak in her current condition.

'I'm sorry, Medusa, but you are wrong,' he replied. 'Gods are never held accountable for anything we do. Haven't you been paying attention for the last few millennia?'

The serpents' hissing grew louder, but Medusa's voice remained chillingly calm.

'Maybe. But you attacked another god. No deity will stand for that.'

'It was you who attacked Poseidon, Medusa. I was there to try to save my poor brother from your fiendish plot.'

Medusa's snakes hissed angrily and Hades smiled, warming to his theme. 'I safely whisked you away before you could kill me or anyone else but was too late to save dear Poseidon. I am simply now trying to return you to the Court of Lore where you will be tried and found guilty of a crime against divinity.

'But – and this is the terrible bit, Medusa – Zeus will attack me and try to take your head in a foolhardy attempt at a coup against the new gods. He has always been jealous of them, you know. I, however, through great bravery and skill, will manage to stop him. Unfortunately, again, during said struggle he will be turned to stone. A terrible tragedy, I think we can all agree.'

Medusa didn't answer at first and Hades smiled, thinking he had impressed her.

'That's a stupid plan,' Medusa said.

Hades frowned. 'It isn't a stupid plan.'

'Yes, it is. It's the stupidest plan I have ever heard.'

'And your plan was so great!' Hades replied defensively.

'At least mine was thought out. It would have worked, too, if Hera hadn't arrived earlier than expected.'

Hades grimaced. It irked him to admit it, but if he had come across the scene Medusa had planned to create, he too would have believed it. Thinking Poseidon was a dirty old pervert was the natural default.

'But it didn't work out like that, did it? And now you are sitting here with your head in a sack, so I think my plan wins.'

'You're just winging it,' Medusa replied. 'You had no idea what you were walking into, and if Cerberus hadn't been there, you'd have been turned to stone along with your no-good brother, and you know it.'

Hades was glad Medusa couldn't see his expression. He *did* know it. When he had entered Poseidon's grotto, he had no idea what was going on. He believed Poseidon had Medusa's head, especially after he had revealed his plans around Pegasus, so *his* original plan was just to beat up the old fish god and make him hand Medusa over. Finding a whole Medusa and her gorgon sisters there had not been part of any plan.

So yes, perhaps he had winged it. A bit. But it was all working out now. 'Well, Fish Pie is petrified and Zeus will soon follow, and I will be 500 million existence points richer. So, all's well that ends well, as they say,' Hades said.

'You're forgetting about Hera,' Medusa hissed from inside the sack. 'She saw you. She knows the truth.'

Yes, he thought, that was unfortunate. His sister's involvement, while useful at the beginning to lead him closer to the reward, was now a definite problem. He should have turned her to stone too, when he had the chance, he realised that now. But he also knew he couldn't really do it. Hades had always been slightly in awe of his sisters, and Hera was no exception, although with Hera the fear was mixed with real affection. He liked Hera; always had. Yes, she was often difficult and meddlesome, but she was also the only one who had stood up for their parents and stopped Zeus and Poseidon from slaughtering them. She was also the only one who, when they were children, had played with him and treated him like a true brother when his older siblings had all made fun of his small frame and constant food allergies. He even found it hilarious when she had consistently uncovered Zeus' many affairs and sexual misadventures, savouring each embarrassment and humiliation she handed out to him. But now that his plans could be spoilt because of her, her detective abilities didn't seem quite so amusing.

On the other hand, the simple fact was Hera was a woman worked in his favour. As powerful as she may be, no one would believe a goddess over a god. Maybe way back when the goddesses were truly powerful she'd have had a chance, but now that male gods dominated all the divine lands, humans and gods alike just instinctively ignored the claims of females, even if they knew them to be true.

He was fairly sure if it came down to her word against his, he could brazen it out against Hera in a court of lore; so there'd been no need to harm her. She was safely locked away and no real threat to him. In fact, if she had time to reflect on it, she may even realise that Hades was doing her a favour. Why she hadn't killed her cheating, lying, mean-spirited old fool of a husband long before was a mystery to everyone. Once Zeus was gone, Hera would see how much better everything would be – may even want to buy Hades a few rounds to show her gratitude.

This thought comforted Hades and he imagined the scene, him and Hera happily drunk, toasting the demise of Zeus and Poseidon. No real loss, either of them! There was just one small problem: Zeus was proving almost impossible to find. After he struck out at the Marrickville house, he had tried everywhere he could think of where the drunken old bastard might hang out: inns, taverns, pubs and strip clubs, brothels, gambling houses, and houses of generally ill repute, on almost every plane of existence – and nothing.

It now occurred to him that Hera would have been useful. She always managed to find the old goat, no matter how he tried to trick her. Maybe he should have enlisted her help instead of locking her up.

Hades kicked himself for not thinking of this earlier. Hera as an ally would be much better than Hera as an enemy. Maybe it wasn't too late. If he didn't find Zeus maybe he would let his sister out and convince her to join forces with him.

As he pondered how he might approach her to take part in the murder of her husband, he realised Medusa's snakes had grown silent. He glanced down to where he had placed the sack, only to realise it was no longer there.

He jumped up and scanned the area. The sack, with its precious contents, was rolling down the hill towards the edge of the Eighth Heaven – making a roll for it off the cloud lands and back to the waiting Earth below.

Hades chased after it, but it had gained a lot of momentum on its way down the hillside and he couldn't catch it, no matter how fast he ran. He could, however, hear Medusa laughing maniacally inside, as the sack spun towards the edge of the cloud plane.

Hades growled at the heavens. She was going to get away!

But then, as the writhing sack flipped over a small bump of cumulus and out over the edge into the empty space below, it was snatched by a perfectly manicured hand that shot out from the fringes of the cloud and caught the trailing silver cords.

Medusa let out a cry of frustration as she was yanked back onto the Eighth Heaven.

Hades was flabbergasted.

Persephone, who had appeared like magic at the boundary of the world, gracefully pulled herself up and held the sack aloft, straightening her Chanel skirt as she turned towards her husband with a look of stern admonishment.

'Honestly, Hades, do I have to do everything?'

Hades' face, already red from the exertion of running, blushed a deeper shade of crimson as he felt his wife's disappointment. 'I just turned away for a minute, darling.'

Persephone waved it away. 'Doesn't matter. I've got it now. Where is Cerbie?'

Hades shrugged and Persephone gave him a withering look, then whistled long and hard. The cloud world shook as the nightmarish hound appeared, galloping over the hillside at the sound of his mistress' call. He barrelled Hades aside and stopped abruptly at the feet of the Spring Goddess, who patted his flank affectionately.

'I haven't found Zeus yet,' Hades said. 'I've looked everywhere. Maybe we should give up on this revenge idea and just turn Medusa in for the reward.'

Persephone looked up sharply. 'We aren't giving up anything. I know exactly where the old creep is. My plan is going to work. I told you it would, and when have I ever been wrong?'

Hades grinned. He loved how Persephone managed to resolve even the most difficult situation. The other gods and goddesses might underestimate her, think her nothing more than a ditzy blonde, but they were idiots. The real Persephone was as sharp, ambitious and ruthless as any of them – more so, if he was honest about it. After all, it wasn't every girl who could work her way up from a little-known spring goddess to one of the most powerful goddess queens in the Greco-Roman pantheon.

The *Zeus Motel* on the fringes of the city was a sad, rundown place. Much, Hades thought, like its namesake, who was currently sitting inside room number 9 eating pizza and watching a Judge Janus re-run.

Pinpointing his room number hadn't been hard after Persephone had flirted with the weedy teenager who manned the motel's front desk.

'How the mighty have fallen,' Hades said smugly as he and Persephone stepped delicately out of the tired reception area and into the asphalt carpark where their Mercedes A-Class was parked. Hades opened the boot and retrieved the hessian sack, now securely bound by some of the Golden Fleece thread.

'You really didn't need to smite that receptionist guy,' Persephone said, using her gold compact to check her lipstick.

'I didn't like how he was looking at you.'

Persephone laughed. 'They all look at me like that.'

'And I'd like to smite every one of them,' Hades replied, slamming the boot and turning to his wife, who even in this filthy, hot carpark managed to look like a Hollywood movie star.

'So, are you sure about this?' he asked her.

'He has it coming,' she replied, powdering her delicate nose before snapping her compact shut. 'Anyway, I thought you liked the idea of getting a little bit of vengeance.'

'Vengeance has never been my thing, my sweet, but if it is what you want then of course I'm in,' Hades said. 'You know I would do anything for you. But he *is* your father. Are you sure you want to kill him?'

'Zeus has never been a father to me,' Persephone answered coldly. 'He denied he even got Mum pregnant until she proved it with a Holy Mary divine paternity test.'

Persephone's face hardened at the mention of her mother's embarrassment at having to prove she'd been seduced and then dumped by Zeus. That was why Hades hadn't been very surprised when, upon hearing of the missing head of Medusa, Persephone had immediately tried to convince him that they should be the ones to retrieve it, and use it to petrify Zeus before handing it in for any reward money.

Hades was certainly not against the idea and, aside from the fact he needed money, he liked the thought of helping his beloved wife make Zeus pay for his abandonment of her and her mother. He needed to pay. How dare he ignore her birthdays and never send her a kind word or a pretty gift.

His beautiful Persephone had been forced, her whole life, to stand silently and watch that rotten brother of his spoil his children, even the other illegitimate ones, while he had given her nothing. Hades thought Demeter had become overly protective of Persephone to make up for Zeus' neglect, but they were both as bad as each other, in Hades opinion, leaving Persephone both smothered and abandoned. No wonder she was vengeful.

'You are the only one who has ever been good to me, Hades,' she said, her face breaking into a radiant smile as she wrapped her arm around her husband. 'You're the only one who has ever understood me. The only one who ever saw me as more than just a silly little spring goddess without a thought in her head.'

Hades took his wife's hand and kissed it. He did know her, better than anyone, and it was one of the reasons their marriage had lasted so long. But he hadn't always known her as he did now. Once, a long time ago, he, like all the rest, had thought her just a pretty goddess with no real ambitions or intellect.

She had been so good at her pretence of a ditzy blonde child, that it was not until she asked directly for his help that he realised she was not the good girl everyone imagined her to be.

They had been sitting and talking by the river near the base of Olympus, as they so often did back in those long-gone days, drinking the tea he made from her sacred flowers and brought her every week. It had become their habit to meet and talk about her life, him giving a sympathetic ear to her teenage woes and infatuations. Their relationship in those days was a closely guarded secret; Persephone had insisted on it, telling him it was important to her to have someone who wouldn't go telling tales on her to gain her mother's favour.

Hades had promised he would never do such a thing, and so she had begun to confide in him, revealing a sharp and thoughtful mind under her crown of golden hair.

During their secret meetings they would share their hopes and dreams. Hades loved every moment spent with the beautiful goddess, but never for one minute tried to fool himself into believing it was anything more than friendship. Women like Persephone did not entertain romantic thoughts about men like Hades. Truth be told, no woman ever really had.

'Mother has promised me to Pan,' Persephone revealed dejectedly one morning as they skipped stones across the river. 'It's not just *like* marrying an old goat. He literally is an old goat! He stinks! And those pipes... he really can't play very well, but all the nymphs say he does because he gets mad if they don't and head-butts them.'

Hades had nodded in sympathy and then poured his niece a cup of sweet-smelling tea and handed her a rose petal biscuit.

'I don't have a choice though; Mother is set on it. She says as the goddess of spring I have to marry the god of the wilds.'

'Well, your mother certainly is a force of nature herself.'

Hades would never openly admit this, but Demeter scared the crap out of him. As the goddess of the harvest, she was one of the most powerful deities in the Greek pantheon and she knew it. It was an open secret that Persephone was Zeus' daughter, but even the great Hera was loath to openly take on her sister the way she'd confronted and humiliated other women who had dallied with her husband.

Only Zeus seemed unafraid of Demeter, which was why he was brave enough to continue to deny paternity, even after it had been proven time and time again. But, because of Zeus' refusal to openly acknowledge Persephone, she had been relegated to merely a goddess of flowers and not a major deity like her half-sisters Aphrodite, Artemis and Athena, who Zeus had openly acknowledged.

Persephone, for her part, hated her half-sisters only slightly less than she hated Zeus, often complaining about how much more attention they got, and having major temples dedicated to them whereas she had nothing.

Hades understood her envy. Persephone was, in Hades' opinion, so much more beautiful and deserving of worship than any of those other goddesses, and he was quick to tell her so at every opportunity. Which was probably the reason she liked hanging out with him so much.

At least that's what he thought was the reason, before she sprang another major surprise on him as they finished their flower tea and prepared to pack up their picnic.

'You know, there is a way I wouldn't have to marry Pan,' Persephone said, so softly he barely heard her over the ceramic clinking of the crockery he was stacking back into the picnic basket.

'There is?'

'I could run away,' she said, staring down at her linen napkin, unable to make eye contact.

Hades shook his head. 'Your mother would find you and bring you back.'

'Yes, maybe...' Persephone nodded. 'Unless I was somewhere she couldn't get to me.'

Hades leaned forward, intrigued at what this lovely young goddess might be proposing.

'And where do you think that would be?'

'Well, everyone knows that the Underworld is impervious to the sight of the gods and goddesses. I could hide down with you and she wouldn't be able to find me.'

Hades sat back on his heels, the implications of Persephone's idea starting to worry him.

'You want to run away to the Underworld – with me?'

'Well, yes. Just until she forgets about this Pan thing and then I'll come back up. It wouldn't be for long, Uncle.'

Hades considered this for a moment.

She glanced up at him coquettishly. 'And I would, of course, be very grateful.'

Hades' not-very-strong resolve weakened, and weakened again when he felt Persephone's outstretched toes playing footsy with him on the picnic rug.

'I suppose—'

She jumped up, delighted. 'I knew you wouldn't let me down,' she cried, enveloping him in a fragrant embrace.

And so, a few weeks later the plan was set. Persephone told him she had organised a trip to pick blueberries, out of sight of her mother's constant surveillance.

When the day came Hades spent an extra three hours getting himself dressed and ready. He terrorised his minions into making the Underworld glow and glisten as much as the dark innermost realms of the planet could. Then he hitched his blackest steeds to his chariot and commanded the ground above him to open up. As the mantle of the Earth formed a huge crevice, he ascended from the Underworld a few feet from where Persephone was gathering her berries.

He grabbed her. But there's often a hole in every plan. Demeter was not as far away as Hades expected and she saw her daughter being taken by the Lord of the Underworld and cried out in horror.

Hades hesitated, but Persephone grabbed the reins and hastened the horses on, down into the depths as the soil, clay and rocks closed up behind them.

Persephone jumped off the chariot and danced around the gates of Hades in joyful abandon.

'We made it,' she cried, gathering Hades up in her arms and making him waltz along the banks of the Styx with her.

Usually morose and solemn, Hades couldn't help breaking into merry laughter at the sight of her happiness. But he was worried.

'Not quite. Your mother saw us. She knows you are here.'

'Oh well,' Persephone responded, picking one of the prettiest lilies growing at the gate and holding it to her nose.

'Persephone, we need to take you back up right away!'

'Why?'

'Because she thinks I have taken you against your will.'

'Oh, that's all right. Gods abduct women all the time. Look at Zeus – no one bats an eye.'

'Except I didn't abduct you. We're just on a holiday.'

'Holiday, abduction – what difference does it make as long as I don't have to deal with Mother anymore?'

Hades wrung his hands in exasperation. There was no way Demeter was going to stand for this. She'd be down there any second and her wrath was something he really could do without.

But Persephone was completely unperturbed, in fact downright happy. She was even humming a tune as she opened the gates and stepped inside.

'Stop! Don't go in there without me,' he cried. 'It isn't safe.'

But the girl was already through the gates as a menacing growl and blazing red eyes announced the presence of Cerberus, the vicious guard dog of the Underworld.

'Persephone! Look out!' Hades rushed to the gate, knowing he had no hope of pulling the great hellish hound off her. He was lucky most days if the horrible beast didn't take a good chunk out of him when he tried to come and go.

Persephone, however, saw the dog and it's slobbery snapping teeth coming for her and, instead of running in fear, she just stood there and clapped her hands in delight.

'Puppy!'

Hades and Cerberus stopped dead in their tracks, both unsure what exactly was going on. Persephone, however, ran up to the mighty beast and wrapped her arms around one of the three-headed dog's massive legs and snuggled her face into its dark fur.

'I've always wanted a puppy,' she said, her voice muffled through the creature's coat. 'But Mummy would never let me have one.'

The dog stopped growling and simply stared at the lovely woman, who was hugging and stroking it, with something akin to wonder. Hades powered up; he was prepared to kill the monster, or at least injure it, if Persephone was in any danger. But, instead of ripping her face off, Cerberus' three heads started licking Persephone and whining for attention. The flower goddess stroked each canine head in turn and then looked over at Hades with shining eyes.

'Can I have him?'

Hades didn't know what to say, so said nothing as the goddess confidently pushed the dog's slobbering faces away and patted it firmly but kindly on the shoulder. 'You are a big boy, aren't you?' She said, taking in the beast's massive bulk.

Then she stepped into the shadowy recesses of the Underworld and Hades swore he saw a faint light emanate from her as she looked around the land of the dead.

Cerberus abandoned his post by the gates, where his job was to ensure none of the deceased tried to make a run for it, and followed his new mistress like a faithful pooch. And Hades didn't really care. So what if a few ghosts escaped? It always livened up the mortal plane when there was a bit of a haunting.

'Are you coming?' Persephone called, moving further into the shadows. 'I really want to freshen up. I need to remove all this soil and grit before it ruins my dress.'

Hades walked away from the gates, but before he could get more than a few steps he was yanked back by his collar and pulled to the ground. He looked up to see his sister, Demeter, standing over him, her fist pulled way back ready to punch his lights out. He was too slow to miss the blow altogether, but his quick movement to the side meant that her fist connected with his cheek rather than his jaw. The cheekbone was probably shattered but at least he retained consciousness.

'You give me back my daughter!' The harvest goddess swung her arm back for another attempt. 'I want her back. Now!'

Hades scrambled backwards and staggered to his feet, his arms up defensively. But Demeter, seeing the gates open, strode up to them and called her daughter's name.

Persephone didn't answer

'Where is she?' Demeter demanded, turning back to her brother.

'Look, calm down, okay,' Hades began, only to be slapped once again across the head, hard enough this time to make his ears ring.

'Don't you tell me to calm down! You think you can just appear up-world and steal my daughter, you lousy old vulture? You wait till her father hears about this.'

'I thought her father has never openly admitted paternity?' Hades replied, realising a moment too late that this was not the best way to respond to his sister's anger.

Demeter's glare turned from raging hot to icy cold in an instant and she leaned forward to grab his head in her hands.

'We both know exactly who her father is, and it doesn't matter, if you have harmed one hair on her head, I don't need Zeus' help to flay you alive.'

'He hasn't hurt me, Mama.' Persephone's voice wafted through the stillness.

Demeter spun around to see her daughter standing in the shadows, just on the other side of the gates.

'Persephone! Sweetheart, are you okay?'

'Yes, I think so,' Persephone said quietly, sounding small and fragile in the gloom.

'Don't worry, Honey, you don't have to stay here. I'm going to take you back home. There is nothing he can do to keep you here.'

Persephone stepped out onto the shores of the Styx and embraced her mother.

'I'm so glad you came,' she said. 'I was so scared.'

Hades' mouth dropped open in stunned surprise. He was about to protest when he caught Persephone's eye and saw her shake her head, almost unperceivably, at him. She then gave him a look that seemed to say, 'don't worry, I got this', before she broke from her mother's embrace and stepped back. She scanned the river for the ferryman, who was waiting patiently to return both mother and daughter to the mortal world.

'Can we go now, Mama? I'm so hungry. All I've had to eat is this pomegranate.' Persephone held out her hand to her mother, revealing the plump, juicy fruit with a number of dainty bites taken out of it.

Demeter gasped and staggered back. 'You didn't take that from in there?' the harvest goddess asked, but her expression showed she already knew the answer.

'Yes, Mama. There's a big tree with lots of fruit on it. Would you like me to get you one?' Persephone made to go through the gate but Demeter pulled her back.

Demeter pinched her daughter's face, forcing her mouth open, and shoved her fingers inside. She felt along Persephone's tongue, hoping to dig out the fruit, but it was too late. The girl had already swallowed.

'You stupid girl! Do you realise what you have done?'

Persephone looked bewildered. 'What's wrong, Mama? Why aren't you taking me home?'

Demeter shoved her daughter aside and strode towards Hades.

'You gave her food? You know if she eats anything in the Underworld, she is unable to leave. You tricked her! She's just a child!'

Hades shook his head. 'As you say, Persephone has eaten from the gardens of Hades, and as a result she cannot leave with you. Now, if you will excuse us, we were just going inside.'

Hades held out his hand to Persephone, who looked at her mother questioningly.

Demeter's shoulders sank in defeat and she nodded at her daughter. 'He's right. There's no way around it. It is a divine law. You belong here now.'

Persephone took Hades' hand with feigned reluctance.

'I am not going to let you stay here, Persephone, no matter what the rules,' Demeter said. 'I won't stand for this. You just have to wait for Mama to solve it, okay?'

'Okay,' Persephone said meekly, then allowed herself to be led into Hades' Underworld by her uncle. 'But don't worry, Mama, I'll be okay. Uncle Hades will look after me, won't you, uncle?'

Hades regarded his niece for a moment and then nodded. 'Always,' he promised.

As soon as they were out of sight of Demeter, Hades said, 'If I didn't know better, I would think you ate that pomegranate on purpose.'

Persephone shrugged her shoulders and smiled her dazzling smile. 'Now why would I do that? I don't have any intention of being kept anywhere against my will.' Persephone opened her fist to reveal two bite sized pieces of pomegranate squashed into her palm. 'I don't even like pomegranate.'

Looking at Persephone now, standing in the approaching twilight by a greasy oil puddle in the carpark of a second-rate hotel, her face a picture of pure determination, Hades knew he had always been at her mercy. Even if he wanted to stop her from killing Zeus, he would never have been able to. Their life together had always gone exactly as Persephone planned it, and he had, he realised, merely been along for the ride.

'C'mon, you stupid old crow,' Persephone called to him. 'We need to get this over with so we can collect the reward. Then we are going shopping! Dior have just announced their new collection.'

Hades hurried over to his wife, who moved aside to let him ascend the stairs first, flinching slightly as the hessian bag hissed at her.

The two-storey motel shimmered in the summer heat, as heavy dark clouds gathered, threatening a thunderstorm that would only trap the humidity. Persephone and Hades were sweating profusely as they climbed the narrow flight of stairs to the second floor.

Number 9 was at the end of a row of identical 50's style motel rooms, the faded pastel-blue door closed and grimy, and its once bright, floral curtains tightly drawn against the last glare of sunlight that bounced up from the carpark and refracted across the aluminium and concrete building. The place was sad and deserted, only the blaring of the television through the thick walls indicated anyone was inside. Hades and Persephone tiptoed up a few doors away from Zeus' room and stopped short. Both shushed the other, then shushed each other for shushing, then, Hades plunged his hand into the hessian sack to grab Medusa's head.

'Ow. Ow. Ow,' he said as the serpents bit him. 'Ow.'

'Shush!' Persephone said.

Hades glared at her but said nothing, grimacing silently as the snakes sank their fangs into his already severely bitten flesh and tangled themselves around his forearm to make the bag difficult to remove.

Eventually he pulled the head free and held it securely out in front of him.

'Where are we?' Medusa asked, her sight still obscured by the glittery pink eye mask, which read: Princess Sleeping.

'Never mind that,' Hades whispered. 'Keep your voice down.'

Medusa frowned and then opened her mouth wide to scream. Persephone, thinking quickly, shoved her Oscar de la Renta scarf deep into Medusa's throat, narrowly avoiding having her fingers snapped off by Medusa's fang-like teeth. The gorgon gagged but could not dislodge the expensive silk material.

'Good work,' Hades said, and Persephone gestured for him to follow her as she crept up to the door of Number 9, the gagged and blindfolded head of Medusa held aloft between them.

25

Confrontation

Persephone pulled a pin from her perfectly coiffed hair and inserted it into the lock. The faintest of clicks announced the door was now unbarred, and the husband and wife gave each other a triumphant look. Persephone kissed Hades on the lips, making him blush in delight.

'Let's do this,' she whispered, and pushed the door open.

Hades' long, skeletal hand lifted Medusa's head in front of them like a shield and, as they stepped into the quiet room, he pulled up the sleeping mask to reveal those terrible eyes.

'Gotcha,' Hades cried as he spied Zeus reclining on the bed.

But the King of the Gods was not alone. Hera, Athena, Euryale, Artemis and Apollo were keeping Zeus company.

'Got you all,' cried Persephone gleefully, whereon the magnificent winged horse standing in front spread her wings to protect them. A dazzling burst of white light emanated from the creature.

Persephone and Hades shielded their eyes, but Medusa's gaze fell upon the horse.

For a moment, all was frozen in time: Pegasus with wings stretched wide, knocking cheap motel lamps to the floor, the gods and goddesses behind her, Hades and Persephone in the doorway with Medusa's head held above them, and the gorgon's paralysing gaze unable to tear itself away from the beautiful shining animal.

Then the world swam back to normalcy with tremendous speed.

The light faded, Hera and Apollo rushed forward to grab Hades who lost his grip on Medusa. Artemis and Athena headed for Persephone who continuted to shake the gorgon's head at her attackers.

Medusa managed to spit the gag out, and cried: 'Ow, my hair!'

Persephone, startled by Medusa's words, looked down and realised that what had been scaly serpents mere moments before, was now thick black ropes of real human hair. She dropped the head in shock and, without thinking, looked directly into Medusa's face. Luckily for Persephone she saw, not the monstrous fanged visage of a gorgon, but the frightened and confused face of a pretty, but very human looking, woman.

Artemis grabbed Persephone's arms and held her securely as Athena placed a pair of golden chains around her wrists. Hera was doing the same to Hades, who was as confused as his wife. A more than slightly drunk Zeus, meanwhile, was completely dumbfounded.

No one, however, was half as bewildered as the disembodied head of Medusa which lay staring up at the ceiling in shock. Pegasus bent down and snickered loudly as she nuzzled Medusa's face, rolling her gently upright so she could see what was happening. It did nothing to help Medusa make any sense of it all.

Euryale guided Medusa's now human body out of the closet, then gently scooped up her sister's head and put her back together, securely tightening the screws on the magical metal collar.

Hera released Hades to Apollo, who was already holding Persephone by one chained arm. 'This arrest will get me a promotion for sure,' he said.

Hades and Persephone struggled against their bonds, even though they knew it was useless. The chains were not ordinary gold, but links forged in the smithy of Hephaestus and designed to hold the divine and the demonic. They had ordered several lengths themselves for some particularly rowdy youths in Hades.

Persephone's gaze settled on Hera. 'It wasn't my idea, Hera, I swear. I had to go along with what Hades wanted. He's my husband. You understand. I had to obey him.'

Hera shook her head as Hades looked sharply at his wife. 'Hades has always been smart, but he would never go up against Zeus. He might have hated him, but they were brothers. It was you who had the ambition and the need for vengeance. When I saw Cerberus attack Poseidon in Atlantis with such accuracy, I knew it couldn't be Hades controlling that dog. We all know he never listens to a word Hades says. The only one Cerberus would follow is you.

'I'll admit, when we visited you, you put on such a good performance, I was unsure if I was right – until I noticed that the hems of your skirt were still damp from the seawater. And you were so intent on getting us to eat something, to keep us out of the way in the Underworld.

'You obviously realised the opportunity the reported kidnapping of Medusa's head offered you, and you took it. You *are* clever Persephone, and I can't blame you for hating Zeus. He was a terrible father to you, and you deserved a lot better. But you are also selfish and cruel, using Hades and Medusa and anyone else you could, not caring about the consequences for any of us. You are truly your father's daughter.'

The sweet, youthful goddess snarled, her face transformed into a picture of ugly wrath as she struggled in her bonds, lurching towards Zeus.

'Why couldn't you have loved me? Why didn't you make me one of the great goddesses like Athena or Artemis? Why was I always second best to you? My only option was living in a dark cavern with that dried-up old skeleton in order to get any power at all.'

Hades flinched to hear his wife speak so, but his face remained stoic and he did not speak out.

Zeus looked befuddled. 'You always seemed all right.'

Athena put her arms firmly, and somewhat comfortingly, around Persephone's shoulders. 'None of us had it easy being a daughter of Zeus, believe me. I had to break myself out of his empty old head after he swallowed my pregnant mother! But if killing him would have solved all our daddy issues, don't you think Artemis or Aphrodite or I would have done it years ago?'

Persephone sank against Athena's shoulder for a moment, then rallied, pasting on her usual enthralling smile. 'I'll be fine,' she said. 'I am always *fine*. I'll be out in a few days. Mama won't stand for me to be in jail.'

Apollo took hold of Persephone's chains and started to lead her and Hades out the door. 'That's up to the Department of Divine Misconduct,' he said. 'Until then, you'll be coming with me to Tartarus.'

As Apollo led them out, Zeus called, 'Hey, Polly.'

The god of music turned towards his father with a questioning look.

'Can you bring me back a couple of beers if you're going out? I have drunk the mini bar dry.'

Apollo glanced at Hera who shook her head, so Apollo ignored his father and led Persephone and Hades out to the approaching EBCU officials.

'You have no idea what just happened, do you, Zeus?' Hera asked.

Zeus looked at her. 'Did we get the reward money?'

Hera snorted. 'You know what? I think maybe you should stay in this hotel room for a while. Have a bit of a think about how much carnage you've created. In fact, when I get the house fixed up, I don't want you back there.'

Hera turned her back on Zeus and caught Artemis' eye. The two goddesses smiled at each other and then Hera went into the bathroom to wash her face and get a bit of distance between her and her husband, before she really let her anger out.

Medusa was already in there, staring at herself in the mirror.

Hera came up beside her and gently stroked her beautiful thick hair. 'You're back to your old self,' Hera said.

'Am I?' she asked, pulling at the dark coils of plaits and locks that tumbled across her elegant shoulders and down her back. She stared at her face, as if trying to recognise a long-lost friend she knew well but whose absence had been so long, their features were almost forgotten. She rubbed her skin, no longer a scaly hue of sickening green, but healthy flesh the colour of darken wood; her teeth, square and perfect, dazzled like stars as she smiled uncertainly at herself. Soft, hazel eyes looked harmlessly back at her from the reflected surface.

'How did this happen?'

'Pegasus.'

The once-gorgon turned to see the winged horse poke her magnificent head in through the door and nuzzle Medusa fondly, crowding Hera against the bathtub, into which she fell with an inelegant thump.

'Who are you?' Medusa asked, as she stroked Pegasus' ivory mane and shook her head in wonder.

'She's your daughter,' Hera replied from her prone position in the tub and the horse snickered in agreement. 'Blood of your blood, the best part of you made flesh.'

Medusa shook her head. 'I don't understand any of this. Why am I no longer a monster?'

'You were never a monster,' Hera replied, pulling herself up to a standing position and leaning against the shower rail. 'You had to deal with monsters, so they made you seem like one. But you were always as you are: a good woman who wanted to protect and be protected.

'That's why we knew you could never hurt your own child, just as you protected Euryale and Stheno, as you protected yourself, as you protected the world from your gaze. You never hurt an innocent or a female – you made sure of it – and we knew you would not allow yourself to hurt Pegasus, your true daughter. The only way to protect her was for you to give up being the monster and find who you truly were. And she helped you become that.'

Medusa looked at herself again in the mirror. 'Well, I've lost my power to protect anyone now,' she said, her face a mixture of emotions. 'Poseidon got his way after all. I'm just a weak, powerless woman once more.'

She turned to Hera. 'How will I protect my daughter from those who wish to do us harm?'

'Poseidon is petrified and so is Perseus. None of us will point any fingers at you. Even if the EBCU wanted to blame you for it, they can't punish your human self for what the gorgon did. The monster they want to destroy no longer exists. This was the only way to make you safe.'

'For now,' Medusa replied. 'But a human woman is never truly safe in this world.'

Hera thought about this for a long moment. She had wrestled with this problem herself when Euryale had shared the secret of Pegasus and the horse's power to transform Medusa back to a human. This was why Poseidon had wanted the horse: as a way to enslave the woman he'd been unable to acquire. Was what she had done to Medusa any better?

Then she remembered something Artemis had told her, long ago.

'Women are the most powerful beings on Earth. We create and nurture life. We weather storms no one else can even imagine. We have our lives stolen by useless men and our own sense of not being good enough. But one thing I have learned: things change. What ruled once will not rule forever, and what we believe in and what we do, is what shapes the world we live in.

'You showed me, Medusa, you showed everyone we can change. And not by being *like* them, those men who use power for selfish ends and the women who allow them to. We can be better than that. You were better than that. Maybe we change the world not by gaining power, but by preventing it from being used for ill. Maybe we do it by protecting each other and working together against those who intend us harm, rather than ignoring or helping them. You had so much power when you were a gorgon, Medusa. I felt it. You could have destroyed the world. But you didn't.'

Hera stepped awkwardly out of the tub, as Pegasus moved aside slightly to give her space.

'I can't tell you how much I admire you. How I wish I could have been like you when I had real power. But I wasn't. I used my position to take my rage and anger out on those who didn't always deserve it, because I was scared that if I focused on the real source of my misery, I would fail. I protected the wrong people and punished those who were victims just like me. You never did that, Medusa. You only ever used your power against those who actively tried to harm you or the ones you loved. You were never the monster.' Hera paused. 'But sometimes I was.'

Medusa looked like she was going to respond, but before she could, Pegasus knocked her with a head nod, as if telling her there was no need to speak. There was nothing she need say. Medusa tearfully hugged Pegasus' neck and buried her lovely face into the horse's white fur. Pegasus encased Medusa in her wings and the two stood, wrapped in each other's embrace, their shared breath fogging up the mirror until both were obscured from view.

25

Back in Court

IN THE COURT OF LORE, THE COURTROOM WAS PACKED FOR THE final verdict. It had been the case of the season, with every known deity presenting in the witness box or jostling in the viewing stalls to see just how Hades and Persephone were to be punished for their crimes.

Because of its notoriety, and Athena having to recuse herself, the case was being heard by Judge Janus himself and being streamed live on Mystic TV to ensure highest possible sponsorship options for the celebrity judge.

Zeus' testimony had been somewhat confusing, as he didn't seem to consider himself in any real danger throughout the ordeal and kept asking who was getting his beer and when Hera was going to let him move back home.

Hera and Athena's information on the stand, though, had been compelling. Athena's inability to lie was a fairly good indication that her version of events in the motel room and those prior was fairly accurate.

Hera was relieved that, because Athena had been locked away during the events in Atlantis, she could neither confirm nor deny Hera's version of what had transpired there. As a result, Hera was able to maintain the myth that Medusa had been merely a pawn in the whole thing, and that Poseidon had been the one to instigate the theft of her head in the first place. A tale that surprisingly neither Hades nor Persephone refuted on the stand.

Now it was the time for the final verdict and the courtroom was electric with excitement.

Janus banged his gavel three times to still the clamour in the courtroom and cleared his throat, indicating that he was preparing to make his ruling.

'We have heard a great deal of quite startling, at times bewildering, but overall worrying testimony throughout this trail. Feuds between gods are common enough, but to put the whole realm at risk like this in this day and age is just not done.'

There was a murmur of agreement in the stalls.

'Since the great Divine Treaty of 1506CE, we have lived with our grudges and familial gripes fairly reasonably, and the court is and always has been the place to settle any such disputes.

'The fact that three such well-known and well-loved deities chose to go outside of this system to settle old scores is something that we cannot abide.

'As Poseidon has already been, some would say, fittingly punished for his role in this sorry affair, it leaves me only to determine an adequate sentence for Hades and his accomplice, Persephone.'

Another murmur rose in the courtroom and the judge banged his gavel to silence it.

'I have heard and accept Persephone's sincere regret at this incident, as well as accept Hades' own testimony that Persephone was merely dragged along as part of her wifely duties.'

Hera and Athena glanced at each other knowingly and shook their heads. Even though they understood this myth served Persephone well, it was thoroughly vexing how willingly she collaborated with the enduring narrative that women were too stupid or powerless to have any responsibility in the events of their own lives.

'As a result, I find you, Hades, God of the Greek Underworld, guilty of attempted divinocide of the Greek God Zeus, and sentence you to exile in your own realm. You may not ascend to either the Mortal or Divine Realm or any other land for a period of no less than 500 years.'

The gallery did a unified gasp at the severity of this sentence. Hades, however, remained absent of expression as he sat by his wife in the dock.

'Persephone, I find you not guilty of attempted divinocide.'

Persephone, sitting beside her husband, was unable to conceal her glee and did a small seated dance in delight.

'However,' the judge continued, 'knowing as I do, from your own testimony, the devotion you have for your husband, which meant you could do nothing less than abet him in these crimes, I rule that you must stay by Hades' side throughout his sentence.'

The blood from Persephone's face drained away.

'You mean I'm stuck down there for 500 years,' she cried. 'With no opportunity to even go shopping? What about the designer sales? You have to be there to get the best bargains.'

The judge shook his head. 'I have had a petition from your mother, and have allowed, for her sake, for you to ascend into the Mortal Realm for three months of every year during which time you will stay under Demeter's care and must not leave her side.'

Hera glanced up to the balcony viewing gallery where Demeter was sitting, majestic and composed.

Persephone cried out in horror but Demeter merely glanced at her and gave her a small, knowing smile.

The judge banged his gavel once more. 'That is my verdict; that is the new lore.' He stood and swiftly left the court as the two prisoners were escorted from the dock.

'I almost feel sorry for Persephone,' Athena said, watching the other gods and goddesses file from the room. 'It seemed like she got a worse sentence than Hades did.'

Hera shook her head. 'I don't feel sorry for her at all. She made that bed now she can lie it in. Persephone is no victim here.'

Athena shrugged. 'You can be hard on women, Hera.'

'Yeah, I know,' Hera said, 'but I'm working on it.'

Hera picked up her purse and began to descend the stairs from the witness gallery. 'I guess I should let the sisters know the verdict. I know they have been a bit worried that Medusa would be implicated.'

'It's good for them that Persephone and Hades didn't dob her in,' Athena replied.

Hera looked at her sharply. 'What do you mean?'

'Hera, you know I'm not stupid. You never did tell me why Medusa and the gorgons were all there when Poseidon was petrified. And it doesn't take a genius to work out what must have transpired. It didn't help that I also saw the gorgon footprints all over Perseus' front yard.'

Hera shook her head in amazement. 'So, you committed perjury?'

'Of course not,' Athena replied. 'I was asked only about what I knew about Poseidon, not what I figured out afterwards. And the fact is I didn't actually see Medusa or the gorgons turn Perseus to stone. Nor attack Poseidon. So, I didn't lie.'

'And you are okay with that?' Hera asked.

'I'm the Goddess of Justice, Hera. And justice has been done.'

Hera smiled. 'You are a good person, Athena. I hope you will judge me as kindly if it ever comes to it. But it is odd that Hades and Persephone didn't try to blame the whole thing on Medusa. It was the obvious defence.'

'It wouldn't have helped their case,' Athena replied. 'By sticking to the story that Poseidon had been the one to abduct Medusa in the first place, that it was he who had attacked Perseus and then accidently petrified himself, Hades couldn't be accused of the attack. So, the only charge the EBCU could really make against them was the attempted divinocide of Zeus. If he had been found guilty of actual divinocide, both he and Persephone would have been executed.'

Hera nodded, realising the sense of this. 'I would guess it was Persephone who figured that out.'

'Oh yeah, definitely,' Athena agreed.

'Give my regards to Medusa and the sisters,' Athena said as the two women parted at the doorway. 'I'd come but I am still so behind on all my cases.'

'Will do,' Hera replied, hugging her stepdaughter before heading off towards the magnificent double oak doors that separated the courtroom from the hallway.

'Oh, I forgot to ask,' Athena called. 'How are the divorce proceedings going?'

Hera turned and shrugged. 'I've given him the papers, and the world hasn't ended. So, I guess I will still exist, even if I am no longer married.'

Athena smiled. 'I'm glad. You are looking happier than I've seen you for centuries.'

Hera nodded. She felt better than she had for centuries – millennia even.

'I'll see you at book club?' Athena asked. 'I think we are discussing *50 Shades of Troy* this week, right?'

Hera sighed. She still hadn't read that damned book!

Epilogue

The heavy gate squeaked as Hera pushed it aside and walked up the cobbled front pathway to the farmhouse. The beautiful meadows and rolling hills of Monster's Realm hinterland stretched out in every direction around her and it felt as though she was as far from anywhere as it was possible to be.

In the distance she saw a woman standing in a field, her face turned to the sky, her arm shading her face from the sun.

Hera approached and the ex-gorgon looked over with only mild surprise at having a visitor.

'Hello, Medusa.'

'I wondered if you were going to show up. Am I going to be arrested?'

'No.'

Hera realised she still avoided looking directly at Medusa. Old habits die hard, she supposed. She forced herself to look the young woman in the eyes and was slightly surprised at how ordinary they now were. Soft mossy green – had they always been that colour? Hadn't they been hazel when the two women had spoken in the motel? Hera couldn't remember.

In her mind Hera always thought of the gorgon's eyes as laser red or acid yellow, the eyes of aliens in 1960s sci-fi comics. But who knew – no one had ever gotten a look at Medusa's eyes when she was a gorgon and lived to tell about it.

Medusa, as unused to being looked at as Hera was of looking at her, fidgeted uncomfortably under Hera's gaze. It was then Hera realised that Medusa was still wearing the fastening collar she had given her so long ago.

'I thought your head was secured properly now?'

Medusa pulled at the collar self-consciously. 'Oh yes. I'm all in one piece. But I feel naked without it.'

She looked at Hera keenly. 'So, are you here to get some kind of revenge? I wouldn't blame you if you wanted to kill me.'

'Why on earth would I want to harm you?'

'I stoned your brother, and your stepson, and almost petrified your husband.'

'Yeah, there's that,' Hera agreed and then smiled.

The two women stood in silence for a moment.

'But I didn't like any of them all that much. Besides my days of vengeance are well and truly over. At least when it comes to anything to do with my feckless, soon to be ex-husband.'

'He's not dead, you know,' Medusa said.

'Who, Zeus? Yes, I know. I just meant "ex" as in we are getting a divorce.'

'No, I meant Poseidon. Or Perseus for that matter.'

'Oh?'

'I'm not sure exactly how it works, but quite a few of the older ones melted back into human form after a few thousand years. Unfortunately, for most of them I was looking at them when it happened and zapped them back. But essentially, they're not dead. Just frozen.'

'Well, I'm sure Poseidon will be relieved to know he's just encased in rock for a few millennia. A kind of an adult timeout rather than a death sentence.'

Medusa looked uncomfortable.

'Don't worry,' Hera said. 'Apollo arranged for the EBCU to move Stone Poseidon into the gardens at Versailles. No one has even noticed a new statue there. Plus, if he is indeed going to come back to flesh at some point, he'll have been racking up a lot of existence points, so you've probably done him a favour.'

Medusa relaxed and Hera looked up to watch Pegasus silhouetted against the sun, swooping and gliding in the periwinkle sky.

'She certainly is a beautiful sight.'

Medusa nodded, the anxiety gone from her face as she watched her daughter prance in the air, revelling in the freedom and joy of being alive.

'Do you want an iced tea? Once Pegasus takes off, she's usually up there awhile.'

Hera nodded and followed Medusa into the neat brick cottage. Inside was exactly as the outside promised: small but comfortable. Hera seated herself on the cosy sunburst-yellow sofa as Medusa disappeared into the kitchen for the refreshments.

'Sugar?'

'Yes please. Six teaspoons should do it.'

Hera heard Medusa opening and closing cupboards and took the opportunity to check out the small living and dining area. The décor was similar to the classical style Medusa had favoured in her cavern home and, Hera noted, also sported a couple of the same petrified victims as ornamental and functional objects. Not as many as before though. Clearly Medusa had picked her favourites – a man with a screaming visage and his hands up in front of his face was a useful coat rack, while another man in a cowering position made quite an attractive coffee table.

Medusa placed a jug of iced tea, a bowl of sugar and two glasses on the granite man's back as she settled down opposite Hera.

'Memories of the old days,' Medusa remarked, following Hera's gaze.

'When did you move out of the cavern?'

Medusa shrugged. 'A few months ago. Not really a place for Pegasus. She needs open spaces and access to the sky.'

'It was a bit dank and dingy,' Hera said. 'Are your sisters living with you here?'

'No. They have their own lives to lead now and have moved into Monsters' Village. Euryale is competing in this year's Tidy Town garden competition; she's a natural with roses. And you know Stheno's married now?'

'Yes, I heard.'

Medusa nodded. 'Funny how things work out. Stheno was always the one who resented being the gorgon. But she is the one who fitted right in, straight away. She's really made a life for herself as a monster and now she refuses to change back, even though Athena explained she could, if she wanted to. She's happily married and Euryale is dating Hydra – which is a surprise to no one really. I'm the one living the life of the human spinster.'

'Do you mind?'

'No. Not really.' Medusa poured the drinks and handed a full cup to Hera. 'Truth is I never really wanted anything to do with men, or romantic engagements of any kind. They were just always forced on me. So, it's all worked out for the best.'

Hera heard the sound of Pegasus' wings beating through the air and the soft thud of her landing gracefully. Medusa stood and looked up at the ceiling happily. Hera placed her cup down and thanked Medusa for her hospitality.

'I'm glad you are happy now, Medusa. If anyone deserves it, you do.'

As Medusa led Hera out to the front gate, Pegasus trotted up behind them and gave Hera a friendly nudge. The goddess patted the horse affectionately and wished them both a fond farewell.

But, just before she closed the gate behind her, Hera decided she had to ask the question that had been bugging her since the showdown in the hotel room.

'Medusa,' she said, biting her lower lip. 'You don't hate me for bringing Pegasus to the hotel that night, for turning you human again, do you?'

Medusa smiled and stroked Pegasus' ivory neck. The horse nuzzled affectionately into her mother's touch. 'How can I?' she answered. 'You gave me back my child.'

Satisfied, Hera left the garden, and Medusa closed the gate securely behind her.

'Anyway, we're not quite human, are we, darling?' Medusa said quietly as she stroked Pegasus' mane and watched Hera leave in a Hermes cab. Pegasus snickered softly and ruffled her feathers as Medusa pushed back her hair and revealed three small snakes writhing under her darkened locks.

About the Author

Gabiann Marin is an award-winning writer in broadcast, publication and multimedia, including several hours of Australian television, three feature film scripts and over 12 published fiction and non-fiction books.

When she isn't writing she is thinking about it or helping others to write – as a story editor, university lecturer and creative mentor.

Gabiann lives in the beautiful Blue Mountains, west of Sydney, where she writes surrounded by the astounding wonders of nature – occasionally interrupted by the whirr of a low flying rescue helicopter searching for lost bushwalkers.

Best known for her children's books, creative non-fiction, and an inexplicable need to volunteer for things she doesn't have time for, *The Medusa Situation* is Gabiann's first novel for adults.

She is completing her PhD in Writing and Mythological Studies.

Acknowledgements

Writing a book is a hard and difficult journey, even as it is rewarding and wondrous. An author cannot do this alone and this new tale of Medusa, Hera, Athena, Artemis and all the other wonderful creatures and characters of ancient myth would not exist if not for the enduring and generous support of many people.

My mother, Jeni Marin, whose intelligence, support and willingness to listen to several versions of this tale over decades was invaluable to its creation.

The incredibly talented Jill Waters who patiently listened to many false starts and helped me figure out so many of the tricky plot questions – she was a critical but non-judgemental sounding board for this zany enterprise of a novel, and one of the main reasons the book got finished at all.

The members of my NSW Writers Centre Writing Group, who gave insightful feedback to the somewhat disjointed chapters and snippets I managed to present over the years.

The indominable Lisa Hanrahan who has believed in me and given me so many opportunities to develop my skills as a writer and editor.

And finally I want to say a huge heartfelt thank you to Lindy Cameron, Publisher Extraordinaire, who saw what I saw in this book, loved and nurtured it through the publication process and has believed in it from the first chapter she read.

Thank you all!

www.ingramcontent.com/pod-product-compliance
Lightning Source LLC
Chambersburg PA
CBHW031059020726
47495CB00007B/1960